Praise for
Christine McGuire's
Until Proven Guilty

"*Until Proven Guilty* transports the reader to [California] to track down a serial killer. Not just your typical maniacal serial killer, mind you, but one with the attributes of Milwaukee cannibal Jeffrey Dahmer. The book has interesting characters, especially an off-the-charts 'investigative' television reporter who makes Geraldo Rivera seem like a student of Mister Rogers' school of gentle broadcasting."

—Arthur Miller, *USA Weekend*

"McGuire brings the kind of inside knowledge . . . and a sharp, observant writing style . . . that makes for compulsive page-turning."

—Patricia Holt, *San Francisco Chronicle*

"McGuire clearly writes from the heart and with the benefit of bitter experience."

—*Yorkshire Evening Post*

"Particularly refreshing . . . McGuire, a former assistant D.A. herself, paints a truly horrifying picture as she describes in shocking detail the crimes of serial killer Russell. . . ."

—Mary Frances Wilkens, *Booklist*

"Until Proven Guilty is a tense, nerve-jangling thriller that should satisfy fans of *The Silence of the Lambs*."

—Edgar Award winner Peter Blauner,
author of *Slow Motion Riot*

"Compelling . . . Christine McGuire has delivered a super read. . . . What sets *Until Proven Guilty* apart from the run-of-the-mill murder mystery is McGuire's experience with the criminal justice system. . . ."

—Biz Van Gelder, *Trial* magazine

Books by Christine McGuire

FICTION

Until Proven Guilty*
Until Justice Is Done*

NONFICTION

Perfect Victim (co-written with Carla Norton)

*Published by POCKET BOOKS

UNTIL JUSTICE IS DONE

Christine McGuire

POCKET STAR BOOKS
New York London Toronto Sydney Tokyo Singapore

This book is a work of fiction. Names, characters, places, and incidents are products of the author's imagination or are used fictitiously. Any resemblance to actual events or locales or persons, living or dead, is entirely coincidental.

A Pocket Star Book published by
POCKET BOOKS, a division of Simon & Schuster Inc.
1230 Avenue of the Americas, New York, NY 10020

Copyright © 1994 by Christine McGuire

First Published in Great Britain by William Heinemann Ltd

ISBN: 0-671-53052-6

First Pocket Books printing October 1995

10 9 8 7 6 5 4 3 2 1

POCKET STAR BOOKS and colophon are registered trademarks of Simon & Schuster Inc.

Cover photo by Valerie Gates/Photonica

Printed in the U.S.A.

This novel is lovingly dedicated
to N.M. for inspiring Emma
and understanding, and to R.B.S.
for his constant help and support.

Acknowledgments

With deep gratitude to Fred Nolan.

I would also like to express thanks to my literary agents, Arthur and Richard Pine.

UNTIL JUSTICE IS DONE

Prologue

The little pig lived in Alameda Heights; she was a slim blonde who reminded him a bit of Michelle Pfeiffer in that movie where she sang on top of the piano. He already knew a great deal about her; he had been inside her apartment several times. The front door presented no problem: he just pushed buttons until someone buzzed him in. A credit card got him into the apartment itself. He had taken his time familiarizing himself with its layout—especially the bedroom; he always spent a long time in the bedroom—flipping through her photo albums, checking the names in her address book, sniffing her cologne, fondling the underwear she kept in the top drawer of her dresser. It was all part of the extended, delicious buildup.

She came out of the building wearing a blue cotton T-shirt, white jeans and leather sneakers. He watched the movement of her breasts under the cotton top as she walked down the path. Bite size, he thought, and smiled, remembering how he had watched her undress through the window. She had no secrets, not from him.

She got into her little Toyota Corolla and banged the door shut. What was she angry about? She drove off, heading across to Lighthouse Drive. He wondered

1

where she was going. Tuesdays she usually met the boyfriend, a big, beefy guy who looked like a prizefighter. She parked outside a pizza place in Española, and he had to drive past; by the time he came around the block she was coming out with a medium-sized flat package. Pizza to go. So the boyfriend had stood her up.

He followed her back and watched as she went in. There was no sign of the boyfriend's car. Mission control, we have liftoff. It would be dark about 9:30. She'd be asleep by 11. And he would go in. The very act of burglary was a symbolic penetration. Not many people realized that. The anticipation as you paused on the threshold: little pig, little pig, may I come in? *It was infantile, but it amused him to think of himself as a wolf and his prey as little pigs living in houses that— as far as keeping him out was concerned anyway— might just as well be made of straw.*

He got back in his car and drove away, smiling. A steady pulse of lust throbbed in his head as he thought about what it was going to be like.

At 10:45 he was back. He put on his "going-in clothes"—a ski mask, work gloves, dark loose-fitting coveralls, tennis shoes one size bigger than his own feet. He moved silently, through the darkness to the rear door of the building. It was too late to use the buzzer trick at the front door and anyway, he couldn't risk being seen. Expertly and silently using a glass cutter and suction cup, he cut and carefully removed a pane of glass from the door.

He reached in, slid back the latch and opened the door just wide enough to ease into the building. The credit card got him back into the apartment. Directly ahead was the living room. He unplugged the telephone line; if anyone called they would simply hear an unanswered ring. The bedroom door opened without a sound—he had oiled it a few nights earlier to make sure it would not make any noise. He smiled his secret smile. She was fast asleep, one arm thrown back over her head, tan against the whiteness of the pillow. The only sound was the steady tock of the quartz alarm. He ghosted across the room and carefully, silently unscrewed the light bulb from the bedside lamp.

Leaving the bedroom door ajar he retraced his steps to where he had parked the car. Now the second part of his ritual began. He stripped off his "going-in" clothes and changed into his "rape clothes"—a different set of coveralls, surgical gloves, different sized sneakers and ski mask. His heart was pounding steadily now and a hard throb of excitement coursed through his body. That was what the dressing-up was for: the actual rape was incidental. What was important was the anticipation, the knowing, the taste in his mouth before the actual taste itself, making the waiting for it last and last and last.

He reached the rear door again. Everything was silent, exactly as he had left it; his entry had not been discovered. If by any chance it had been, he would have left immediately and begun the ritual again at one of the other homes he had been watching. He had chosen this one because it was the easiest. The second little pig was a birdlike woman who worked as a legal secretary for Santa Rita Operations whose husband traveled a lot. He had crossed the third one off his list when her husband came home unexpectedly while he was casing the house. That was another rule: never push your luck, always be ready to abandon the plan.

The bedroom door was still ajar. He could hear the young woman's soft breathing. He eased over to the bedside and stood looking down at her. This was the moment, the best moment. He felt enormous. Hold it off, hold it off. He started the countdown: ten seconds. One-elephant, two-elephants, three, four. When he got to ten he straddled the woman's thighs with his legs like a man getting on a horse and clamped his hand down tight on her mouth. He felt her go rigid beneath him, saw her eyes flare wide with sudden terror. She made a stifled noise under his hand. He smiled.

"Hello, little pig," he said. He ripped her nightgown open with his free hand. Then he bit off her right nipple.

1

"All rise!" the bailiff snapped as the judge appeared through the doorway to the right of the bench. Here we go again, Kathryn thought. She only half-heard the bailiff's monotone as he chanted the ritual words that precede the opening of every session of court.

"Ready?" she whispered, stealing a look at her companion. Dave Granz was one of the DA's homicide inspectors. The best one, in her opinion, which was not unbiased.

"Sure," Dave nodded. He looked worn and she knew why; the homicide investigation he was working with the SO detectives was taking it out of him.

"You okay, Dave?" she whispered.

When you were in trial you wanted your inspector on the firing line with you, anticipating whatever moves the defense might make, ready to come up with the right police report or the correct piece of physical evidence. But some things couldn't be helped.

He gave a half shrug. "I'm fine," he said. "Just tired."

"Tell me about it," Kathryn murmured to herself. As usual, the night before opening statements she had hardly slept and this morning her stomach was uneasy.

It wasn't like on TV, where all you had to do was deliver a nice, neat, two-minute speech that demolishes the defense and conclusively establishes the defendant's guilt. In real life, courtroom victories came from careful preparation, from attention to detail, from determination. Win the skirmishes and you won the battle; win the battles and you won the war. A case started out being a jumble of facts. It was up to the prosecutor to shape those facts into a picture of truth.

The trouble was, there just never seemed to be enough hours in the day. Meetings, phone calls, interviews and filings ate away time that could have been spent painting that picture of truth. She was always on the run, always feeling she was doing no better than patting the problems on the head as they came by, never really solving any of them.

You got used to it, of course. There wasn't any choice. Her days were always hectic, never comfortable, sometimes unbearable; and when she was in trial, worse. Every trial triggered incipient paranoia. Self-doubt plagued you; unanswerable questions rattled around in your head like a button in a vacuum cleaner: had you prepared enough, would one of your witnesses recant or become amnesiac, would the defense blindside you? There was no time for reflection, no time for measured judgment. You just went out there and did it.

"Is the prosecution ready to proceed, Ms. Mackay?" Judge Spencer asked.

With his iron-gray hair and deeply lined face,

David Spencer looked every inch the impartial jurist, although many of the ADAs found him biased in favor of the defense. Plenty of judges let a jury know their biases one way or another. Sometimes the rulings they made against the prosecution were so biased it became impossible to get a conviction, no matter how obvious the defendant's guilt. And since prosecutors cannot appeal an acquittal, there wasn't the same kind of restraint on a judge who favored the defense as there was on one who favored the prosecution.

"Yes, Your Honor."

"Let the record show the defendant and his counsel are present," Spencer said. "And that the jury is seated. Ms. Mackay?"

Kathryn stole a quick final glance at her notes, then stood up and walked empty-handed to the podium, carefully placed a few feet from the jury of six women and six men, and two female alternates. She smiled at them, hoping her nervousness wasn't apparent.

These days the old-fashioned, flowery "ladies and gentlemen of the jury" form of address was considered *passé;* the style now was get out there and get straight to the heart of it.

"The evidence will show that Bradley Jasen and Margrit Riker, the defendant's wife, had a personal relationship—a sexual relationship, to be precise. This sexual relationship began shortly after Bradley hired Margrit to be his administrative assistant. When Margrit separated from her husband, Karl, Bradley moved Margrit into his guesthouse. Dieter, Margrit's younger brother, moved into the guesthouse a few days later. Within three weeks, Bradley Jasen was missing."

A pause; let it sink in. She glanced across the courtroom to where the defendant, Karl Riker, sat next to his attorney, public defender Paul Bradley. Tall and well-built, Riker wore a green sweater over a white striped shirt, jeans and brown shoes with soft crêpe soles. His thick brown hair had a high left-hand parting; he had high cheekbones, small, dark, liquid brown eyes beneath heavy brows, a snub nose, a neat moustache. His face was completely expressionless.

"In the early morning hours of Sunday, February 15, Deputy Kennedy found a body in a dumpster at the Santa Rita shopping mall. The body had no head, no hands and no feet. A few days later, however, a man walking his dog found a hand wrapped in a plastic shopping bag. He brought the hand to the sheriff's department, who in turn delivered it to Dr. Morgan Nelson, the county's forensic pathologist. Dr. Nelson forensically matched the hand to the torso from the dumpster. Next, he fingerprinted the hand, then matched those prints to prints on file belonging to Bradley Towne Jasen."

Another little pause. You were telling a story. Beginning, middle and end. Go too fast and you would lose them. Go too slow and they would doze off. At the defense table, Paul Bradley made a show of impatiently tapping a pencil on the legal pad in front of him. Kathryn ignored it; she knew his tactics. His specialty was distracting the jury, especially when someone else held center stage.

Among his other tricks were the brooding looks with the left hand to the lower lip, the puzzled frowns as he ran a hand through his receding thatch of black curly hair, the frequent sighs of affected exasperation and, while busily polishing his tortoiseshell-frame glasses, the expression of utter lack of interest. Today he was wearing an off-the-rack three-piece suit in navy blue, a light blue shirt with a button-down collar and a dark-blue tie with a single knot.

"With the body identified, detectives had a place to begin their investigation. Police questioned Margrit and Dieter. They claimed to know nothing. Detectives made inquiries about Margrit and her brother, beginning with family members. Among them was Margrit's young daughter Carla, who was interviewed at school. She told detectives that her father, Karl, had made her mother and her uncle Dieter leave their home after he found them together in her parents' bed.

"With a connection between Karl Riker and Bradley Jasen—and a possible motive—established, the police investigation focused on Karl. Detectives searched Department of Motor Vehicles records and discovered that around the time Bradley Jasen was reported missing, Karl had sold his Dodge station wagon. Detectives located the station wagon's new owner. Crime scene investigators using a laser light examined the inside of the station wagon; they found bloodstains on the liner at the rear of the wagon.

"The liner was pulled up, packaged and sent to the crime laboratory, along with tissue specimens collected from the torso of Bradley Jasen during the autopsy. Forensic scientists at the crime lab examined the bloodstains to see if there was a DNA match."

She wished she could take a drink of water, but she made no move toward the counsel table. It was a rule she never violated; once she began her opening statement, she did not leave the podium until it was finished. She wanted the jury's absolute attention on what she said, not what she did, especially when she was explaining some of the more complex aspects of investigation.

"Such examinations are based on the fact that each individual has a unique genetic pattern," she continued. "DNA—deoxyribonucleic acid—is the material found in the nucleus of body cells which contains that genetic pattern. Scientists are able to extract DNA patterns from blood, semen, hair or tissue. Patterns from blood or tissue for example, can then be compared to see if they match. You may have heard the process referred to as 'genetic fingerprinting.'"

She watched the jurors carefully; one or two of them nodded, as if in agreement. She had got the theory across; good.

"Scientists isolated and extracted DNA from the bloodstains and the tissue samples. The DNA extracted from the bloodstained liner matched the DNA extracted from the tissue of the torso, proving beyond doubt that it was Bradley Jasen's blood on the liner of Karl Riker's station wagon.

"Next, detectives got a warrant and searched Karl and his home. A detective saw blood on Karl's watchband so he seized it and sent it to the crime lab for testing. Scientists extracted DNA from the blood on the band and determined that it matched Bradley Jasen's DNA.

"When Karl Riker was arrested for the murder of Bradley Jasen and placed in custody, Margrit felt safe enough to come forward. She told detectives she was having an affair with Bradley that continued when she separated from her husband and moved into his guesthouse. Then when Dieter moved into the guesthouse, the three of them began a sexual relationship.

"Karl tracked her to Bradley's guesthouse, where he encountered Bradley. Margrit, who was inside, heard their raised angry voices. She feared Karl had learned that she was sexually involved with Bradley. Then she heard gunshots, followed by the sound of a vehicle pulling away. She never saw Bradley Jasen again."

One last pause. Had she taken too long? Had she given them enough? Too late to worry about that now. Tell them what you want, right up front.

"Ladies and gentlemen, in a moment I will sit down. The next time I'll speak directly to you will be in closing arguments. At that time I will ask you to find the defendant guilty of murder. Now the defendant's attorney, Mr. Bradley, has the opportunity to make his opening statement. Listen very carefully to what he tells you, but do not forget the facts you have just learned."

As she stepped away from the lectern she felt the release of her own tension. The jurors felt it too and relaxed visibly. She looked up at Judge Spencer, who glanced at the clock.

"It's ten forty-two," he announced. "We'll take a twenty minute recess at this point. Please be back here two minutes after eleven. Now, ladies and gentlemen of the jury, I am going to admonish you during this recess, and every recess that follows throughout this trial, not to discuss this matter among yourselves or with anyone else. And you will keep an open mind until you have heard all the evidence. Court will stand recessed."

The bailiff snapped "All rise!" and everyone stood as Spencer disappeared into his chambers in a swirl of black robe.

Kathryn sat down at the prosecution table and took a grateful gulp of the iced water Dave Granz had poured her from the thermos, glancing at the defense table, where Paul Bradley was whispering into his client's ear. Riker was watching Kathryn as he listened, his glistening button eyes unblinking. She wondered if Bradley was explaining her tactic to him.

She had told the jury that Bradley had an opportunity to speak to them next, if he wished to take it. She knew, however, that he preferred to reserve his opening statement until the beginning of the defense case. If he declined, it might set the jury wondering why he needed to wait.

"Well?" she said to Granz.

"Great opening," he said, automatically.

"That bad, huh?"

His lopsided grin looked as if he had to work to put it on. "Sorry," he said. "My mind was on something else."

"I hope the jury's wasn't."

"You were fine, really. We're going to put this asshole away, aren't we, Kathryn?"

"We'd better," she said, only half-joking.

Over the past few months, the DA's office had been taking a beating. Two important murder trials had ended in an acquittal and a hung jury. Although she had not tried either case, Kathryn knew her boss, district attorney Hal Benton, was looking to her to bring in a guilty verdict. He hadn't said anything, but the pressure was there all the same. It went with the job.

"I want this guy as badly as you do, Dave," she told him, "but there are no sure things in a trial. You know the saying."

"If you want a guarantee, buy a toaster, right?" He stood up. "I have to make a call."

Kathryn nodded. "Get back before the judge takes the bench if you can. You know how he bitches about late appearances."

"No problem . . ."

She turned around in her swivel chair so she was facing Eleanor Jasen, sitting in the front row of the spectator section, and smiled encouragingly at her. Having the victim's sister in court was another psychological weapon. The jury would come to know who she was. Her presence would be a constant reminder to them of the reason Karl Riker was on trial. And perhaps knowing Bradley Jasen's sister had come to terms with her brother's sexual practices would help the jury to do so as well.

She glanced at the clock. Court would reconvene in ten minutes. Her first witness would be Jerry Kennedy, the deputy who had found the body in the dumpster that rainy February night. He would set the scene for everything that followed.

To Kathryn Mackay this evidence, all the evidence, was like building blocks. She would place them carefully one atop another until they eventually formed an enclosure so strong, so high, that the defendant could never escape. She looked across at Riker and felt the rancor coming off him like heat off a stove.

She shrugged; that went with the job too.

2

"Going to be another hot one," Helen Corcoran observed as the children clambered noisily aboard the school bus. Kathryn Mackay watched as her daughter Emma found her usual seat next to Helen's daughter Julie. The doors shut with a hiss and the bus moved off. Kathryn waved and Emma wiggled her fingers goodbye. She's growing up, Kathryn thought. In her head she heard the words of an old song, "Sunrise, sunset."

"What was all that with the posters?" Helen said as they walked across to their cars.

"Emma's running for pet helper at school."

"She doesn't waste words. 'Pet Helper. Vote for me.'"

"She's very serious about it. She bought candy to hand out. Even wrote a speech."

"She's a winner," Helen said, smiling to take any sting out of the words. "Like her mother. Well, gotta run. Tennis game."

"Have fun," Kathryn said.

Helen was all ready to play, in a short white dress and white Reebok Tennis Pro shoes, her state-of-the-art Wilson racket on the back seat. She looked cool and elegant as she got into her white Mercedes 190. It must be nice sometimes to have no more to worry about than a game of tennis followed by lunch at the club, Kathryn thought. She tried to imagine herself doing it and smiled at the thought. Sorry I missed that one, partner, but I was up all night interviewing a rape victim.

County Communications had called at 3 A.M. A rape, the unemotional dispatcher told her. Victim Karen Esterhaus, nineteen, abducted from her Marina Beach Village apartment, taken to some nearby lot where she was raped and sodomized, then forced to orally copulate her assailant. She had been taken to County General for examination.

Road signs loomed like the credits in an old horror movie as Kathryn's little red Mazda sped through the thick mist coming in off the ocean. At this time of morning there was hardly anything moving on the highway. She took the Cabrillo Park exit and turned north toward County General. The hospital stood on the crest of a hill above Santa Rita.

DA's Inspector Michael Gaines was waiting for her in the lobby. He was in his mid-thirties, a husky six-footer with light brown hair and green eyes. He was wearing a light blue polo shirt, navy Dockers and Topsiders. He needed a shave and there were dark shadows beneath his eyes.

He stood up as she came in and Kathryn concealed a smile. Michael might be one of the newer breed that was coming into law enforcement these days, college educated, working on his master's, computer literate, but all that education hadn't quite eradicated the heritage of his Texas boyhood.

"How long have you been here?" she asked.

"About ten minutes. I checked upstairs. The SANE on duty is Marianne Dickens."

The acronym SANE translated as Sexual Assault Nurse Examiner. Marianne Dickens was a member of the Sexual Assault Response Team—SART—which was activated immediately a rape was reported. Kathryn had worked with her many times. Marianne was a pro, sympathetic without being gushy, supportive without being patronizing.

"How about the victim?"

Gaines shook his head. "She's just about holding herself together. I don't know how long it will last."

"You think maybe we could interview her while Marianne is doing the rape kit?"

"Be good if we could," Gaines said. They both knew the faster they could get a detailed description of the perp and the crime from the victim, the quicker the cops could identify and apprehend the suspect. Set against this was the need to place before everything else the victim's physical and emotional well-being.

"Let's go talk to Marianne," Kathryn said.

They took the elevator to the second floor. The corridors were silent, the rooms on each side dark. Overhead dome lights spilled circular pools of brightness on the shiny green composition floor. Gaines's rubber-soled shoes squeaked as they turned into the SANE office.

The nurse examiner was a small woman in her mid-forties with a round face and short hair. Under the white jacket, she wore a cotton ribbed sweater and houndstooth trousers. She met their eyes as they came in and then pointed with her chin at the young woman in the examination room.

Karen Esterhaus was sitting on a chair wearing a white hospital gown, a blanket draped around her slender shoulders. Her lips were swollen, her face a mass of bruises. Shame still burned in her dark, wet eyes. The bright fluorescent overhead lights made her look drawn and haggard.

"How is she?" Kathryn asked.

"She hasn't said much. I didn't push. She's in her sophomore year at the University. I gather her parents live in El Paso."

"Have they been told?"

Marianne shook her head. "She doesn't want them to know."

"Did she say why?"

Marianne shrugged. "Her father's a captain in the Army at Fort Bliss. I get the feeling she thinks he wouldn't be . . . understanding."

"Have you taken a history?"

Marianne nodded. She had already filled out a two-page medical report covering Karen's description of the rape. Next would come a medical-legal exam using the rape kit—a sexual assault victim evidence kit that would take between three and four hours to complete.

"Marianne, what about if I interview her while you're doing the exam?"

Marianne frowned. "I don't usually . . ."

"The faster we give the detectives something to work with, the faster they can catch this bast . . . the rapist. Mrs. Dickens," Gaines said urgently. "In four hours he could be in Nevada."

17

Marianne made an impatient sound. "I appreciate that, Inspector. But my first consideration must be for the victim."

"She needs something to hang on to, Mrs. Dickens," Gaines said. "Maybe we can give her that."

Marianne Dickens looked at him thoughtfully, as if she was seeing him for the first time, then nodded. "All right," she said. "We'll give it a try. But if I see any sign she's hurting, you're out."

"You call it, Marianne," Kathryn said. "Whatever you say, we'll do."

They went together into the examination room. As they came in, Kathryn smiled reassuringly; Karen Esterhaus didn't smile back. Her eyes were puffy and red from crying. She's just a kid, Kathryn thought. She looked uncertainly from Kathryn to Michael and then to Marianne Dickens.

"Karen, my name is Kathryn Mackay," Kathryn said. "I'm head of the Special Prosecutions Unit of the district attorney's office. This is Inspector Gaines from my office—a kind of detective—who has been assigned to your case."

"We know a terrible thing has happened to you, Karen," Michael said. "Probably the last thing you want to do right now is talk about it, but it's very important we get as much information about what happened as we can while everything is still fresh in your memory. You understand?"

Karen turned her head away, her face covered by the long dark hair. She extended one arm away from her body, the hand palm out, as if to ward off something only she could see. Kathryn gave Gaines a signal: stay with her. The big man gave an infinitesimal nod of assent; for a moment Kathryn thought she saw pain in his eyes. He's probably just tired, she thought. We all are. And getting pulled out at 3 in the morning didn't help.

"Is there anything you need, Karen?" Gaines said softly. "Anyone you would like me to contact?"

"I don't know," the young woman said. "I wish Art was here."

"Who's Art?"

"Arthur Olivas. He's my boyfriend."

Michael glanced at Kathryn; she shook her head imperceptibly. Boyfriends often took news like this very badly. She inclined her head to one side and Marianne Dickens followed her into the office, out of earshot of the young woman on the chair.

"How are we going to work this?" Marianne asked. "Doesn't your inspector need to hear what she says?"

"I thought, if we could set up some screens?" Kathryn offered. "Michael could sit on the other side, hear everything."

Marianne Dickens looked at Gaines thoughtfully through the office window. "Funny," she said, almost to herself, "you don't expect some big hunk of a cop to be so . . . gentle." She opened a wicker hamper and took out a folded white hospital gown. "Put this on and we'll go on in. I may have to move you around some while I'm working."

"Thanks, Marianne," Kathryn said. "I'll try not to get in your way."

They went back into the examination room and Kathryn helped Gaines wheel screens into a semi-circle around the examination table. Then he went around to the back. She heard a chair scrape.

"Can you hear okay, Michael?" Kathryn asked.

"Fine," he said. "Go ahead."

"Come on over here, Karen," Marianne told the young woman. "Just sit on the examination table. Kathryn is going to talk to you while I do your nails."

Karen frowned. "Do my nails?"

"I'm going to clip your nails." Marianne told her. "You may have scratched the man who attacked you. If you did there may be tiny fragments of his skin under your nails that can be used to identify him."

"Ugh," the young woman said, shivering.

"Lie down on the table, just relax. Make yourself comfortable."

As Karen lay back, Kathryn slid a chair beside the table on the opposite side to the one Marianne Dickens was working.

"I'm going to ask you quite a lot of questions, Karen," she said. "You may feel some of them are . . . invasive. But you mustn't feel embarrassed. You've done nothing wrong. What happened to you was not your fault."

"I know. It's just . . . oh, God, I hate all this."

"We all understand that," Kathryn said. "But if we are going to catch this man, we need to talk about it. Would that be okay?"

"No, I . . . I want to help." Karen Esterhaus's voice was hesitant, but determined. "To catch him. Yes."

"Karen," Marianne Dickens said softly. "I need to remove your gown. It will only be for a moment."

Karen looked at her and nodded. Marianne unfastened the ties of the hospital gown and laid it aside. In the cold overhead light the bruises on her body were a shocking blue-black against the pale tan of her skin.

Marianne Dickens handed Karen a pair of protective goggles.

"Put these on," she said. "You too, Kathryn." Donning a third pair herself, she picked up a squat device about the size of a cellphone.

"What's that?" Kathryn asked.

"Technology marches on," Marianne said. "This is an Omniprint 1000 scanner. Compared to this, using the old Woods lamp is like lighting a candle. Watch."

She flicked off the lights, then switched on the Omni. It gave off a low buzz and a bright, hard, blue light. She passed the scanner downwards slowly along Karen Esterhaus's body. The fluorescence turned her fine body hair a brilliant orange. The bruises on her chest, stomach and inner thighs appeared as bright irregular patches, oddly reminding Kathryn of the skin of burn victims she had seen.

"That's amazing," Kathryn said.

"Blue enhanced high-intensity metal vapor arc lamp, three hundred and fifty watts," Marianne said. "It'll show up hairs and fibers you'd have completely missed using a Woods lamp. Even fingerprints. Karen, I want you to lie on your stomach, please."

Karen Esterhaus moved as if something inside her was broken. A stifled sob escaped her lips as she turned over. As she had done so many times with so many victims, Kathryn tried to imagine the nightmare of the young woman's experience. No matter how many rape victims she interviewed, she never failed to be surprised by the mind's ability to swathe itself in a protective cocoon of non-reality during an attack, as if what was happening was being done to some unreal other self while the real self somehow stood aloof, unviolated.

"Doesn't look as if there are any external semen stains, or for that matter anything else we can use," Marianne remarked, interrupting Kathryn's reverie as she flicked on the lights and reached for swabs. Kathryn shrugged. The absence of semen meant little or nothing. Many rapists were sexually dysfunctional. Others failed to ejaculate, or wore a condom to preclude DNA typing.

"There," Marianne Dickens said. "How do you feel, Karen?"

"I'm all right," Karen said, turning over. "What happens next?"

"I need to check your mouth," the nurse said. "Like a dentist. Sit up and open wide, please."

Kathryn watched mutely as Marianne swabbed the area in and around the mouth, making notes on the clipboard beside the table as she worked. Next she started to prepare two dry mount slides.

"Karen, while the nurse is busy let's talk a little about what happened," Kathryn said. "You don't have to go into detail unless you want to. Just tell me in your own words anything you remember. Start at the beginning. How it happened, what you saw, what you heard, that sort of thing. We can go through it more fully later. Okay?"

It was a technique she used often, a way of giving the victim a little room to move around before they came face to face with the real trauma.

"I was asleep in my bedroom," Karen said, turning her head away. Her voice was a monotone, like someone talking in their sleep. "I woke up. I saw a shape. A man. He must have touched me."

"Did he say anything?"

"He . . . he put a knife against my throat. He told me not to make a sound or I was dead."

"Were those his exact words? 'Don't make a sound or you're dead'?"

"That's right."

"What happened then?"

"He told me to get up. He gagged me."

"Do you know what he used to gag you?"

"They found it . . . there. Where it happened. A towel. From my bathroom. I told all this to the deputy already."

"I know. We have to go through it with you as well. Just to make sure nothing gets missed."

"I wish I didn't have to do . . . all this." She made a gesture that encompassed the examination room and everything about it. She drew in a long, quavering breath. "He told me to get up, walk. He said, 'Don't try to run, I'll be right behind you. Try to get away and I'll kill you.'"

"What were you wearing?"

She was wearing a cotton nightgown. Although it was a warm night, she was shivering uncontrollably. He made her walk barefoot across the parking lot into the scrub bordering it on the far side. Sharp stones cut her feet but she was afraid to cry out.

"He told me to lie down and take off my nightgown. Then he . . . started doing it. Like I was . . . an animal. But I was too frightened to make a noise. Then he stopped. He said, 'Am I hurting you?'"

"He asked you in those words?"

Karen nodded. "I said, 'No, it's all right' and it . . . he went mad. He hit me and hit me . . . Oh, God, Oh, God, Oh, God!" She buried her face in her hands and

23

sobbed. Kathryn felt a touch on her shoulder; it was Marianne Dickens. They stepped to one side, out of earshot.

"I think she needs a break, Kathryn," she said. "Before I . . ." She gestured at the instrument tray.

"Of course," Kathryn replied. "Shall I . . . ?"

"No, stay. She may be glad to have you here." She took some tissues from a box, went over and handed them to Karen. "That's it, Karen," she said softly. "That's the girl. Come on now. Dry your eyes. We need you to help us."

Karen Esterhaus blew her nose and combed her hair away from her face with her fingers. "It's okay," she said. "I'm okay now."

"Good," Marianne said. "Good. Now then, let's get you ready for your examination, shall we?"

Kathryn saw the look in Karen's eyes as she glanced at the stirrups and the instruments on the tray. She yearned to reassure the young woman, but there was nothing anyone could do or say that would make what was going to happen next pleasant. Karen lifted her legs wide apart and fitted them into the stirrups.

"Ms. Mackay," Karen said, her voice not much more than a whisper. "Kathryn?"

"What is it, Karen?"

"Could you please . . . would you mind holding my hand?"

Kathryn slid her chair closer to the table and took the young woman's hand in her own. It was cold. She wanted to say something comforting, but she couldn't think of the right words.

"I'm here," she said and hoped it would be enough. She watched silently as Marianne closely examined the young woman's genitalia for injury and then briefly switched off the lights again to scan with the Omni lamp. Using tweezers, she collected fragments of leaves and dirt, dropping her findings in separate envelopes labelled with the source. She cut away some of the matted pubic hair before slipping a paper sheet under Karen's buttocks and combing the remaining hairs with a one-time comb, depositing Karen's loose hairs into another paper envelope.

"What's that?" Karen said apprehensively, as the nurse moved a piece of equipment nearer to the bed.

"It's called a colposcope," Marianne replied. "It's basically a binocular microscope on an adjustable stand with a light source used to magnify and photograph the walls of the vagina."

"You're going to put that . . . inside me?"

"It won't hurt," Marianne said, squeezing Karen's hand. "I promise."

"Try to relax, Karen," Kathryn said quietly. "Just let yourself go limp."

"I . . . I'm trying," Karen said.

As the nurse did what she had to do, Karen Esterhaus lay silent, tense against the alien intrusion, staring unblinkingly at the huge circular overhead light as the shutter of the colposcopic 35mm camera made its almost imperceptible sound.

No matter how much you recognized the necessity, Kathryn thought, it was another kind of rape. But it had to be done, even when you felt, as Kathryn often did, that the law demanded far too much from the victim and nothing like enough from the perpetrator.

She looked at Marianne and raised her eyebrows. The nurse nodded confirmation; they still had a lot to do. Fifteen to twenty samples of head and pubic hair would be taken as controls: they had to be plucked, not cut. Samples of blood would be drawn for tox screening and blood typing.

Kathryn sighed. It was going to be a long night for Karen Esterhaus. For all of them.

Her reverie dissolved as the car phone made its distinctive sound. Can't it wait? she thought irritably.

"Kathryn?" It was Michael. "Sheriff's Office just made an arrest in the Karen Esterhaus rape." She could almost see the triumphant expression on his face.

"That was fast."

"She gave us some pretty good info to follow up on," Michael said. "SO checked known sexual offenders through the Department of Justice Command Center and came up with some possibles residing in Santa Rita. At the same time we ran the partial license number she gave us through the DMV computer in Sacramento to see if we could come up with a Dodge Dart—there aren't that many of them out there any more. We got one registered to a guy named John Paul Bitzer. He was one of the possibles on the DOJ printout. So SO picked him up."

Bitzer, he reported, was a twenty-eight year old from the Liberty area south of Santa Rita who had a history of sexual assaults.

"Where is he now?"

"In the SO interview room."

"Meet me there in ten minutes," Kathryn said.

26

3

Ten minutes after she took the call from Michael, Kathryn parked in her numbered space in front of the County Building in downtown Santa Rita. County, as everyone called it, was an uncompromising hulk of gray concrete that looked more like a nuclear command bunker than a government center. Five stories high, it stood between Pacific Street and a children's playground flanking the river that Kathryn could see from her office window. She took the stairs to the third floor and turned right into the Sheriff's Office. The clerk at the counter saw her coming and buzzed her in. A couple of detectives leaning over a desk looking at some crime scene photographs said hello as she hurried past. Gaines was standing outside the door of the interview room. He was still dressed in the same shirt and pants.

"Jeez, Michael, you look even worse than I feel," she said. "Didn't you get home at all?"

He rubbed his stubbled chin and made a wry face. "I needed to do some things," he said, without elaborating.

She looked over his shoulder toward the suspect interview room. The cops called it Hell's waiting room. It was a windowless box with a table bolted to the linoleum floor and sheetrocked walls covered with scratched graffiti. *JHT was here. Suck my dick pig.* The suspect was sitting slouched over one of the scarred tables smoking a cigarette. He looked older than twenty-eight, with thinning sandy hair and dark, resentful eyes beneath jutting brows. He had on a dirty white T-shirt and faded jeans. The detective interviewing him was Harry diStefano. Short, balding, overweight, he looked more like a TV cop than most TV cops did.

"What's happening inside?" she asked.

"They read him his rights. Shit, he knows them better than they do. He refused to waive. Just sat there saying 'I don't want to talk.'"

"We'll need to schedule a lineup," Kathryn told him. "Better get him a PD." Following the arrest of a suspect, the DA's office had forty-eight hours to file charges; Kathryn's first priority was to contact a municipal court judge to request the judge to appoint a public defender to represent him at the lineup.

"Already done," Michael told her.

"You doing my job as well as your own?" Kathryn said.

Gaines managed a tired grin. "I just used your name. Strong men wilted."

"What about the PD?"

"Ernie Oppicelli's been appointed. The lineup's set for two-thirty this afternoon by the way."

Ernie Oppicelli was a partner in the law firm of Burke, Hansen, Oppicelli and Slade. They handled most of the County's public defender work on a contract basis.

"You've notified Karen Esterhaus?"

"I'm picking her up from the hospital at two."

"Think she's going to be all right?"

Michael lifted a shoulder in what might have been a shrug. Maybe, maybe not, Kathryn thought. She knew, and Michael knew, that the trauma of rape affected every victim differently. A woman who had been cooperative and expressive in the course of one interview could become anxious and guarded in the next. A woman who had declared herself determined to name and face her rapist could suddenly become anguished and panic-stricken when faced with doing it.

"It's still early," Kathryn said. "You need a shower, a shave, some clean clothes. Why don't you take off, get some sleep and come back for the lineup?"

"Look, I want to stay on this, okay?"

The anger in his voice was totally unexpected. For no particular reason Kathryn remembered the moment at the hospital when she had seen what she had thought was pain in his eyes. It was hard to contain the emotions a rape victim's injuries could arouse in you. Maybe it was that. She held up her hands in the surrender position. "Okay, Michael, okay."

"Oh, shit," he said wearily. "I'm sorry, Kathryn. It's just . . . it's like things are coming at me from every angle. You know how it is."

"Sure," she said. "I know how it is."

They said if you worked in law enforcement it only came at you two ways: lousy or rotten. Cops like Gaines saw more tragedy in one day than a lot of people saw in a lifetime. You could care too much. Or not enough. Some cops grew cynical, authoritarian and emotionally withdrawn—the "John Wayne syndrome," they called it. Others became so calloused by what they did that the sight of a dead body or a raped child meant less to them than what to have in their lunch-time sandwich. Many—far too many—just burned out.

"Maybe we'll get an ID," she said, trying to lighten his mood.

"Yeah," he said glumly. "And maybe it'll snow."

It was as if every summer the hot weather somehow escalated the crime rate to new heights. Not only were Lt. Walt Earheart and the detectives of the Sheriff's Office buried, but the sheer volume of crime had doubled the workload of every prosecutor in the DA's office, most notably its senior trial attorney—Kathryn. At times like this you forgot you had a private life.

"I've been meaning to ask you, how's Jenny?" she asked. Jenny Frazer was Michael's fiancée, a good-looking, long-legged blonde with a sunny personality.

"Good," Gaines replied absently. "Fine, fine."

Michael and Jenny had announced their engagement the preceding Easter, but the wedding plans seemed to have gone on hold; something to do with her studies, Kathryn had gathered.

"We ought to get together," Kathryn said. "How about if Emma and I cooked dinner one night? Maybe Dave could join us."

Michael walked over to the window and looked out at the street below. "I'll talk to Jenny soon as I get a chance," he said without turning around. "Let me get back to you, okay?"

"Okay. Are you sure you don't want to take off?"

"I'll survive," he said and moved his shoulder again in that typical manner he had. "Look, there's no point both of us hanging around here. I'll let you know if they get anything from the suspect exam. Otherwise, see you at the lineup, okay?"

She hesitated. "You sure you're okay, Michael?"

"Sure," he said and forced a grin. "Only, hey, Kathryn? You ever wish you were in some other line of work?"

She smiled, recalling her own thoughts about Helen Corcoran.

"Sure," she said. "Every time I get called out in the middle of the night."

She walked down the stairs to her office, stifling a yawn. Once there, she switched on her computer. While it booted up, she made some tea and glanced quickly at the local paper. The details of last night's rape were briefly covered. A familiar three-two tap on her half-closed door made her look up. Only one person knocked that way.

"Hi, Dave," she said. Today Granz wore a cream-colored shirt and a dark-brown jacket, tan pants and tan loafers.

"Well, well," Kathryn said, measuring out the words.

Dave smiled self-consciously and ran a hand through his beach-bum mop of blond hair. "Aren't you the one who always used to tell me I should take more interest in how I look?" he parried. There was something more than the words in his eyes; she decided to ignore it. The past was the past.

"What happened, your rich aunt die?"

"Overtime," he said. He picked up one of the photographs on Kathryn's desk. "How's Emma?"

"Smarter every day. And tougher to ride herd on."

"I haven't seen her for ages. When was this taken?"

"Last month," Kathryn told him. "A friend of mine

got married. Emma was a flower girl. Is that what you came in here for, to ask about Emma?"

He looked uncomfortable. "You see Gaines upstairs?"

"What about him?"

"Come on, Kathryn, you must have noticed. He looks like shit."

"So do I. We had a rough night, Dave."

"Not just this morning. All the time."

"He's bushed, Dave. Under pressure. Everybody is."

"I like the guy. I don't like to see him beat to shit."

"I thought you two were friends. If you think he's got a problem, why don't you ask him yourself?"

Dave was silent for a moment, as if he wanted to say more, but when he spoke it was about something else. "I heard SO made an arrest in that rape case you were out on last night."

The Sheriff's Office was always Dave's first stop in the morning. He kept tabs on everything, not just the cases he was assigned to but whatever murder or rape was breaking. A DA's inspector walked a sort of line: his job was to assist and support the SO detectives, without ever making them feel he was telling them what to do or how to do it. Nobody was better at that than Dave.

"Bitzer, yes. He looks good for it."

"Good job. That bastard needs taking off the streets."

"I'm putting him in a lineup at two-thirty," Kathryn said. "Want to come hold my hand?"

He smiled. The scars on his face and neck, put there by a serial killer they called the "Gingerbread Man," were almost invisible now; because of them, his smile had become even more lopsided than it was before. It wasn't unattractive; unexpected, maybe.

"You don't need anyone to hold your hand," he said.

"Sometimes I do," she said. "Sometimes everyone does."

For some reason the unhappiness she thought she had seen in Michael Gaines's eyes came back to her.

"You'll be fine," he said. "You always are. Kathryn, listen, I have to go."

"Anything else happening up in SO I ought to know about?" Kate asked as Dave reached for the door to leave.

"Do you remember a guy named Piselli?" he said. "Francis Norman Piselli?"

Kathryn frowned. "Piselli, Piselli. Why do I know that name?"

"Gaines arrested him about three months ago for rape. He had cocaine on him when he got busted."

Pulling the file in her memory, Kathryn recalled that Piselli had "worked off" the cocaine charge with BNE, the Bureau of Narcotic Enforcement, and without a positive identification by the victim, the rape charges against him were never filed. "I remember. What about him?"

"He was found dead. Electrocuted."

Kathryn frowned. "So?"

"Doctor Death has some concerns."

"Dammit, Dave."

Granz ducked and held up an arm as if to ward off a blow. "Sorry. It just slipped out."

Dr. Morgan Nelson was the forensic pathologist

employed by the County as its coroner. Some years ago, one of the local newspapers had dubbed him "Doctor Death" and it had stuck. "Forgetting" how much Kathryn disliked the nickname—Morgan was one of her closest friends—was one of Dave's little games, a way of letting her know he felt he still had an interest in her affections.

"All right," Kathryn prompted. "Morgan is concerned because?"

"He thinks it could be an autoerotic accident."

Simply put, an autoerotic accident was a death that occurred during masturbation. The problem with them was, more often than not they were actually suicides or even homicides.

"Who called it in?"

"Some old guy who lives in the same building with him hasn't seen Piselli for a few days, he gets worried and gets the manager to open up the apartment. Whoof, the smell nearly knocks them down. Piselli is lying on the floor up against a radiator. He's wearing briefs and an undershirt and socks. Now get this: he's got an electric floor buffer between his legs. And it's still turning."

"An electric *floor* buffer?"

"It looked pretty straightforward. The guy is fixing the buffer, holding it between his legs to steady it, only he doesn't know it's got a faulty plug, no ground prong. He switches on, zap. Then when Doc got there he noticed that the switch on the buffer was held in the 'on' position with tape, there's ejaculate on the briefs. Doc figures what happened was, while he was enjoying himself, Piselli touched the radiator with his bare shoulder and made a circuit."

"You're telling me all this for a reason. I imagine."

"Yeah. Doc's setting up an autopsy. Just to be on the safe side. He wants us to sit in."

"When?"

"He thought maybe Thursday night. You know Doc, he loves to work while the world sleeps."

"Tell him if he makes it before midnight, okay. We're in trial and I need my sleep."

"You got it."

"I wonder if Michael knows," Kathryn mused aloud.

"About Piselli? Sure. He said if he had his way, he'd cut the bastard up and use the bits for rat poison."

"That's pretty rough," she said. "Even for you guys."

"He's got a hard edge on him these days," Dave agreed. He got up out of the leather chair and left. As the door closed behind him, Kathryn looked up at the clock again, pushing the matter of Piselli's death out of her mind for the moment and concentrating on the police reports in front of her. Next time she looked up at the clock it was time to get ready.

No matter how many times she organized them, she still experienced the same unsettling unease preceding lineups. What you were hoping was that it would go smoothly: the victim would walk in, look through the window and unhesitatingly identify the suspect. What made you uneasy was the knowledge that sometimes witnesses got frightened, or became unsure of themselves, or were intimidated by the atmosphere. There was a big difference between a traumatized victim's confused recollection of the suspect while he was attacking her and seeing him with five other clones in prison garb beneath the harsh, bright lights.

Well, no use borrowing trouble; you could only do what you could do. She drew in a deep breath and let it out. She put Michael's interview notes with Karen Esterhaus into her briefcase and checked her make-up in the mirror behind her door.

It had to be just right; too much overpowered the face. The idea was to look natural—just a touch of color on the eyes and cheeks. Today she was wearing a double-breasted blazer, a mid-length gabardine skirt and a white silk shirt. She wasn't into power dressing, but how she looked was an integral part of the role she played. Justice might be blind, but nobody else was.

4

"I don't believe it," Dave said. "He walked?"

"Right out the door. Laughing at us, the bastard."

They were in Kathryn's condo at Seaview Heights overlooking Shelter Island. The balcony door was open and a soft, warm breeze moved the drapes. Dave put down his wine glass, went over to the window and stood looking out at the ocean. The sun was down now and dark purple shadows were creeping across the water.

"Jeez," he said. "You must feel like shit."

"That's one way of putting it."

"You want to tell me what happened?"

"Nothing much to tell," Kathryn said. Lineups were always the same: routine, time-consuming, but unpredictable. Bitzer's had been par for the course.

Michael Gaines drove Karen Esterhaus in from County General and brought her to the viewing area, a small, cramped, airless room in the jail building.

"Hello, Karen," Kathryn said. "Thank you for coming in. How are you feeling?"

"I'm all right," Karen said. She looked wan and tense; the bruises on her face were stark against the pale skin. Her voice was very controlled. Kathryn recognized the signs; she had seen them many times before. Karen Esterhaus was frightened. But why? Was it the lineup? Or something else?

"We'll try and make this as easy for you as possible," Kathryn told her. "Just relax and don't be afraid." She tried to make the words reassuring but she was only too aware how empty they sounded.

"Karen's read the witness instructions," Michael told Kathryn, handing her the signed document. "She understands what's going to happen."

Everything was ready. Prior to Karen's arrival Harry diStefano, the SO detective, read Bitzer the standard lineup admonition advising him of his rights. After Bitzer signed it, the lineup participants were photographed individually and as a group. Each was assigned his position by random selection, then led into the viewing room to await the arrival of the witness.

"This way," Kathryn said gently.

The young woman looked around apprehensively as she entered the viewing area. It wasn't much bigger than a walk-in closet, featureless except for the drawn drapes on one wall. Two men stood waiting inside. Kathryn moved to one side as Michael introduced them.

"Karen, this is Mr. Oppicelli," he told her. "He's a public defender appointed by the court. The other gentleman is Mr. Segrist, an investigator with his law firm."

Oppicelli nodded expressionlessly. He was a short man, slightly overweight, dressed in a creased cream linen jacket and tan slacks, carrying a leather brief-case. The thin, horse-faced man standing beside him blinked like a lizard.

"We ready to begin here?" Oppicelli asked. His voice was brusque. Kathryn just looked at him.

"I'll let you know when we're ready," she said.

She took her position facing the curtains, placing Karen Esterhaus on her left. Michael Gaines moved to the other side. Kathryn pulled the drawstring; the curtains parted and light flooded in through the one-way glass. Six men in orange prison jumpsuits were seated shoulder to shoulder on a bench in front of them. Kathryn heard Karen draw in her breath sharply.

"They can't see us, Karen," she said. "It's a one-way mirror."

Karen nodded, her eyes fixed on the scene before her. With the exception of Bitzer, who held the card with number three on it, all were inmates of the county jail, selected because of a general physical resemblance to the suspect. Scrupulous care was taken to ensure that each was dressed identically, right down to socks and footwear. Even their plastic ID bands were checked to ensure no one had his on a different wrist from the others. Each man held a card at chest level with a number on it: one through six. Detective Harry diStefano sat on a stool to their right, wearing his usual expression of terminal boredom.

"Number one, move forward," he intoned. The man wearing the number one card stood up and stepped forward. He stared straight ahead, shifting from foot to foot.

"Turn," the detective droned. The man shuffled around to his right so his left profile was displayed. After a suitable interval, the detective told him to face right again so his back was turned to the viewers, and then once more to display the right profile. The procedure was repeated identically with each of the men in the lineup. *Turn, turn, turn, turn. Turn, turn, turn, turn.* Kathryn glanced at Karen Esterhaus; she appeared to be staring intently at one of the men. But which one? Which one?

When the lineup was completed the men remained seated on the bench staring at nothing. They would remain there until CSI photographed them exactly as viewed by the witness. Kathryn drew the drapes to close out the scene.

"Okay, let me just refresh your memory, Karen," Michael said. Kathryn marveled at how gentle his voice was. He had a wonderful instinct for each victim he worked with. "You have the witness form. Everything you need to know is on it. If you can identify someone in this lineup, put a circle around that person's number on the form. You're not obligated to select or identify anyone from the lineup if you cannot do so. Any questions?"

Karen made a small movement of her head that could have meant either yes or no, then turned away from the one-way window.

"Could I talk to you for a moment, Michael?" she said. Her voice was almost inaudible. "In private, please?"

Oppicelli and his investigator were listening alertly. Michael looked at Kathryn and frowned. She gave a small shrug and opened the door leading into the corridor outside the viewing area.

"What's the matter, Karen?" Michael said softly. "Is something wrong?"

"That bastard," Karen said. Her voice was thin and tense. "Number three. The one who . . . raped me."

"Are you identifying number three as the man who raped you?" Michael said.

Karen shook her head. "I want to know something first," she said. "I want you to tell me now, Inspector. If I do—if I say it was him—will you protect me?"

"If you identify him, we'll do our best to make sure he goes to prison for a long time," Michael promised her.

"That wasn't the question. If I identify him, can you guarantee my safety? Yes or no?"

"What's happened, Karen?" Michael said. "Why are you worried about your safety?"

"You don't know," she said. "You don't know what he did."

"I want to help you. Tell me."

"That . . . animal. He called me. He called me on the telephone at the hospital. Collect." Her laugh was bitter. "He told them he was my boyfriend, so they put him through. How is he able to do that? How can you allow that to happen?"

"Karen, we didn't know—" Kathryn began.

"Bitzer called you?" Michael asked sharply, interrupting her. "Why didn't you tell me this before? What did he say?"

"He said, 'I know where you live. I know where you work. I know everything about you. If you identify me I'll come back and get you. And . . . next time . . . next time, I'll really . . . I'll really . . .'" Her voice broke and tears filled her eyes. She shook her head helplessly. "He beat me and he raped me and he . . . you . . . you let him say things like that to me?"

"He's threatening you because he's afraid, Karen," Kathryn said. "Don't let him scare you."

"That's easy for you to say," Karen replied, her voice bitter. "But what about me?"

She turned to Michael. He looked at Kathryn helplessly. Karen saw the look and her expression altered. "Don't bother to answer," she said. "I can see it in your eyes."

"Karen, we can't guarantee your safety indefinitely," Kathryn said. "Nobody could. It just isn't possible."

"Can't, won't, what's the difference?" Karen said harshly. "What you're telling me is, this . . . this filth can come back and rape me again, tomorrow, next week, next year, whenever he wants—and there's nothing you can do about it, right? And after he's through with me, you'll tell me the same things all over again. How sorry you are. How much you sympathize."

"Karen, when we convict him—and I promise you

I will do everything in my power to see that he gets convicted and goes to prison—I can't get him sent away for the rest of his life," Kathryn said. "There isn't anything law enforcement can do to insure he never comes out of prison."

"Law enforcement," Karen said bitterly. "That's a good one. Law enforcement hasn't helped me much, has it?"

"Unless you identify the man who raped you, there's no way we can," Kathryn said.

"I'm not going through with it," Karen said abruptly.

"Karen, please, don't be hasty—"

"No!" There was a touch of hysteria in the young woman's refusal. "No more! Just tell me what I have to do to get out of here."

"Karen, please don't do this," Michael said. "You're making a mistake."

"No," Karen said and there was anger in her voice now. "I already did that. My mistake was trusting you people. I won't make it again."

Dave went over to the refrigerator, took out the bottle of wine and poured himself another glass. "Doesn't she realize that if he's on the street she's just as much at risk as if she'd ID'd him?"

"Michael tried to explain that to her. But she wouldn't listen. She said if we couldn't protect her, she wasn't going to cooperate. And damn it, Dave, I couldn't disagree with her. Sometimes the system just doesn't work."

"Sometimes it doesn't," Dave said. "But you can't blame yourself for that."

"You should have seen Michael," Kathryn said. "You know how he is. He knew he had the bastard. And then to watch him walk."

"Look, it happens," Dave said. "He'll be mad as hell for a while. But it'll pass."

"He's so like me . . . and you, Dave, he just hates to lose."

"But lose he will from time to time, Kathryn. We can't win 'em all. No matter how bad we want to."

"I suppose so," she said wearily. "Sometimes I just get so tired."

"Hey," he said, putting an arm around her shoulders. "This isn't like you."

"I'll be all right," she said. "Thanks, Dave. I'm glad you stopped by."

He went over to the sink, rinsed out his glass and stood it on the drainer. He picked up the jacket he had slung over the back of the sofa and went to the door, turning to lift her chin with his forefinger so he could kiss her good-night the way he used to do. To Kathryn's surprise she found herself responding. The kiss went on for what seemed like a long time.

"You want me to stay?" he said softly. Just for a moment she wanted to say yes, to let go, let it all go, let someone else make the decisions.

She pushed him away. "No," she said. "We tried that once before, if you remember."

"I remember."

"It didn't work then and it won't work now," she said. "Get out of here, Granz."

"Ah, the DA's back in control," he said. "For a moment there I thought you were someone I used to know."

She touched his scarred face with her hand and smiled. "You're one of the nicest men I know, Dave," she said softly. "I admire you and I'm very fond of you. And I think I'd like to keep it that way."

He nodded. "You could change your mind."

"True," she replied. "But not tonight."

After he was gone she threw off her clothes and rolled into bed, but sleep refused to come. Although he didn't know it, Dave had touched an exposed nerve. One of the things she worried about constantly was that there was so little inside her that was soft any more, so little that was feminine. The longer she played the hard-edged role of prosecutor, the tougher it became to turn it off and on. She lay there for a long time, staring out of the window at the stars and wondering if maybe she had forgotten how to be in love.

5

On the fourth day of the trial Kathryn called Dr. Morgan Nelson to the stand. She watched him swear to tell the truth, trying to see him not as one of her favorite people, but as the jury would, middle fifties, tall, cropped gingery hair, dressed in a white Oxford shirt, dark-gray sports coat, charcoal slacks and suede shoes. She smiled as she walked across to face him in the witness stand.

"Please state your name and spell your last name for the court reporter."

"Morgan Nelson. N-e-l-s-o-n."

"What is your occupation?"

"Forensic pathologist for the Sheriff/Coroner of Santa Rita County."

"Dr. Nelson, please describe to the jury your education, training and experience which qualify you to be a forensic pathologist."

"I have a doctorate in Medicine. I completed a two-year rotating internship. I did six years' post-graduate training in pathology. I am Board Certified in anatomical forensic pathology."

"Doctor, could you back up for a moment and explain to the jury exactly what forensic pathology is?"

"Of course. Forensic pathology entails interfacing with law enforcement agencies in assessing trauma and conducting autopsies."

"How many autopsies have you conducted, Doctor?"

"Over seven thousand."

"Have you qualified as an expert witness in forensic pathology in courts throughout the State of California?"

"Yes, several hundred times."

The performance she and Morgan Nelson had just given was exactly that, a performance. They had done it a hundred times or more; to them, it was almost routine, but the jury was seeing Nelson for the first time and they had to be made aware of the range and depth of his experience. She had learned that from Morgan a long time ago.

"People ask me what I do, and I say, 'I'm a pathologist, I work for the county.' And they say, 'Oh, you mean like a coroner?' Now you and I know a coroner is a politician who probably has as much appreciation of forensic pathology as an orangutan, but the jury doesn't. So it's up to you to explain the difference."

"Dr. Nelson, were you notified of a body located in a dumpster at the Linda Vista Mall on February 15 of this year?"

"Yes, at approximately five A.M. on that day I met with detectives at the service area to the rear of the stores. Sprawled on garbage bags inside a dumpster was a headless torso of a man. It looked as though it had been thrown into the dumpster in a heavy duty plastic garbage bag that had been torn open by whatever animals had got in there."

"Did you examine the torso?"

"Yes, I did."

"Where did you conduct the examination, Doctor?"

"I conducted a preliminary examination at the scene, before the body was removed. I conducted a more extensive examination of the body after it was received at the county medical facility."

"Doctor, why did you conduct an examination at the scene where the body was found? Wouldn't it have been better to wait until you were at the medical facility where you have better equipment and working conditions?"

She knew perfectly well why an examination was

made at the scene, but she wanted the jury to hear it from Nelson.

"It's standard procedure, Ms. Mackay. You see, there are certain factors and information detectable at the death scene which will be changed or lost altogether as a result of moving the body."

"Can you be more specific?"

"Certainly. It is often vital to an investigation that the approximate time of death be established. The critical factors in determining time of death are algor mortis; livor mortis; and rigor mortis. Temperature of the body is a primary determinant in the development of these three conditions. Lividity was fully advanced and rigor mortis was diminishing but still present. Body temperature, determined by use of a rectal thermometer, was fifty-one degrees."

"Can you explain this in terms we can understand, Doctor?"

"As I said, I took the temperature of the body at the scene using a rectal thermometer and found the body temperature to be fifty-one degrees. The ambient temperature—the air temperature, if you will—at that time was slightly over sixty degrees. Since we know that an inert object such as a dead body can't cool to a temperature lower than the surrounding air temperature, I knew the body had been there at least during one night when the air would have been colder.

"Lividity is the tendency for the blood to settle at the lowest part of a body, after death, due to gravity. If we know the temperature of the body and the environmental temperature, we can estimate very closely the length of time it takes for this phenomenon to occur.

"Rigor mortis is the temporary stiffening of the muscles after death, followed by a relaxation of the muscles after a period of time. The body was left naked in the open where body heat would dissipate rapidly. Cold retards the onset, and especially the departure, of rigor mortis. Again, by knowing the ambient temperature and that of the body we can determine the length of time that has passed since death occurred."

"And do you always conduct an examination at the death scene?" Kathryn said.

"Almost always. Moving the body to a warm environment in a heated building such as the morgue would alter the temperature patterns and make our measurements much less accurate."

"So, based on your examination at the scene, did you make a determination as to the approximate time of death?"

"Yes. In my opinion the post mortem interval was approximately forty-eight hours."

"You said you conducted a further examination at the medical facility after the body was removed. Would that be the autopsy?"

"Yes, I conducted an autopsy to determine the cause of death."

"Did you determine cause of death and if so, what was it?"

"The cause of death was left hemothorax, which is a collection of blood in the left chest cavity, due to multiple gunshot wounds. One shot punctured the left ventricle of the heart and one severed the aorta. Either wound would have been fatal."

"Did you determine a contributory cause of death?"

"Yes, decapitation of the head and dismemberment of the hands and feet."

"Let me stop you for a moment, Doctor. Did you take, or cause to have taken, photographs during the autopsy to illustrate your . . . ?"

Bradley was on his feet before she had finished her question, but Judge Spencer forestalled his objection with a raised hand. "Approach," he said.

Kathryn and Bradley approached the bench as the judge turned off his microphone and nodded at Bradley, proceed.

"The autopsy photos are cumulative of the testimony of the pathologist and any probative value is outweighed by their prejudicial impact," Bradley stated, keeping his voice down so the jury could not hear.

"Mr. Bradley, the prosecution is not obliged to prove the details of the homicide solely from the testimony of its witnesses," the judge whispered. "The jury is entitled to see how the physical details of the body support her theory. Murder is seldom pretty and photographs in murder cases are almost always unpleasant. Objection overruled. Step back."

Kathryn returned to her position in front of the witness box, where Morgan Nelson sat patiently, hands clasped in front of him. "You may answer the question, Dr. Nelson," she said.

"Yes, people's exhibits 14 through 16 show the head having been removed by cutting through the soft tissue and intervertebral discs. People's exhibits 17 through 20 show how the feet have been disarticulated at the ankle joint. People's exhibits 21 through 25 show the hands having been disarticulated at the wrist joint."

"Doctor, what kind of cutting instrument was used to decapitate and dismember the body?"

"The decapitation and dismemberment were accomplished with a very sharp instrument in an almost professional manner; there was very little gashing of the flesh, and no broken bones."

Kathryn looked first at the jury, and then at Dr. Nelson with raised eyebrows. "Doctor, I'm a little confused. You said the decapitation and dismemberment were done *professionally*. Are you telling us that it was a physician who severed the head, hands and feet?"

One of Kathryn's favorite examination techniques was to feign puzzlement to elicit further explanation from the witness. In this case she knew exactly what Nelson meant, but she wanted the jurors to think she was as confused as they were.

"No, that's not what I mean at all. Let me demonstrate."

He raised his left arm for the jury to see and rotated the left fist to emphasize how the wrist joint works. "Anyone with medical training—a physician, nurse, dentist, or a veterinarian—knows exactly how the joint works and exactly where to insert a cutting tool between the rounded bones of the joint, here, so as cleanly to sever the connecting ligament and disarticulate the joint with virtually no damage to the surrounding tissue."

Nelson had been through this routine many times. He was careful to look at Kathryn during his testimony so it didn't appear he was "playing to" the jury.

"I said the decapitation and dismemberment were accomplished in an *almost professional* manner," he continued, "without *extensive damage* to the surrounding tissue. However, there was more damage than I would expect to see if the incisions had been made by a medical professional with extensive anatomical knowledge. There were gashes in the tissue around the disarticulated joints and a number of small but distinct cuts and chips in the bones of the joints. Nevertheless, the manner in which the dismemberment was performed indicates, in my opinion, a degree of anatomical knowledge far superior to that possessed by the average person."

"Doctor, would an experienced butcher have sufficient anatomical knowledge to have decapitated and dismembered the body in the manner which you have described?"

"Objection." Bradley jumped to his feet. "Lack of foundation."

"I'll rephrase," Kathryn said smoothly. "Margrit Riker testified previously that her husband Karl worked as a butcher in Germany before immigrating to the United States. Are the articulated joints of other animals, such as cows, pigs and sheep significantly different from the joints of a human?"

"No, they work almost identically. In fact, in medical school most anatomical work is performed on exactly those animals."

"In your opinion, Doctor, who—other than a medical practitioner—might possess sufficient anatomical knowledge of cows, pigs, sheep . . ." Kathryn paused for effect ". . . and human beings, to be able to decapitate and dismember a body, without extensive damage, consistent with the manner in which this victim's body was decapitated and dismembered?"

Bradley jumped to his feet again. "Same objection, Your Honor," he snapped, his tone attempting to convey to the jury his frustration at liberties he wished them to believe Kathryn was taking.

"May we approach, Your Honor?" Kathryn wanted to argue for allowing this crucial testimony without the jury hearing it. She couldn't afford to let this line of questioning go unanswered.

"There is no need for that, Ms. Mackay. I'm prepared to rule on counsel's objection."

Judge Spencer tolerated no unnecessary delays in his court.

"Your Honor, counsel *must* approach." Kathryn strode toward the bench. Whenever a judge appeared ready to deny her request to approach the bench and to sustain the defense objection, Kathryn used this tactic to force the judge to hear her argument.

Bradley beat her to the bench. He was all too aware of Kathryn's reputation for aggressive edge-of-the-envelope prosecutorial tactics. "This is ridiculous," he said in an urgent whisper. "Nelson can't testify as to whether a butcher could make those cuts. He has no training or experience in meat cutting."

"I'm inclined to agree, Ms. Mackay."

"Judge, everyone knows what a butcher does—he carves up cows, pigs, sheep and chickens. A butcher probably dismembers more animal bodies in a year than most surgeons do in a lifetime. However, if you wish I can subpoena a butcher as an expert witness and ask him to describe to the jury how he cuts up animals; and how it is that he knows exactly how the joints and connecting ligaments work; and how he obtains training from other butchers and from books and charts which describe in detail the structural anatomy of all mammals, including humans. Then I'll ask him if he could disarticulate a joint as efficiently as the defendant did. If defense counsel wishes I can even arrange for a meat-cutting demonstration right here in court. But all that would take more time than Dr. Nelson's testimony, Your Honor."

"All right, Ms. Mackay, you've made your point," Spencer said. "I'll overrule the objection. Now, step back."

"Your Honor!" Bradley clearly wasn't happy with this turn of events.

"I've made my ruling, Mr. Bradley," the judge growled. "Step back! Now!"

Bradley slouched back to the defense table while Kathryn resumed her place in front of the witness stand. She waited for the judge's explanation to the jury.

"Ladies and gentlemen," Spencer said, "at times an issue, which does not affect the jury, comes up and must be discussed between myself and counsel. After considering counsels' argument, I have overruled Mr. Bradley's objection." He turned toward Nelson. "You may answer the prosecution's question, Doctor."

Kathryn nodded; she intended to reap full benefit from the court's ruling. "Your Honor, would you please ask the reporter to read back the question."

The court reporter read directly from her tape.

"In my opinion, an experienced butcher would have sufficient anatomical knowledge to dismember a human body the way the victim's body was dismembered," Nelson answered.

"Thank you. Now showing you people's exhibit 10, is this a photograph of a hand you examined?"

"Yes, detectives turned the hand over to me for examination a few days after I autopsied the torso. I

X-rayed the hand for comparison with the stumps of the unidentified torso. Although it had been wrapped in a plastic shopping bag and jammed between some rocks away from sunlight, there was marked decomposition. However, the tendons and extensors were in good shape—"

"Let me stop you there for a moment, Doctor. Please explain to the jury what tendons and extensors are."

"Think of them as the ropes and pulleys of the hand. The tendons—their medical names are *flexor digitori* and *carpi radialis*—run through the palm and fingers. These clench the hand, so." He extended his right hand and clenched it. "The extensors on the back of the hand straighten it out, like this." He spread his fingers wide.

"Thank you. Go on, please."

"The tendons and extensors were severed at roughly the point where the radius and ulna meet the carpals—the eight bones that form the wrist. The instrument that was used had a small notch on the cutting edge. The marks it made on both sides of the cut were clearly visible under the microscope. The hand was a perfect match to the arm stump."

"Just a few more questions. You said the hand was decomposed. Did the decomposition prevent you from fingerprinting the hand for identification purposes?"

"As you can see from people's exhibit 10, the epidermis—the skin—had already begun separating from the muscles beneath," Nelson said. "It was loose, something like a glove. However I was able to fingerprint the hand and later make a comparison with missing persons prints on file."

Kathryn looked up at the judge. "That's all I have, Your Honor."

Judge Spencer nodded briskly. "It's ten after noon," he said. "Unless anyone objects, I think we'll take a recess here." He glanced at the clock again. "Court will reconvene at two o'clock. Members of the jury, I again admonish you not to discuss this case among yourselves or with anyone else."

"All rise," the bailiff snapped. As Spencer went through the door into his chambers, the air of tension in the courtroom abated. Morgan Nelson stepped down from the witness stand and walked out of the courtroom without stopping, but Kathryn caught the eye signal as he passed her table. As soon as the jury had left the courtroom she hurried outside into the corridor where Nelson was waiting.

"Seemed to go okay," he observed.

"You were fine, Morgan," Kathryn said. "Thanks."

"See you tonight?" he asked.

Kathryn frowned. "Did we have a date?"

"Francis Piselli," Morgan said. "I'm doing the autopsy tonight, remember?"

"What time?"

"About ten, ten-thirty?"

"I'll be there."

"You look tired, Katie."

Morgan was the only person who called her Katie. The way he said it always reminded her of her father, although there was not the slightest resemblance between the tall, spare pathologist and the short, stocky Irishman she remembered from her childhood. She had a subliminal flash of Patrick Mackay, sitting in front of the TV with a can of beer in his fist, watching a Royals game. *Look at that, Katie, will you look at that fumbling eejut! Did you ever see the like in all your born days?* So few memories: he had died when she was fourteen.

Kathryn shook her head to banish the ghosts. "It's coming at me from every direction right now, Doc. The trial, some bad rapes. It's like God's trying to see how much I can take."

Morgan touched her shoulder and smiled. "He always did have a poor sense of humor," he said. "See you later."

She watched him as he walked briskly off along the crowded corridor toward the exit. She would always be grateful to him for his friendship during her probationary period in Santa Rita. They had hit it off right from their first meeting, as if there were no difference at all in their ages. Now Morgan was one of the closest friends she had, a cross between father and shrink. And, it had just occurred to her, she didn't even know where he was born.

6

The autopsy began at a little after 10:30 P.M. The fact that Morgan Nelson preferred to work late at night made it difficult for Kathryn to attend as many of his examinations as she might have done if she had had no daughter to look after, but she always made a special effort if Morgan requested her presence. As with her insistence on being at as many crime scenes as possible, it was her way of achieving empathy, of understanding the hurt done to the victim.

"The body is that of a well-developed white male, identified by a coroner's identification band bearing the name of Francis Norman Piselli present on the right ankle," Nelson began, busy with a flexible tape measure as he spoke into his mini-cassette recorder. "Height five feet, seven and a half inches. Weight one hundred forty-eight pounds, apparent age between thirty and thirty-five."

There were just the three of them in what Nelson called the VIP room, the smallest of the three autopsy suites; the pathologist, Granz and Kathryn. You couldn't count the body: there was always a not-there-ness about the dead. Apart from the sound of constantly running water, the place was—Kathryn smiled as the thought occurred to her—as silent as the grave.

There was a routine procedure for dealing with bodies arriving at the morgue. First they were brought to the staging room, put on a gurney and weighed. They were then meticulously photographed before being taken to one of the three autopsy suites.

The largest of these had three stainless steel tables with the usual weighing scales, sinks, sluices, steel lockers, tools and soundproof booth for dictating notes. The second, for cases requiring special study, had only one table. It was known as the VIP room.

The third suite was used for autopsies on bodies with known or suspected infections or diseases, or which were in an advanced state of decomposition. Here special air-conditioning systems vacuumed out the noxious gases and directed them into an incinerator. Also on the same level were a complete X-ray and color photo processing lab.

"There are second degree burns on both inner thighs halfway between crotch and knee," Nelson continued. "There is a similar burn, roughly circular, on the right shoulder."

He switched off the recorder and gestured them over. "Katie, Dave," he said. "Come and look at this."

He picked up the dead man's right hand, holding it between finger and thumb and reticulating it so the arm turned.

"I can't see anything," Dave frowned.

"Me neither," Kathryn said.

"Here, on the back of the wrist. On the other arm too. About an inch of skin has been depilated. I noticed it at the scene. When I got the body here, I swabbed the areas and found traces of adhesive on the skin. They were consistent with surgical adhesive tape."

"Meaning what?"

"Sometime prior to death, Piselli taped his wrists together—or someone else did. Not unusual if he was into bondage, however."

"Is it significant, Doc?"

"On its own, it isn't."

"But?"

"I did an autopsy a few weeks ago. Guy called Croma. Paul Alfred Croma. He was found naked at the bottom of an empty silo on a small farm in Catalina. Deputy coroners called me out. Lying next to the body we found a piece of rope with one end frayed. The rest of the rope was hanging from the ceiling of the silo. I realized what we had right away. The rope Croma used to pull himself up with when he had enough had been chafed so much it just came apart, broke in two.

"When I got him back here, I found the same thing, this depilation of the skin, but just above the wrists. I wrote him up as an autoerotic accident."

"Did it look as though he had been bound the same way you think Piselli was bound?" Kathryn asked.

"Yes, but there was no way of knowing when," Nelson replied. "There was no trace of adhesive tape at the scene, nor was any found among his personal belongings."

"They didn't find any at the Piselli death scene either," Granz said, flipping through the coroner's report he had picked up while Doc was speaking.

"Hell, it's probably not significant," Morgan said, laying Piselli's arm alongside the body. "It could have been done a day or two earlier. But then again, it could be foul play."

"Is there anything else unusual?" Kathryn asked.

Nelson shook his head. "I just thought you ought to know."

"Let's get back to Piselli," Dave said wearily. Since his brush with death at the hands of the Gingerbread Man, Dave had grown increasingly uncomfortable with autopsies, as if viewing them made him reflect a little too intensively upon his own mortality.

"My preliminary findings indicate the cause of death is ventricular fibrillation; manner of death— accident. However I haven't completely ruled out suicide or homicide."

"Okay, let's back up," Dave said. "How long has he been dead, Doc?"

"Only one way to be sure of that," Nelson replied.

"Yeah, be there when it happens," Granz half-grinned. "And even then you have a small margin of error."

"You know the three guidelines we use," Nelson said. "I went through them in court today. Algor, livor and rigor mortis. I estimated time of death not less than twenty-four or more than forty-eight hours. I'll run some vitreous potassium tests later to see if I can refine that."

"So we're saying what—he died the day or night before he was found?" Dave said.

Nelson nodded. "For what it's worth, my guess would be the night," he said.

He turned away from the body to pick up several long-bladed surgical knives and, one by one, began carefully whetting each of them, taking his time, testing the edges first with a finger, then by slicing a piece of paper.

Sometimes, Kathryn knew, he made a little production out of this necessary operation. Especially when there were first-timers in the audience. Nelson called it his Sweeney Todd routine. He said if merely watching the knives being sharpened made onlookers queasy, no way were they going to make it through the autopsy.

"You said he died of heart failure caused by electrocution, right?" Kathryn asked. "So what else are you looking for?"

"I'm not looking for anything in particular. I have a completely open mind. But it seems such a bizarre way to die, I just want to be absolutely sure that's the way it happened," Nelson replied. "Let's see what we find when we open him up."

He picked up the long-handled scalpel lying on the bench and sank it into the left shoulder of the corpse, making a sweeping curved cut down to the pubis. He repeated the procedure from the right shoulder to the sternum, then, grunting with effort, peeled the flesh away so that it lay curled back, the yellowish subcutaneous fat looking like nothing so much as the lining of an unzippered winter coat.

A quick cut with the Stryker saw parted the sternum; two slightly longer runs severed the ribs on each side. These were lifted away and after careful examination laid aside; the internal organs glistened in the bright fluorescent light.

"What a piece of work is man," Dave said, almost to himself.

"Amen to that," Nelson said. "I never do an autopsy without thinking what incredible machines we are. The way we're put together."

"Seems like a shame to deconstruct it," Kathryn said.

"He won't mind," Nelson told her, the bright lights glinting on the round granny glasses as he separated and sliced. He removed the stomach and emptied its contents into a glass jar.

"Looks like he hadn't eaten for some hours prior to death," he said. "Smells like there was some alcohol in there. I'll have tests run later."

"Frank Piselli," Dave said thoughtfully. "You know anything about him, Doc?"

"Will soon," Nelson said with a tight grin.

"His specialty was rape," Dave told him. "Then threatening the victim with violence if she testified against him. I'd never have figured him for an autoeroticist."

"Nevertheless."

"I always thought autoerotic deaths were caused by asphyxia," Kathryn said. "Sort of not knowing when enough was enough. Not some guy electrocuting himself with a floor buffer."

"Absolutely right," Nelson said, lifting the intestines out of the body and dropping them into a plastic bucket. "But that's only one aspect of it, Katie. Look, the term autoeroticism is just a fancy way of describing sexual pleasure obtained without the participation of another person. Typically, the autoerotic death is caused by asphyxiation. But there are plenty of other ways to die. The inhalation of anaesthetic gases, nitrites—what they used to call 'poppers'—or bondage, or self-mutilation, or electrocution . . . When it comes to sexual behavior there's no limit to the human imagination."

"It's a kind of erotic risk-taking," Dave said. "The nearer you go to the line, the more exciting it gets. That's a turn-on, too. Problem is, the more dangerous the game, the easier it is for something to go wrong. Right, Doc?"

"That's why among the bondage community it's called 'terminal sex.'"

"And you're saying that was what Piselli was into?"

"He lived alone," Dave said. "No way of knowing for sure. It's a solitary vice."

"Years ago, I consulted on a case out of San Francisco," Doc said. "The guy was an actor, quite well known. The cops found him suspended from a hook in the ceiling by leather wrist restraints. He was wearing pantyhose and a woman's silk slip. He'd written all his bad reviews in lipstick on his body.

There were clothespins on his nipples and he'd tied a red ribbon in a bow around his penis."

"Good grief, Morgan, do we have to?" Kathryn said.

"Just making a point, Katie," Nelson smiled. "That one had 'autoerotic death' written all over it. Some aren't quite so obvious, but they're a lot commoner than people think. Far too many are written up incorrectly because the cop at the scene doesn't make the connection between what he sees and what he finds."

He straightened up as he removed one of the dead man's lungs prior to weighing it and beckoned Dave over. "Here's something for you to think about," he said, pointing with the blade of the knife. "Look at the tissue discoloration. Mr. Piselli was a real heavy smoker."

"I'm cutting down, Doc," Dave said defensively.

"Quit altogether," Nelson said. "You'll live longer."

"Like this guy, you mean?" Granz grinned. "What about his heart?"

"Pretty much as I imagined," Nelson said, lifting out the second lung and stooping down to peer at the chest cavity. "They reckon a hundred and ten volts isn't lethal. Tell that to Frank Piselli."

Kathryn looked at the clock. It was after midnight. "Dave?"

He shrugged. "What do you say, Doc?"

Nelson spread his rubber-gloved hands. "Sorry I dragged you up here for nothing. But those adhesive tape marks bothered me."

"Nobody minds the occasional wild herring, Doc," Kathryn said with a smile. Nelson was fond of quoting his home-made aphorism to the effect that nobody who ever achieved anything worth a damn didn't occasionally chase after a wild herring or a red goose.

"Okay, there's nothing else to suggest it didn't happen just the way it looked," Nelson said, smiling behind his little nose-cone mask. "Unless I find a bullet in his brain when I open the skull, I'll write this one up as accidental death while engaged in autoerotic activity."

Kathryn tapped Granz on the shoulder and pointed at the door. He nodded, looking around the room. "Nice place you got here, Doc," he said to Nelson. "Shame about the floor show."

Nelson looked up, eyes twinkling. "Get out of here, you two. Go get some beauty sleep."

Kathryn stretched and put on her jacket. "Sounds good to me," she said and headed for the door. "Don't stay up too late, Doc."

Morgan grinned. "Who, me?" he said.

7

Of the original twelve defendants who had been brought into Department Thirty of the Los Angeles Superior Court after the morning recess, only two now remained in the jury box awaiting arraignment. Jack Hallam looked impatiently at the clock to the rear of the courtroom. It was almost noon. The way things were going he would miss his plane. He drummed his fingers on the table as Judge Braithwaite called the next case: *The People* v. *Guajardo.*

Luis Ray Guajardo was twenty-nine years old, short, squat and ugly, with greasy black hair and eyes like a cobra. He was a typical Los Angeles street criminal, his origins a witches' brew of Hispanic, Haitian and Oriental blood. IQ of an avocado, foresight of a housefly. Dressed in the usual orange jumpsuit, his ankles shackled, Guajardo shuffled over to the podium beside his PD, a young woman named Sharon Mendoza who looked as if she hadn't been out of law school more than about ten days.

Rich Baumgasser stood up as the judge looked his way. A prosecutor, like Jack Hallam, he was one of almost a thousand lawyers working for the L.A. District Attorney's office. He was assigned to the Guajardo case.

"It's a solid case and Mendoza knows it," he had told Jack as they sat together earlier, "but she won't even waive time."

Sentenced to eleven years for manslaughter in June 1988, Guajardo had served five and been paroled this month. The stupid sonofabitch hadn't been on the street two weeks when he tried to rob a 7-Eleven at gunpoint and shot a cop who responded to the clerk's 9-1-1 call.

"Are you going to cut him a deal?" Jack asked.

The L.A. District Attorney's office prosecuted a hundred thousand felonies a year and even criminals as stupid as Guajardo knew a trial for every defendant was an impossibility. Which meant a chance at a plea bargain, that seemingly magical process by which a DA took a plea to a lesser charge now instead of a trial later. For all its faults, however, plea bargaining had some benefits. To begin with, the victim was not required to testify at trial; a plea was guaranteed. Even more important, there was no chance of an acquittal. A plea was final; the defendant could not appeal to a higher court for a new trial.

"No way," Baumgasser replied, walking over toward the podium as the judge read the Information and asked the defendant what his plea was. Guajardo shrugged as if none of what was happening concerned him. Next, Braithwaite asked Baumgasser how he wished to proceed and Rich told him to set it for trial. The judge had a flat, mid-western voice that made everything he said unimpressive, dull and monotonous.

Come on Judge, Jack thought impatiently, get this asshole back to the jail where he belongs. The whole arraignment shouldn't have taken more than five minutes, but Braithwaite was taking it slowly to help out the defendant's PD.

Jack's case—a residential burglary—would be the next one called. The PD was offering to plead to the burglary as a "no state prison." If Jack didn't take the offer and convicted him at trial, Braithwaite would find a way not to send the defendant to prison. Either way he ends up doing local time, he thought. Better to take the plea.

He ran his own timetable again: drive to the airport, catch the shuttle to San Jose, arriving there an hour later. Twenty minutes to pick up an Alamo rental, allow an hour—it was Friday—to drive over the hill to Santa Rita, he ought to be there by 5. He had no intention of being late if he could help it; Kathryn always made him feel inadequate.

In fact, given a choice, he would as soon have skipped the entire experience of taking Emma to visit her grandparents, but it was all arranged. Tom and Elaine Hallam enjoyed seeing their granddaughter as long as she didn't stay too long. He felt she sometimes disconcerted them, she was so direct and open. He smiled as he remembered her asking his father how much money he earned. In all the years they'd been married, his mother had never dared to ask the old boy that one.

The phone gave its muted ring; he watched apathetically as Don Carmody, the deputy acting as bailiff nearest the door through which the custodies entered and left, picked it up, listened for a moment, wrote something on a slip of paper, then ambled across to put the message on defense counsel's table. As he retraced his route past the podium, Guajardo, who was shackled but not cuffed, swivelled around and clumsily snatched Carmody's gun out of his holster.

"A'right, I'm outta here!" he shouted, brandishing the weapon wildly. "Everybody get back!"

Jack Hallam froze, astonished. Everything seemed to be moving in slow motion. People were screaming, scrambling wildly over the benches toward the door. He saw the judge slide off his chair and disappear behind his bench, Rich Baumgasser and Sharon Mendoza backing away from Guajardo with their hands up like extras in a Western.

As Guajardo shuffled toward the door, Don

Carmody took a step forward, his hand outstretched. He was trying to appear confident, but every line of his body betrayed his fear.

"Give me the gun," he said.

"Back off!" Guajardo screamed.

Carmody made a lunge for the gun and Guajardo started shooting, the explosions like thunder in the enclosed space. Carmody staggered backwards then went down, his legs thrashing. In the same moment, Jack Hallam felt a blow on his chest, as though someone had kicked him. He looked down and saw blood on his shirt. Then the room tilted. His legs buckled beneath him and he collapsed, his head half under the prosecution table.

"Shit!" he said angrily. This was going to screw up all his plans. There was a roaring in his head and he couldn't see properly. He tried to call for help but it felt as if something very heavy had fallen on his chest. Everything started to go away, very very fast.

As Guajardo reached the rail dividing the court from the spectator area the doors of the courtroom burst open. Two deputies rushed in, a burly older cop and a dark-skinned younger one. They saw the gun in Guajardo's hand and split apart, straddled, guns forward in the firing position.

"Drop the gun!" the old one shouted. "Drop it!"

Guajardo turned to face them, bringing the weapon up. Both cops fired simultaneously and he folded over the wooden railing, his eyes emptying of life. The younger of the two deputies ran nimbly forward and kicked the dropped gun out of reach.

Gun trained on the fallen inmate, the other deputy edged closer till he had the muzzle pressed against Guajardo's temple. He bent down, pressing his fingers against the man's carotid artery, then looked up, nodding at his partner. A small frown of concern creased his forehead as he saw the look on the younger deputy's face. "He's dead," he said. "You okay?"

"Sure," the young cop said, although he looked rocky. He picked up the weapon that had fallen from the dead man's hand and went over to check on the bailiff. The judge appeared from behind his bench, his face as white as a sheet. He looked at the three bodies sprawled on the courtroom floor.

"Jesus Christ," he said. "Jesus Christ."

Richard Baumgasser and Sharon Mendoza got to their feet from behind the rail of the jury box where they had taken cover, their faces white, bewildered. People were boiling into the courtroom now, lawyers, jurors, reporters. "Get these people out of here!" the judge yelled to one of the deputies. "And get an ambulance here!"

"Tell them to get the coroner, too," the older deputy said. He looked across at his partner, who had sunk into a chair at the defense table, his head in his hands.

"Pete?" he said.

"Just give me a minute," the younger cop replied without looking up.

"What about Carmody?" the judge asked.

"He's dead," the deputy sitting down said dully.

"And the . . . other one?"

The big deputy was kneeling down by Jack Hallam. "Anybody know this guy's name?" he said over his shoulder. The judge shook his head.

"Hallam," Rich Baumgasser said hollowly. "His name is Jack Hallam. He's with the DA's office."

"Not any more he ain't," the deputy said.

8

Kathryn put down the phone and stared at it for what seemed like a very long time, not thinking, as if her mind had been emptied, numbed.

Dead.

The word hovered inside her brain like a great black bird. How could Jack be dead? How could anyone be taken from life so suddenly, in the snap of a finger, in the single beat of a heart? The very randomness of it was like an insult. Like God, or Fate, or whatever you believed in, was saying, Nobody counts. Anybody can go. Any time.

You knew of course, everyone knew, it could happen. Courtroom shootings were becoming an occupational hazard. A disgruntled husband kills his wife's lover at a divorce hearing; an outraged mother puts a bullet through the brain of the man accused of molesting her child; a judge is shot to death by a witness called to testify. You just somehow never envisioned someone you knew being killed. Yet it happened to Jack. All in a few seconds, the Chief Deputy at the L.A. DA's office told her. A careless deputy, a prisoner who grabbed a gun. Nothing anyone could have done, he said. As if somehow that made it easier.

Poor, dear Jack. They had got married straight out

of law school. It was the beginning of everything then, for both of them. All the years ahead were going to be full of that hope and enthusiasm. But hope and enthusiasm had died, replaced by jealousy and indifference. Maybe it was my fault, she thought. Maybe I should have tried harder. No. She had grown up and Jack had not. She had wasted all those years thinking it was she who needed him; only to find out at the end it had always been he who needed her.

She wondered whether Jack's parents had been told yet. It would hit them very hard. He had been an only child; Tom and Elaine Hallam always acted like their son was the Los Angeles District Attorney rather than just one of the county's thousand assistant DAs. Maybe I should call them, she thought. There would be the funeral to arrange, and people who would have to be told, and . . .

Emma.

Oh, dear God in Heaven, how was she ever going to break the news to Emma?

Kathryn called the school and told them she was coming over to pick up her daughter; and why. She was no nearer to an answer to the question when she got into her car and headed over La Loma. Emma was waiting for her at the school entrance.

"What happened? Did something happen? Mrs. Thompson said you were coming to pick me up early, why have you come early?" she said, as she clambered into the car. "Is it about going to see Gramma and Grandpa, is it?"

"I'll tell you when we get home, sweetheart," Kathryn said.

"Is it so I can get all packed and everything? Is that why you came early?"

"No, it's something else," Kathryn said.

"Mom-my!" Emma said, affecting exasperation. *"Tell* me!"

"Not now, honey," Kathryn said. "We'll talk about it when we get home."

She drove automatically, concentrating on not letting anything show as Emma prattled on about school and about going to see Gramma and Grandpa.

"What kind of house do they have, Mom, what kind?" she asked.

"It's a vacation cabin, sweetie," Kathryn said.

"Is it big?"

"No, not big," Kathryn said. "Just a little place up in the Gold Country where they spend vacations."

"I'm so excited," Emma said. "I can't believe I'm really truly going."

Kathryn turned right into Lighthouse Drive and then left up the hill toward her condo. She parked the car and they went up in the elevator. Emma ran into her room to dump her backpack on the bed the way she always did. Then she came into the room where Kathryn was sitting on the sofa. "I better start getting packed, right?" she said. "I bet Daddy will be here soon."

Kathryn shook her head. It was no use. She couldn't pretend any longer. "Listen to me for a moment, sweetheart," she said. "Just listen, okay?"

Emma looked at her and saw something in her expression. Apprehension widened her eyes. "Has something bad happened?" she whispered. "Is that what it is?"

"Do you remember when you were really young and you wanted to know why I had to go out, sometimes in the middle of the night, to do my job, and I told you it was because someone had done a very bad thing to someone else? Do you remember that, Em?"

Emma nodded, her eyes never leaving Kathryn's. "And you had to catch whoever did the bad thing and send them to jail."

"Criminals. You know what criminals are, don't you?"

"They shoot other people. Like on TV. Only real."

"That's right. But sometimes . . . sometimes criminals do very bad things to . . . people we know. People we love."

"Oh, Mommy," Emma's voice was fearful. "I'm scared of what you're going to say."

"It's your daddy," Kathryn blurted. "He's been shot, sweetheart."

Emma stared at her for a long, long moment. Then she turned away, her expression blank. "I don't want to hear this," she said, as if she was angry. "You're going to say he's dead and I don't want to hear it."

"I know, sweetheart. Neither did I. But it's happened and we've got to deal with it."

Emma put her hands over her ears and turned away. "Don't tell me. Don't tell me. Don't tell me!" she shouted.

"Daddy was in court, Em," Kathryn said, conscious of the futility of explanation. "One of the criminals tried to escape. He got a gun, started shooting. He shot your daddy."

"Is he . . . is he . . . ?" Emma couldn't bring herself to say the word so Kathryn said it for her.

"Yes. He's dead, Emma. Your daddy is dead."

"Oh," Emma said. Her voice was almost inaudible. "Oh, no."

"I wish I didn't have to tell you this, Em," Kathryn said. "I wish it wasn't true."

"But it is!" Emma wailed, as the tears finally came like a torrent. "It is! Why did he have to shoot my daddy? Why?"

"I'm sorry, oh, baby, I'm so sorry," Kathryn said, putting her arms around her daughter. Emma was trembling, her whole body shaking. Kathryn hugged her close, close, stroking her hair. Over and over, over and over, Emma repeated the same single word. No. No. No. *No.*

"We have to be brave, sweetheart," Kathryn said softly. "We both have to be very brave."

No. No. No. No.

"I need you to help me, Em," Kathryn whispered. "I really need you to help me get through this. I can't do it on my own."

Gradually, almost imperceptibly, the shivering stopped. They sat in silence, arms wrapped around each other.

"What's going to happen?" Emma whispered.

"We'll be very sad for a while," Kathryn whispered, fighting to hold back her own tears. "But it will be all right. We'll get through it. Somehow. We still have each other."

"I'm afraid, Mommy."

"I know," Kathryn said. "I am too."

Emma sat in silence, her head bowed, the dark hair hanging like a curtain over her eyes. Kathryn held her close, hoping desperately she was saying the right things, using the right voice. How could you know? How could you ever know?

"Why did it happen? Why?" Emma whimpered.

Sobbing herself now, Kathryn held her sobbing

daughter close, rocking her in her arms like a baby. If the words to answer her question existed, she did not know them.

The next day was a Saturday. It gave her a breathing space, a little time to work out what to do. Over breakfast Emma was listless, wan. She toyed with her food, ate practically nothing. When the sun came through midmorning, Kathryn went into her daughter's room and found Emma sitting on the bed, swinging her legs, staring out of the window.

"How about a walk on the beach?" she suggested.

Emma shook her head. "Couldn't we just stay here and watch TV?" she said.

"I think we need to get out for a while," Kathryn said. "We can't just sit here all the time."

"I'm not just sitting here, I'm thinking about Daddy," Emma said, and the sadness in her young voice brought the tears back to Kathryn's eyes.

"That's good, sweetheart," Kathryn said gently. "That's what I'm doing, too. Thinking about all the things we used to do together. He used to like to go down to the beach, you remember that? He'd probably like it if we were thinking about him while we're walking. As if we were all together."

Emma sighed and got off her bed and Kathryn suddenly saw in the slender, dark-haired, freckle-faced child before her the beautiful woman her daughter would become. It was quite unnerving.

"I feel very strange," Emma said. "Like everything that's happening isn't really happening. Do you feel that way, too?"

"No," Kathryn said. "But I understand what you

mean. It's how we deal with bad things. With things we don't want to believe."

"Maybe there was a mistake," Emma said hopefully. "Maybe it was someone else who got . . . hurt. Not Daddy."

"No, sweetheart," Kathryn said sadly. "There was no mistake. It's even in the newspaper."

"I don't want to see that!" Emma said, her voice rising sharply. "I don't want to see it!"

"You don't have to," Kathryn said. "Come on, let's go down to the beach."

They drove along the Esplanade, then crossed the bridge to Shelter Island. It was a narrow spit of land running parallel to the coastline, no longer really an island—it had long ago been linked to the mainland by infilling—with fine white beaches on the ocean side. Holding hands, Kathryn and her daughter walked toward the lighthouse in its little park on the western end of the promontory.

As they came level with the sand dunes, a picture of a young woman's body, sprawled head-downward on the rain-wet sand, flashed through Kathryn's memory. She always tended to associate places with crimes. It had been on Shelter Island they had found the first victim of the serial killer called the Gingerbread Man. Was it really more than a year since then? Was it really more than fifteen years since she had married Jack Hallam straight out of law school? Where did the time go?

The sun was hot and comforting as they trudged through the fine, white sand; the very normality of the scene helped to dispel dark thoughts. There were kids splashing in the ocean, making like they were surfing. The smell of food wafted on the soft breeze from the hot-dog stand in the park. Further along the beach a crowd of young people was playing a noisy game of volleyball. An arrow of pelicans flew over, aimed at the Monterey peninsula.

"It's like nothing happened," Emma said, angrily. "Everything's just like always. How can that be? All these people playing like nothing happened?"

"Because it didn't happen to them, sweetheart," Kathryn replied softly. "It happened to us."

Emma let go her hand and stared furiously at the ocean. "Why?" she shouted. "Why did it have to happen to us?"

An elderly couple walking along the footpath turned at the sound of the anger in her voice. They looked at Kathryn as much as to say, How can you let a child act like that?

"I don't know, sweetheart," Kathryn said wearily. "Nobody knows."

"It's not fair," Emma said and started to cry. "It's not fair!"

"Come on, Em," Kathryn said, taking her daughter in her arms. "Let's go home."

Emma knuckled the tears away and looked intently into Kathryn's eyes. Her defenselessness was poignant.

"Mommy, do you think Father Murphy might know?" she said.

Father Sean Murphy was the parish priest. Emma had received her first communion from him earlier in the year. He was great with children; they all loved him. He had a special rapport with Emma. My wild Irish rose, he called her.

"We'll ask him," Kathryn replied, trying to sound confident. "Tomorrow."

Maybe it was cowardly, she thought, but tomorrow was better than anything else she had to offer her daughter right now.

9

He wore dark blue Lee jeans and a light blue cotton short sleeve shirt. Of medium height, strongly built—he worked out with weights—he had dark, naturally wavy hair, dark brown eyes and a long, vulpine face. The big bad wolf. He was thirty-eight years old and by his own count he had raped twenty-three women.

He worked at it the way other men work at golf, devoting all his spare time to perfecting his skills. It was a dangerous game. Mistakes were not allowed; you could profit from the fact that the cops were overworked and sometimes careless, but they weren't stupid. Anybody who thought they were was taking a shortcut to the penitentiary.

The watchword was know the enemy. *Find out his strengths, his weaknesses. Learn how he thinks. The college bookstore supplied him with a list of textbooks for their criminal justice classes. From them he learned that cops investigating rape cases looked at what they called "core behavior": how the rapist maintained con-*

trol over his victim, the amount of force used during the rape and what he made the victim do.

Knowing that made it easy: all he had to do was turn their rules upside down. If rapists got caught because they conformed to a certain pattern of behavior, the first rule was to have no pattern. Always vary the method of control. Exercise different levels of force. Vary the sexual acts. Change the conversation. Never strike in the same area twice.

And from the rules grew the technique. First, find a victim. Then target it. Then strike. People were stupid. Women especially. They won a prize, they earned a college degree, they got married, bam, they put their pictures in the paper. Full names, where they worked, everything, like, hey, come and get me. Well, if they wanted to serve themselves up as if the local paper was some kind of menu, fine. It made everything that much easier.

From each paper's Living section he would select three women—three little pigs—whose workplace was identified. He would follow them home from work, check out the security of the building if it was an apartment, and which of them lived with parents, or a partner, or alone. Over the next couple of weeks he would familiarize himself with their patterns of behavior—visitors, sleeping hours, hours away from home. Three little pigs who had no idea they were being watched, and watched, and watched by the Big Bad Wolf.

Like the *guapa*, the little *señorita* he was watching now as she leapt and shouted and screamed and laughed with her friends, playing volleyball on La Loma Beach. Her name was Lisa. Lisa Hernandez.

She was in her twenties; they all were. Husky young guys and pretty girls, mostly University students. He didn't really see the rest of them: his attention was fixed on the slender figure of the Hispanic girl in the bathing suit, the way her breasts lifted when she jumped for the ball, the play of the muscles of her upper thighs.

He walked away after a while. People tended to remember a man standing alone. He went back to his car, parked where he could watch where they went after they finished their game and sat waiting, saying the girl's name aloud, running it across his lips as if tasting it: Leeeess-a, Leeeess-a.

After a week of watching, he knew a great deal about Lisa Hernandez. He knew she was a student at the University and a member of its championship volleyball team. She lived with her parents and three brothers and two sisters in a recently restored Victorian home. Her father was an engineer and her mother was a teacher.

The sounds of the volleyball game carried to where he sat. He smiled. If Lisa stuck to her usual routine, she would play until about 3, drive home, take a quick shower, change and leave for work; during vacations, she worked part-time, 4 till 9, six nights a week in a department store at the Mall. Her boyfriend, who worked part time at a record store in the Mall, would usually meet her after work and drive home with her. Couldn't be too careful, right? He smiled again; why did people think it could only happen late at night?

As Lisa Hernandez came up the steps from the beach he put his car in motion; he was behind her seven-year-old Subaru all the way back to her house. He continued on down to Cliffside Park Drive, stopped to pick up a pastrami sandwich and a cup of coffee, then doubled back and parked where he could watch the Hernandez house. Forty minutes later Lisa came out and got into her car. Off to work, he thought.

He followed her to the Mall, and was right behind her when they reached the ticket barrier at the parking facility. He stayed about three car lengths back as she drove into the cool darkness, waiting for her to signal, as she always did. He watched her turn into a space, and as she came to a stop, slid the BMW into a space a few cars further along. He was out of the car and moving purposefully as she got out of the Subaru.

He glanced over his shoulder; no one in sight. He pulled the nylon stocking over his head. He was level with her now and as she bent to put the key in the door lock, she heard, or sensed, or felt something and started to turn. Too late, little pig, he thought and spun her around, hitting her in the belly with his fist. She slammed back against the car, her unfocused eyes huge with horror, an ugly retching sound coming from her throat, holding up her hands to defend herself. Stupid bitch. He grabbed the car keys from her slack fingers and hit her again, this time on the right side of her face. She collapsed in a sitting sprawl, blood running from her open mouth, her face paper white with pain and shock. She was trying to say "no" and it amused him.

He took the front of her cotton shirt in his fist and hauled her to her feet, jerking the door of her car open. He shoved her across the front seat, bundling her into the passenger side like a sack of potatoes. She looked about wildly and he saw her throat tense and her mouth move to scream. He hit her again without mercy, this time just below her ear and the hinge of the jawbone. She bounced off the window and her head fell forward, smacking meatily against the dash. She lay unmoving like a bundle of wet wash. He checked her eyes, her pulse. Out like a light, he told himself. He took off the stocking, started the car and drove out into the sunshine. The whole thing had taken less than half a minute.

He looked at the helpless figure of the girl next to him, remembering the movements of her body as she played. Oh, this was going to be a good one, he told himself. Maybe even extraordinary. Lust sang in his blood. Images flickered in his mind. He could smell her, he could almost taste her. He headed up Highway Seventeen, thinking about all the things he was going to do to Lisa Hernandez. She'd better not spoil it.

In the hall outside the cafeteria in the basement of the County Building were Coke and candy machines and a newspaper stand. Kathryn put in change and took a copy of the *Gazette*. There was a piece by Mike Berry on the rape that had happened the preceding night, while Kathryn was in Los Angeles.

"You going to lunch?"

She looked up to see Michael Gaines smiling at her. Why is it even when he smiles, he looks sad? she wondered. Today he was wearing tan Dockers and a beige shirt. He still looked like he needed a good night's sleep.

"I said, are you going in or coming out?"

"Out," she said. "Sorry. I was miles away."

"I need to talk to you. About this."

He gestured at the headline on the *Gazette* in the rack: UCSR STUDENT, 22, ABDUCTED, BEATEN, RAPED.

"Come up to my office," she said. "No time like the present."

"Let me get a sandwich and some coffee," he said. "I haven't had a chance to eat since the rape was called in."

"See you upstairs," Kathryn said. Michael went into the cafeteria and she walked up the two flights of stairs to the DA's office, where the receptionist buzzed her in. Ten minutes later, Gaines came in with a sandwich in one fist and a cup of coffee in the other. He straddled the arm of one of her leather chairs like it was a saddle, giving her a fleeting glimpse of the little boy he had once been.

"Lisa Hernandez," she prompted.

"What the media call a good rape," he said, harshly. "Good for them. Bad for us."

Newspaper and TV reporters classified crimes "good" and "bad." Cops saw things differently. What the media deemed a "good" murder, the cops called "bad." It wasn't anything to do with how difficult it might be, how many days or weeks or even months of investigation it would consume. It was bad as in brutal.

The same rules applied to rape; and as Michael outlined the circumstances of the attack Kathryn realized this one was as bad as they got. The victim, Lisa Hernandez, was a young woman of twenty-two. She was walking to her car in a three-story parking lot at the Mall when a man spun her around and struck her again and again in the face and stomach with his fists.

"He shoved her into her car," Gaines continued, "and drove her to an isolated canyon somewhere up in the hills above Cathedral Heights. He told her to strip. When she hesitated with the buttons, he struck her again and ripped off her clothes. He forced her into the back seat and performed oral sex on her, biting off a chunk of skin from the inside of her thigh in the process. He made her perform oral sex on him. Then he raped her. It took a long time. He kept telling her to shove her ass, help him out."

When he was finished with her, the rapist dragged the battered, bleeding victim out of the car and rolled her into a roadside ditch. She was found by a passing motorist, wandering along the highway, naked and in shock.

"He broke her nose, fractured her jaw and cracked three of her ribs," Gaines said, anger showing in the set of his face. "He knocked out some of her teeth. Both her eyes are swollen shut. Her body's a mass of bruises. Jesus, he really worked her over, Kathryn."

Sometimes the depth of his empathy with rape victims surprised even her. Telling him not to become so emotionally involved in his cases was like telling a writer not to become so involved with his characters. You couldn't do the job any other way. She laid a sympathetic hand on his arm. It felt as hard as a block of wood. "We'll get him, Michael," she said softly.

"Damned right."

"What about her car?"

"Found abandoned in a Safeway parking lot in Highland Valley," Michael told her. "CSI is examining it now."

"Anything from the rape kit?"

"Some pubic hairs that don't look like hers. Maybe semen on the vaginal swabs."

"When can we talk to her?"

"I'm going up to the hospital at four. Are you free?"

"I'll make myself free," Kathryn said. "Had she seen him before?"

Michael shook his head. "No."

"Did she give us a description?"

"Yeah—white, medium height, dark hair and eyes, thirtyish. Well spoken. She noticed his hands particularly. Definitely not a manual laborer, she said. I thought with that and his MO, it might be worth running it through the VICAP computer for a possible match."

VICAP—the acronym for Violent Criminal Apprehension Program—was the national data center which collected, collated and analyzed information on violent crimes and determined if similarities existed between the individual case reported and those in the VICAP data base.

"Go ahead," Kathryn said. "Unless you want to wait until we talk to her?"

"Wait? That bastard is walking around out there and you want me to wait?"

"Hey, this is me, remember?"

"Oh shit," he said, smiling his awkward-boy smile. "I'm just mad at the whole goddamn world. I keep seeing that poor kid with her broken face, lying there sobbing, and I think, how can this happen? Doesn't anybody care?"

"And you know the answer," Kathryn said quietly. "A lot of people care. You and me for starters."

He stood up and sighed. "You're right. Sorry I lost it."

"Forget it."

"Listen," he said. "About . . . your ex. I'm sorry."

"You heard what happened?"

"It was on the news. I didn't connect it to you until Dave told me. It must have hit you pretty hard."

"It didn't seem . . . real. It still doesn't."

"Is there anything I can do?"

Kathryn shook her head.

The funeral had been an ordeal, as she had known it would be. Tom and Elaine Hallam had spared no expense: mountains of flowers, the most expensive casket, a fleet of limos from the church to the cemetery.

Afterwards there was a catered gathering at their home: uncles and aunts, cousins and old school friends and colleagues from the DA's office. Seeing them all again made her realize how much she had changed, how irretrievable the past really was.

Tom and Elaine listened with icy disbelief to her explanation that Emma was still too upset to come to the funeral. She could see they felt it was Emma's duty to be at her father's graveside, regardless of what traumas the experience might inflict upon the child herself.

She stayed for as long as she could. As she left, Tom Hallam embraced her perfunctorily, like a man bidding thankful farewell to a tiresome guest. Elaine came to the door to say goodbye. The tailored black suit and crisp white silk blouse made her look severe and disapproving.

"I'm sorry you won't stay longer, Kathryn," she said frostily. "We haven't had a chance to talk."

What was there to talk about? Kathryn wondered.

"I'll try to come down again soon," she said. "With Emma."

"I don't suppose we'll see much of her now . . . now that . . ."

"I wouldn't keep her from you, Elaine," Kathryn said, perhaps more sharply than she intended.

"Of course not, my dear," Elaine said smoothly. "It's just we know how busy you always keep yourself."

She's pleased she got under my skin, Kathryn thought. They had never really been friends; from the start Elaine had never troubled to conceal her belief that her expensively educated son could have done a lot better than marry a lower-middle-class girl from Kansas City.

"How is Emma handling it?" Michael's question brought her back to the present.

"As well as can be expected. I need to spend more time with her. But there's . . . this."

She waved her arms to encompass it all, the building, the job.

"I know," Michael said. "I know what you mean."

"I can't let it affect Emma."

"You won't let it," he said. "She'll heal, Kathryn. Give it time."

Time, she thought. How much time would it take? "Sorry," she said brusquely. "I didn't mean to . . . lean on you."

He looked surprised. "I can't imagine you having to lean on anyone," he said. "You're as solid as the Rock of Gibraltar."

"Five feet four inches high."

Michael shook his head doggedly. "What I'm trying to say is, we all admire you. When it comes to sex crimes, damn few prosecutors are crusaders."

If only you knew, she thought, how exhausting it was being a crusader; trying to create a small piece of justice for victims of rape and having to fight for every inch of that piece. "Get outa here," she grinned. "Before you turn my head with all this flattery."

"Okay. But, hey . . . Kathryn?"

"What?"

"Tough cookie like you," he said. "Ever thought of becoming a lawyer?"

He ducked out a second before the pencil she threw at him hit the door.

10

Mornings were always a rush; Kathryn often felt like she'd done a day's work before she even got to the DA's office. Make breakfast, pack Emma's lunch, do a load of washing, iron, empty the dishwasher, then into the car and up to Lighthouse Drive to catch the school bus. It never went smoothly.

"You ready, Emma?" Kathryn called, collecting her briefcase and laptop. There was no answer. Frowning, she got up and went through to her daughter's bedroom. Emma was sitting on her bed staring at the floor.

"Come on, we're going to be late," Kathryn said.

"I'm not going," Emma said without looking up.

Kathryn was taken completely aback. "What?"

"I don't want to, I don't want to go!" Emma said stolidly. "I don't want to go to school!"

"Sweetheart, what is it?" Kathryn said, sitting down and putting her arm around her daughter's shoulders. Her body was stiff. "Don't you feel well?"

"I just don't want to go, that's all," Emma said. "I want to stay with you."

Kathryn took Emma's hands in her own, turned her to face her. "You funny thing," she smiled. "You can't stay with me. I have to go to work. You have to go to school. Like we do every day."

"You let me come to work with you when they had that day," Emma said. "Why can't I come today?"

"That was different, Em," Kathryn said. "That was a special day. All the moms took their daughters to work with them that day."

A year or so earlier, the Santa Rita Board of Supervisors and the Ms. Foundation had sponsored a "Take Our Daughters To Work" day designed to boost self-confidence and introduce girls to jobs they might not normally consider.

"I want to do it again," Emma said. "Today."

"Look, sweetheart, I'm sorry, but the answer is no. You have to go to school. So let's not talk about it any more."

"I don't want to go," Emma shouted, tears springing to her eyes. "I want to be with you!"

Her distress was real, but Kathryn didn't have any

more time this morning to deal with it. "Just go get in the car, Emma."

"Please? Pleeeeease, Mommy, pleeeeeeease?"

Kathryn shook her head. "In the car," she said. "Now."

Emma looked at her angrily, then picked up her backpack and stamped out, banging the door behind her. When Kathryn got down to the garage, she was sitting in the passenger seat staring furiously ahead.

"Are you going to tell me what's wrong?" Kathryn said as she started the car. "Are you going to tell me what this is all about?"

"You don't care!" Emma said. Her face was wet from the tears. "You don't care."

"Darling, if you'd tell me—"

"You don't care if I'm all on my own."

"Emma, I don't understand. Tell me what's upsetting you and then we can talk about it."

Emma sat moodily silent as they drove up the hill. Kathryn pulled over by the bus stop and switched off the engine. Emma made no move to get out.

"Look, there's Julie," Kathryn said. "Don't you want to go say hello?"

Emma gave her a pitiful look. "I want to be with you, Mommy," she wailed. "I want to stay with you."

"You have to go to school, sweetheart," Kathryn said firmly. "Come on, we'll walk over to the bus stop together."

She got out of the car. Emma still sat unmoving. Kathryn walked round and opened the door. Her daughter looked up at her with the same entreaty in her eyes. Kathryn just waited until, with a huge sigh, Emma picked up her backpack and got out of the car.

Kathryn tried to take her hand but Emma snatched it away. "I don't want you to hold my hand!" she said, running away. "I hate you!"

Stunned, Kathryn watched her daughter climb on to the bus. Emma had never used that word—hate—before in her life. She sat by the window staring straight ahead and did not return Kathryn's wave as the bus drove off.

"Everything all right, Kathryn?" Helen Corcoran's voice was concerned.

"Why do you ask?" Kathryn fenced.

"Things looked a little . . . tense between you and Emma."

"She didn't want to go to school," Kathryn said. "That's all."

"Oh, that," Helen smiled. "I've had the same thing happen with Julie. They have a fight with a classmate or they take a dislike to one of the teachers, suddenly they don't want to go to school. Take Julie—every day she tries to think of an excuse to stay in bed another ten minutes. Do you know what she said to me the other day? "I'm trying to get up, Mommy, but the blanket is heavier than usual this morning.'"

"That's cute," Kathryn said automatically, her mind on her daughter's untypical behavior.

"You have a good one, now," Helen said and got into her car.

An hour after Kathryn reached her office, Michael Gaines came in. His clothing looked wrinkled and his eyes were puffy from lack of sleep. "I need to update you," he said. "SO's got a new rape. DiStefano went out on it."

Kathryn automatically glanced at the clock. Rape could happen at any time, of course, but a little after 9:30 on a bright, hot summer morning it was disconcerting.

"You want to brief me?" she asked, as he slumped down into one of her leather chairs.

"First the bad news," he said, "it's four days old. The victim's a prostitute. She wasn't going to report it at all—figured nobody would believe her anyway—but a friend finally convinced her she should call the cops."

"What happened?"

"She picked up this guy, had a few drinks. She took him back to her place. They smoked some pot. When she asked him for money up front, the guy beat the shit out of her and then raped her."

"Was she taken to County General?"

Michael shook his head. "She wouldn't go to the hospital," he said. "Not that it matters—there's no point doing a rape kit after seventy-two hours anyway. Any trace evidence would be gone. Plus, she took at least two baths since the attack."

"You said he beat her up."

"She's still black and blue," Michael told her. "And before you ask, she's already been photographed."

"That's something," Kathryn said. "Where is she now?"

"DiStefano brought her in. I'm going up to the SO interview room now to talk to her."

"What about the suspect?"

"That's the good news. She ID'd him already. SO will pick him up."

"Let me get a legal pad," Kathryn said.

* * *

Harry diStefano met them in the doorway. Over his shoulder they could see the victim sitting hunched over a table smoking a cigarette. Her face was swollen and she had a split lip that looked angry and sore. There were also bruises on her thin, bare arms. She wore a half-defeated, half-defiant expression that somehow touched a chord of empathy in Kathryn.

"Full name Francesca Jaramillo," diStefano told them, keeping his voice down so the victim couldn't hear him. "Frankie, for short. Age twenty-eight, she lives in Catalina."

"You run her rap?" Michael asked.

"She's got a string of misdos long as your arm," diStefano grunted, using the cop shorthand for misdemeanors. "About what you'd expect. Soliciting, possession, DUIs. Nothing serious."

"Her statement still the same?"

"Yup."

"What about the guy who raped her?"

"They're bringing him in now. Name of George Zabrowski, lives down in Liberty. He claims he doesn't even know her."

"Any record?"

DiStefano shook his head. "We're just running his rap now. He claims to be your average, everyday John Citizen," he said.

"Except he rapes women," Kathryn said.

After an interview with Frankie Jaramillo that lasted almost two hours, Kathryn and Michael returned to her office.

"What do you think?" he asked.

"She's telling the truth," Kathryn replied, "but that's not the question is it?"

Gaines sighed and shook his head. Neither of them needed to put it into words. As Harry diStefano had already sourly pointed out, it wasn't a question of whether she was telling the truth but whether anyone would believe her.

Kathryn considered her options. A defendant charged with a felony—and rape was a felony—had the right to a preliminary hearing within ten court days of his arraignment. Alternatively the DA could take the case before the grand jury to seek an indictment.

There was no guarantee that a grand jury would be able to see past Frankie's demeanor, criminal history and the way she earned her living, to the real crime that had been committed against her. A grand jury was just a representative cross-section of the community, nineteen average citizens. And Frankie was what was known in the system as a "bad victim." "Good victims" have jobs, are well educated, articulate and presentable. "Good victims" are attractive, demure. "Bad victims" are drug and alcohol abusers, prostitutes, anyone who could be expected to elicit biased or negative feelings from the average juror. To make matters worse, Frankie wasn't very likeable. She was sullen when she could have been sympathetic. Before Kathryn could make a decision as to how to proceed, the phone rang. It was Mrs. Thompson, the principal of Emma's elementary school in La Loma.

"I'm grateful I caught you," Mrs. Thompson said. "Can you come to the school right away? It's Emma."

An icy hand clutched Kathryn's heart. "What's wrong?" she whispered.

"Please, don't worry . . . she's not hurt. But I'm

afraid you'll have to come and get her. She's been crying on and off all day. Says she wants you, wants to go home."

"I'll be right there," Kathryn said. She put the phone down.

"It's Emma," she said to Michael. "Tell my secretary I'll be at her school." She headed for the door.

Twenty minutes later she walked into Mrs. Thompson's office at La Loma School. It was a light, airy room looking out on to the playground behind the main school building. The walls were covered with bright, cheerful children's paintings. The principal was a middle-aged woman, perhaps forty-five, with short, dark hair and a thin, earnest face made more studious by dark hornrimmed spectacles.

"We didn't want to over-react," she told Kathryn. "But knowing what had happened to her father, we were . . . concerned. How did Emma react when you told her?"

"She cried nonstop for days. Then she seemed to face up to . . . what happened. The crying stopped. We talked about Jack. Her father. And how she felt. I tried to help her come to terms with his death. It's . . . you never know quite how much of what you're saying makes sense to a child. How much they understand."

Mrs. Thompson moved her head, as though she had intended to say something and then thought better of it. "How about school? Has she said anything?"

"We had a difficult time this morning. She wanted to stay home, not go to school at all."

"Did she tell you why?"

"She said she wanted to be with me."

"Yes, but did she say why?"

Kathryn frowned. "No."

"Let me tell you then, Ms. Mackay," Mrs. Thompson said. "She's afraid someone is going to shoot you."

"What?"

"That's what she told her teacher. She said bad people get into courtrooms with guns. Like the bad person who shot her daddy. She was very needy and clingy in class."

"What can I do, Mrs. Thompson?" Kathryn asked. "Do you have any ideas on how I should handle this?"

"She may want the lights left on and the doors left open. Give her an opportunity to talk. Reassure her that you're not likely to be hurt in the courtroom."

"The truth is, Mrs. Thompson, there isn't enough money available for the county to secure the courtrooms. There are no metal detectors in place at the entrances. Lighting is inadequate inside and outside the courthouse after hours. Jurors find people camped out in restrooms during the rainy season. The other day, an 'in custody' pulled a wire hook from under his arm and struck his defense attorney twice. By the time the bailiff got over to the defense table, blood was running down the attorney's face on to his shirt."

"Then reassure her as realistically as you can. You might discuss practical safety procedures or go over phone numbers with Emma, how to page you in an emergency."

"Anything else?" asked Kathryn.

"Perhaps it would be helpful if Emma talked to a psychologist. I could give you names of two or three who specialize in child and family therapy."

"Thank you, I'd be very grateful."

"Now, let's go get Emma."

Emma was sitting alone in the infirmary. When she saw Kathryn she jumped to her feet and ran to her, throwing her arms around her and hugging her fiercely. "Oh, Mommy, I'm so glad you're here, I'm so glad!" she said. "I was thinking about you and thinking about you all morning."

"Mrs. Thompson said you were crying," Kathryn said, kissing her. "What were you crying about?"

Emma buried her face in Kathryn's shoulder, moving her head from side to side.

"Come on, sweetheart," Kathryn coaxed. "Maybe if you tell me, I can help."

"It's all right now that you're here," Emma said, holding on tight. "I just want to go home. Can we go home, Mommy?"

"If Mrs. Thompson says it's okay," Kathryn said. She looked up at the principal, who nodded.

"I'll leave the names and numbers on your voice mail at the office," the principal said. "See you tomorrow, Emma?"

Emma smiled but did not reply. Kathryn thanked Mrs. Thompson and took her daughter out to the car. Emma got in and stared straight ahead, her hands in her lap, her lips set in a firm line. Her body language was explicit: don't ask me questions.

"How about going to Espanola to get pizza?" Kathryn said, brightly. "We haven't been there in ages."

"Could we just go home, Mom, please?" Emma said. "Just straight home?"

"You know this is all wrong, don't you?" Kathryn

97

said. "Me having to leave work to come get you at school and you not telling me why."

Emma said nothing.

"So do I get to find out what happened?" Kathryn asked.

Still no reply, just the fixed stare straight ahead through the windshield.

"Mrs. Thompson said you were crying in class."

"Pussyface." Emma's voice was almost inaudible.

"What?" Kathryn said, not sure she had heard correctly. "What did you say?"

"Nothing," Emma muttered. "I didn't say anything. Mom, could you just let me alone, okay? I don't want to talk."

"You have to, Em," Kathryn said as gently as she knew how. "You can't keep bottling it up."

"I can if I want to," Emma said, turning her head away to stare furiously out of the side window. She did not speak again all the way home.

To Kathryn's surprise, Dave Granz was waiting outside the condominium in his car. He got out as she pulled to a stop.

"I was in Laguna Heights," he said. "Thought I'd drop by. Hello, Princess. What are you doing home from school so early?"

"Hi, Dave," Emma said, apathetically. She didn't answer his question.

"Hey, you know what the Mother strawberry said to the Baby strawberry?"

"Don't get in a jam," Emma said, without enthusiasm.

"Aw, you heard it," Dave grinned. "Hey, how about

I take you and your mom to Espanola beach? You remember how we used to go there all the time?"

Emma sighed. "I'm real tired, Dave," she said. "Could we go some other time?"

"Sure," he said. "You just say when."

"You two go on up," Kathryn said. "I'll park the car."

She watched as Emma slipped her hand confidently into Dave's and they walked over to the front entrance. In a lot of ways Dave knew Emma better than Jack ever had. Ought she have tried harder to make their relationship work for Emma's sake?

She shook her head exasperatedly. Come on, Kathryn, she chided herself. Calling it off had been hard, remaining good friends even harder; but they had somehow managed both. In many ways they were closer now than they had been as lovers.

Dave and Emma were sitting on the balcony when she came up from the garage. She could hear them talking but not what they were saying. With a shrug she went into the kitchen and put on a kettle to make some tea. After a while, Emma came in. She looked grave but composed.

"What were you talking about?" Kathryn asked her.

"Things," Emma said offhandedly.

"Do you want something to eat?"

Emma shook her head. "Dave wants to talk to you. It's private."

"Sounds mysterious."

"I wish he wouldn't smoke."

"So do I, honey."

"Why does he do it?"

"That's a hard question. Cigarettes are a kind of drug, Em. You want to quit, but you can't."

"Couldn't you get him to stop?"

Kathryn smiled. "I don't think so, Em. I don't think anyone could get Dave to do something he didn't want to do."

"I wish he'd quit," Emma said. "Before something happens."

Now she's worried about Dave dying, Kathryn thought. There must be a way to deal with her fears, but how?

"He's a pretty healthy guy," she told Emma. "Don't worry about him."

Emma went to her room and Dave came in from the balcony.

"Did you hear any of that?" Kathryn asked.

"Enough," he said. "I'm touched."

"So quit smoking."

"Maybe I will," he said.

"You weren't up in Laguna Heights at all, were you?"

"Marcia told me you'd had a call from the school. I put two and two together and came over here."

"What were you and Emma talking about for so long, anyway?"

"She asked me if it's really true people go to Heaven when they die."

"Why would she ask you that?" Kathryn wondered. "I've never known her to have a moment's doubt about it before."

"I don't know. But that's what she asked me."

"And what did you say?"

"I told her the truth. I told her I didn't know. You know what else she said?"

"Tell me," Kathryn said, sipping her tea.

"She asked me if I would take care of her if a bad person killed you."

Kathryn felt like someone had punched her in the stomach. But before she could say anything Dave went on. "Listen, Kathryn, I have an idea. Something that might help take her mind off everything. That's the real reason I came over here."

"I knew there was something," Kathryn said.

"I bought her a present."

"Dave, that's not going to—"

"It's a puppy," he said.

"What?"

"A puppy. I bought her a puppy."

"Are you serious?"

"Look, it's not as crazy as it sounds," Dave said. "He'll need someone to look after him. It's a full time job for a few months. I thought if she had to take care of a puppy, maybe she wouldn't worry about . . . everything else so much."

"A puppy," Kathryn said, shaking her head. "That's not the answer, Dave. Emma is grieving. Grief hurts. We can't—she can't gloss over it, or hurry through it, or deny it. Grieving over someone really important in your life takes time."

"I understand that, Kathryn," he said. "It was just—"

"Right now Emma is scared something will happen that will take me away from her as well. I have to let her work through that. I have to allow her to be sad or angry or depressed, to deal with her grief. Not be distracted from it by a puppy."

"What kind of a puppy?" asked Emma coming into the room.

Dave hesitated, then replied. "This puppy I brought over to meet you. He's a golden Labrador."

"Where is he, where?"

"I'll go get him," Dave said.

He glanced over at Kate then disappeared and she heard the door open down below. A couple of minutes later he came back. Out of his jacket poked a soot-black nose, two brown eyes and a golden muzzle. Emma's eyes widened as she saw the puppy.

"Say hello to Sam, Emma," he said, handing the puppy to Emma.

"Hello, Sam," Emma said. The puppy twisted and wriggled with pleasure, wagging its tiny tail energetically as it tried to lick her face. Emma looked up at Dave, her eyes shining.

"Is he a present? He is, isn't he? He's for me, isn't he? Isn't he, Dave?"

"Well, that depends," he said gravely. "You'd have to promise to look after him. A dog isn't just for while he's a puppy, you know. He's part of your family."

"Oh, I will, I would," Emma said breathlessly. "I would really truly, Dave."

"Well," he said, as if reluctantly.

"Can I keep him, Mom, can I?" Emma asked. "Can I please?" She squinched up her eyes with delight as he started to lick her face.

"It's a big responsibility," Kathryn said. "You have to be sure you want to take it on."

"Oh, I'm sure, I'm sure," Emma said. "Please, Mom, can we, can we?"

"Come on, Kathryn, he'll be fun," Dave said.

As he spoke Emma put the puppy down on the

floor, where he immediately made a puddle. "Bad dog, Sam," she scolded. "Bad dog."

The puppy wagged his tail enthusiastically as Kathryn grabbed some paper towels to soak up the mess, scowling over her shoulder at Dave. "Fun, huh?" she said.

11

Four nights later Kathryn convened the grand jury. At 6:30 P.M., the nineteen jurors filed into Superior Court Two. The foreman, a stocky individual in his mid-fifties with the deeply lined face of someone who has spent most of his life outdoors, took the chair usually occupied by the judge. The others found seats in the jury box and looked expectantly at Kathryn.

She glanced around the courtroom. She knew it the way a fighter knows the ring: the wood-paneled walls, the light oak furniture, the swivel chairs. On the wall behind the judge's high-backed leather chair hung the carved wooden Great Seal with the state and national flags below it. To the left of the bench was a blackboard. The jury box was on the right-hand side of the room, a sectional bookcase on the facing wall.

Tonight there was no judge, no defendant, no

defense attorney, no spectators. The room was empty except for herself, the jurors—one of whom acted as a secretary, another as a sergeant-at-arms responsible for guarding the door—and a court reporter to record the proceedings. Apart from any witness under examination, no other person was permitted to be present. The prosecutor acted as court clerk, bailiff and judge. It was demanding and often exhausting work.

"We are on the record with the Santa Rita County criminal grand jury," Kathryn began, addressing herself to the foreman. "We have taken the roll. For the record, please state how many grand jurors are present."

"Nineteen," he said.

"The case we are going to consider tonight is entitled *The People* versus *Zabrowski,*" Kathryn said. She had already checked to see that Michael was in his office upstairs with Frankie before beginning. "We will be calling only one witness, Francesca Jaramillo. If any of you think you might know her, please indicate by raising your hand."

There was no response. Kathryn then asked the foreman to read the admonition required by Section 939.5 of the Penal Code. The foreman put on his glasses and cleared his throat self-importantly.

"I shall require any member of the grand jury who has a state of mind in reference to the case which would prevent him or her from acting impartially and without prejudice to the substantial rights of the victim or defendant, to retire," he droned. He took off his glasses and looked at Kathryn as if he expected applause.

"In regard to that statement is there anyone present

with such a state of mind?" Kathryn asked. Again no one moved. "The record will show that no hands are raised and that no one has offered to retire," she said and picked up her notes on the Zabrowski rape.

"Ladies and gentlemen of the grand jury, the charge in the case of *The People* versus *Zabrowski* is a violation of Penal Code Section 261: rape."

As always, she emphasized the word and paused to let it sink in.

"Rape," she said again. "We will show that on June 17, the defendant George Zabrowski brutally beat and raped Francesca Jaramillo. Before I call her to testify, however, there is something you need to know about the victim. She is a prostitute."

The jurors were watching her closely. Well, at least they knew the worst, she thought. It was vital to her presentation that Frankie's way of life was on the table right from the start. Right or wrong, the outcome would rest on the way the victim told her story. She drew in a deep breath, like someone preparing to plunge under water.

"I call my only witness—Francesca Jaramillo."

As she picked up the bailiff's phone to call Michael she surreptitiously scanned the faces before her in the jury box. None of them showed any emotion. That was something, she supposed. Within minutes Michael was at the door with Frankie. They had found her a printed rayon dress and dark pumps. She looked almost pretty. As she came into the courtroom, Kathryn went to meet her and led her across to the witness stand. Frankie sat down and stared defiantly at the men and women in the jury box.

Tread softly, Kathryn reminded herself. And hope

the jury does, too. After Frankie was sworn, and gave and spelled her name for the record, Kathryn began her examination.

"Your name is Francesca but everyone calls you Frankie, is that right?"

"Yes."

"Frankie, tell the jury where you were on the evening of Thursday, June 17."

"In Mario's."

"That's a bar on Solano Street in Catalina."

"Right down the street from where I live."

"And what time was this?"

"Eight, eight-thirty, like that."

"Go on."

"This John—this guy sittin' at the bar. He look over at me, you know, give me the eye. I smile. He send a drink over."

"Did you know him?"

"Seen him around."

"I show you people's exhibit 1—can you identify the person depicted in the photograph?"

"Yeah, thass him. George Zabrowski."

"Let the record reflect the witness identified a photograph of the defendant, George Zabrowski," Kathryn said. "Did he speak to you?"

"He came over and said, 'You a good lookin' woman.' I said, 'Ain't that the truth?' He laugh and sit down and we have some drinks."

"How many?"

"Many?" Frankie said. "I don't remember. Five, six."

"What were you drinking, Frankie?"

"Tequila. Margaritas," she said

"Would you say you were intoxicated?"

Frankie bristled. "Just feelin' good. I don't get drunk."

"What happened next?"

"He ask me, 'You got any grass?'"

"Is that exactly what he said, 'Have you got any grass?'"

"No. What he say is, 'I bet you got some shit stashed.'"

"And what did you say?"

"I tell him yes, I got some over my place. And he say, 'Less go, what the fuck we waiting for?'"

"So you went back to your apartment together. What time was this?"

"'Round nine-thirty."

"What happened when you got back to your apartment?"

"We real friendly, you know, a few more drinks, smoke some pot. Then he . . . it change. He start to get mean."

"Exactly how did he get mean?"

"I sittin' on the sofa. He stand up and he say, 'Party time, baby.' Like, mean, you know. He unzip his pants and say, 'Come on, cooze, suck on this. Give me some head.' An' I say, 'That cost you twenty dollars.'"

"Stop there for a moment, Frankie," Kathryn said. "Did Zabrowski know you were a prostitute?"

"Yeah, course he know."

"What happened when you asked him for money?"

"He go crazy," Frankie said. "He grab my hair and throw me against the wall. Then he start hittin' on me."

"I show you people's exhibits 2 through 10," Kathryn said. "Can you identify them?"

"They pictures the cops took of me when I come in to the Sheriff's office."

"Let the record reflect the witness identified photographs taken by CSI on June 19," Kathryn said, handing them to the jurors for inspection.

She turned back to face the witness. "What happened after Zabrowski hit you?"

"I musta black out," Frankie said. "Next thing I know I on the floor and he's rippin' my clothes. I start shoutin', screamin', I don't know. Then he start hitting me again, and this time it real bad. And while he hittin' me he sayin, 'Twenty dollars,' bang, 'fucking bitch,' bang, 'twenty dollars,' bang, 'fucking bitch.'" She drew in a breath that sounded like a sob. "Just hittin' on me an' hittin' on me."

"We know this is painful for you, Frankie," Kathryn said gently. "But please go on."

"I tryin' to crawl away but he come after me, he tear my pants off. I tryin to get him to stop, I mean, I screamin' 'Jesus, don't hit me no more, tell me what you want and I do it for free.'"

"You offered to give him sex if he would stop hitting you? What did he say?"

"He say, 'Fucking-A you will.' He got me up in a corner hittin' on me and yellin', 'Lie down and spread your fucking legs, you bitch. And lift up your ass.' Then he stick it in . . . he did it."

"He penetrated your vagina?"

Frankie looked startled for a moment, as if the word was a surprise to her. "Yes. Thass right."

"Then what happened?"

"When he all through he grab me around the throat. He say, 'You better keep your mouth shut about this.'"

"Were those his exact words?"

"No."

"Tell the jury exactly what he said."

"He say, 'You breathe one fuckin' word of this, I come back and cut your fucking throat.'"

"What did you do then?"

Frankie shrugged. "I just lay there maybe half an hour, thinkin' what I gonna do, you know, did I ought to call the cops. Then I figure, with my record, why would they believe me? So I run a bath. Hot, hot. I sit there I dunno, two, maybe three hours till the water gone cold. Like I, you know, someplace else? Then I went to bed."

"How long did you stay in bed?"

"All the next day. I stiff all over, couldn't hardly move my legs. My face all swelled up, can't see out of my eyes. And I hurtin', you know . . . there."

"Did you call a doctor?"

Frankie displayed astonishment. "You think any doctor gonna come down to Harbor Park see a beat-up whore? On'y time you see a doctor down there, someone dead. What happen is my friend Tania come around that night. She say I got to report what happened. I say he kill me if I do. She say if I don't tell nobody, that sonofabitch—'scuse me—he gonna do the same thing to someone else. So next day I call the cops."

"Thank you, Frankie," Kathryn said. She turned to face the jury box. "That concludes my examination. Do the grand jurors have any questions they would like to ask this witness?"

"Yes, I'd like to ask a question."

The speaker was a blond, beefy man of about thirty, dressed in a white cotton shirt, tan slacks, white socks, and Reeboks with green, purple and blue trim. He had a beer belly and the bad color of someone who spends all his time under artificial light.

"Did this man Zabrowski at any time tell you he wanted sex for money?" he asked. Frankie looked at him in disbelief.

"In them words? No."

"And when he attacked you, how did you resist? Did you fight back? Scream? Call for help?"

Kathryn saw Frankie's anger kindle. "Listen, mister, he beatin' the shit out of me. I didn't want to get killed. I just lay still till he finished."

The man nodded, disbelief plain on his face. Frankie gripped the edge of the witness box tightly and leaned slightly forward, her lips pressed together, as an older woman sitting in the back row of the jury box held up a hand. "I have a question," she said. "Could the witness tell us how long she has been a prostitute?"

"Fourteen years," Frankie said flatly.

The woman nodded primly, her face flushed, her lips a straight line. "And has . . . this . . . ever happened to you before?" she asked.

"Before?" Frankie said, her voice breaking angrily. "Course it never happen before!"

"Then why did you wait four days to report the attack?" a middle-aged man in the front row asked.

"The witness has already explained her reasons for not reporting the rape, sir," Kathryn pointed out, before Frankie could reply. The hostility of the questions was unexpected.

"Yes, but what I'm trying to get at is, how do we know she isn't doing this, you know, to get revenge or something?" the man persisted. "I mean, has this man Zabrowski ever been in trouble for anything like this?"

"That isn't a question the witness can answer, sir," Kathryn replied.

"You said you've been . . . on the street fourteen years," a man in the front row said. "Did you run away from home?"

"I'm sorry, sir, that's irrelevant to the charge," Kathryn said.

"I answer him," Frankie said, making no effort to conceal her anger now. "I tell him. Yes, I run away from home. You wanna know why, I tell you. My daddy start screwing me when I eight, mister. Then he start bringin' friends back to the house. I fourteen then. So I run away. That answer your question?"

The silence was palpable. Kathryn let it lengthen, hoping Frankie's angry outburst might just work for her. On the other hand, of course, it might have completely alienated the jury; there was no way of knowing.

"If there are no more questions . . . ?" she said, looking around. Nobody spoke. She smiled at the witness. "Thank you, Frankie. You may be excused."

Frankie Jaramillo looked at the jury and walked out of the courtroom; Kathryn could see anger and contempt in every line of her body. The jury saw it too. As the door opened, Kathryn saw Michael standing outside; they would wait there until she joined them. She turned now to face the jury. They stared back at her—almost defiantly, she felt.

"Ladies and gentlemen of the grand jury, I want to thank you for being so patient and attentive, and also for your pertinent and perceptive questions. There are just a few things I want to say to you before you retire to consider the indictment."

Pertinent and perceptive questions, my ass. But you caught more flies with honey than vinegar.

"Rape is a crime of power and control. It's violence with sex as the weapon. Anyone can be a victim of rape—children, teenagers, mothers, grandmothers, even nuns. But rape victims also include dope dealers, crackheads, junkies, thieves—and prostitutes. It doesn't matter whether the victim is a nun, or like Frankie Jaramillo, a prostitute. If she's been raped you have a duty to indict."

She paused, trying to gauge their reaction. There was no feedback, nothing. Was she getting through to them?

"You swore that you would be fair and follow the law. The law doesn't say prostitutes can't be raped. It doesn't matter whether you approve of how Frankie Jaramillo makes her living. If you decide here tonight that the evidence shows the defendant raped Francesca Jaramillo, you must—you *must*—return an indictment against George Zabrowski.

"Think of a rapist as a predator. Like any predator out there, a rapist wants easy prey. And a prostitute is easy prey. Why? Because the rapist is gambling that no jury is going to believe the word of a prostitute. Prove him wrong."

She stepped back and let it sink in. The jurors looked at her stonily. Come on, try, damn you, she thought.

"I will now leave you to deliberate," she said. "If you have any questions of a legal nature, I will be waiting outside the courtroom."

She left the room and sat down on the bench outside next to Frankie Jaramillo and Michael Gaines. It was almost dark outside.

Frankie's face was still set in anger. "How long do they usually take to decide, anyways?" she asked.

Before Kathryn could reply the courtroom door opened and the sergeant-at-arms nodded to her. The grand jurors had completed their deliberations. Fast, she thought. Too fast. She squeezed Frankie Jaramillo's hand and went back inside. The faces of the members of the jury were unreadable as she took her place at the prosecution table.

"In the case of *The People* versus *Zabrowski,* has the grand jury reached a decision?" Kathryn asked.

"Yes, we have," the foreman replied, avoiding her eyes. "The grand jury cannot find an indictment against the defendant."

Kathryn stared at the jury and they stared back at her. Damn it, she thought, I lost them. She thanked them again, then turned on her heel and went out, letting the door bang shut loudly behind her. Michael and Frankie looked up expectantly as Kathryn came out into the corridor. When he saw her expression, disappointment clouded Michael's face.

"They refused to indict?"

"I'm sorry, Frankie," Kathryn said. "I'm truly sorry."

"They didn't believe me, did they?" Frankie said. "I knew they wouldn't. You can't rape a whore, right?"

"Frankie, it wasn't that," Kathryn protested. But what was it and how could she explain it?

"Goddammit, Kathryn," Michael said, angrily.

"Let's prelim it and take it to trial. We know Zabrowski raped Frankie."

Kathryn shook her head. "Michael, a grand jury is no different from any other kind of jury. If this one won't indict, what makes you think taking it to trial would change things?"

"You're just going to drop it? Let another rapist walk?"

"Let's ask Frankie," Kathryn said. "How do you feel, Frankie? What if I took it to a preliminary hearing?"

"Forget it," the woman said flatly. "I mean, I 'preciate what you tryin' to do here, but no way I goin' through that again, fat cow asking me how many times I been raped, like I do it for a hobby. Pardon my French, Ms. Mackay, but fuck it, I'm outa here."

She stalked off towards the door, every line of her body stiff with anger and hurt. Michael started after her but Kathryn laid a hand on his arm.

"Let her go, Michael," she said. "It's over."

He shook his head frustratedly. "Jesus, I hate this," he said fiercely. "I hate to lose like this."

"You think it makes me feel good? You think I'm happy that Frankie didn't get justice?" Kathryn snapped back.

Gaines was immediately contrite. "Hell, I'm sorry, Kathryn," he said. "You did your best."

"We all did our best," she said. "It just wasn't good enough. There are still times when society judges the rape by the victim rather than the perpetrator. This was one of them. So let it go."

"Okay," he said. "I'll let it go. But nobody said I have to like it."

12

As Granz got into his car the cellular phone rang. He picked it up and spoke his name.

"Dave, this is Morgan Nelson. Where are you?"

"Alameda Heights, Doc."

"I'm in South Alameda. Something I want you to see. Can you get over here right away?"

"Give me the address."

It was an apartment house on Laguna Boulevard, easy to identify because the white coroner's van was parked at an angle near the curb outside the building. Granz slid his car into the space on its left.

"Second floor, turn right top of the stairs," the deputy coroner said as he met Dave at the car. "Follow your nose."

The reason for his macabre humor became obvious as Granz got to the upper landing and the all-too-familiar coppery tang of death assailed his nostrils. The door of the apartment was open. He went inside and saw Morgan Nelson bending over the body of a man lying on a rumpled bed.

White, mid-thirties, Granz judged. The man lay naked on his back, dressed only in pantyhose and a bra. His eyes were wide open, bulging as if in rage.

The skin of his face, neck and upper chest had a cyanotic tinge. Both hands were bound at his sides by a braided cord that looked as if it might have come from a robe. A sanitary pad was wedged in his mouth and held in place by a pair of panties wrapped around his head.

"Do we know who he is?" Dave Granz asked.

"Tell him, Dougherty," Morgan Nelson said to the deputy coroner standing near the door.

"Name's Harry Bosendorf," Dougherty said, referring to his clipboard. "Age thirty-two. Unmarried."

"Who found the body?"

"The landlady came by for her rent. Couple of days pass, he still doesn't answer. She uses her passkey. There he was."

"How long has he been dead?"

Morgan shrugged and stuck out his lower lip. "I'd put it at four, maybe five days."

"What exactly happened here?"

"Another autoerotic fatality," Morgan told him briskly. "The sanitary pad inhibited his intake of oxygen, but not completely: he could breathe through it while it was dry. Look, see how slack the cord holding his arms is tied. He could slip his feet between his arms and pull it down to free them. Then he could remove the gag before it got dangerous."

"But something went wrong."

"The petechial hemorrhages of the conjunctival and laryngeal mucosa suggest to me he'd reached a stage of asphyxia that impaired his judgment. He couldn't coordinate his movements to free his hands, take out the gag. It got soaked in saliva and expanded, blocking the trachea. Goodbye, Charlie. Or in this case, Harry."

"Okay, so you've got another autoerotic death. What made you think I'd be interested?"

"Go on, Pat," Morgan told the deputy.

"The guy's got a rap sheet," Dougherty told Granz. "Goes back a couple of years. All sex-related stuff, you can see it escalating. Arrests for prowling, burglary, assault, battery and rape."

Granz looked at the pathologist and shook his head impatiently.

"Bear with me, Dave," Nelson said. "Go on, Pat."

"Last August, Harry here and his buddies picked up a seventeen-year-old girl at the boardwalk, took her to a local motel and gang-raped her. She made a positive identification of his buddies but couldn't identify Bosendorf. Eventually the buddies went to prison. With no ID and no physical evidence to hold him, Bosendorf was released."

"So?" Granz said to Morgan Nelson.

"Doesn't it bother you?"

"Doesn't *what* bother me?"

"You remember the Piselli autopsy?"

"Piselli electrocuted himself. You saying there's a connection to Bosendorf?"

"No. A coincidence. An unusual one. Bosendorf walked on rape charges too."

"Coincidences happen, Doc."

"I accept that. I merely wished to draw it to your attention."

"Why?"

"So I wouldn't have to lie awake worrying about it."

"And so I can?"

Nelson frowned. "Something like that. Will you do the psychological autopsy for me?"

"Aw, shit, Doc, gimme a break here!" Granz said. "I'm in trial with Kathryn and working with the SO on a murder investigation."

Nelson said nothing, waiting.

"Look, is there anything about this—anything at all—that makes you think it wasn't an accidental death?"

"Not based on what I've seen so far," Morgan said. "It's almost a textbook case, right down to the ejaculate on the pantyhose. But I won't know for sure until I conclude the autopsy."

"Okay, if you come up with anything during the autopsy, I'll follow it up," Granz said.

"Okay, Dave," Nelson said equably.

Granz shook his head in vexation. "Dammit, Doc, you knew I'd say that, didn't you?"

"No," Nelson said over his shoulder as he examined the body on the bed. "But I hoped you would."

"Coincidence," Kathryn said. "It can't be anything else."

"That's exactly what I said," Dave told her. "But you know Doc. He spots things ninety nine out of a hundred pathologists wouldn't even notice. I mean, here's Bosendorf, he's been four days in a warm room, most pathologists would say shit, let's get this done and get out of here. But not Doc. He notices the hairs on the dead man's arms have been torn out, you remember the way Piselli's wrists were? Sometime before his death, the guy's arms were bound with adhesive tape."

Kathryn frowned. "I thought we agreed that wouldn't be unusual in an autoerotic fatality?"

"Well, yes. We know these autoerotic freaks tie

themselves up all sorts of weird ways, but they don't usually rip off the bondage before they even get started on the sex."

"You think there might have been another person involved?"

"That's untypical too. The essence of the experience is that it's secret, solitary."

"What, then?"

Granz shrugged. "It's just . . . two autoerotic deaths. Both of them one-time rape suspects."

"What are you saying?"

"Nothing," Granz said, perhaps more emphatically than he had intended. "I've told Doc if anything out of the ordinary turns up during the autopsy, I'll do the PA."

Death came officially in only four forms: natural, accidental, suicide and homicide. Unless clearly one of the first two, all fatalities were treated as suspected homicides until it was established through investigation that the deceased had—whether deliberately or inadvertently—taken his own life. This was done by means of what was called a PA, a psychological autopsy. The procedure had a great deal in common with a homicide investigation.

"You don't have enough work?" Kathryn said, raising her eyebrows. "You want me to find you something to do?"

"How's Sam?" he asked abruptly, getting up and walking across to the window.

"Messy," Kathryn said. "And according to our neighbors, he barks nonstop all the time we're out of the condo."

"What about Emma?"

"She adores him."

"You know what I mean."

"She has mood swings. Bright one minute, dark the next, like the sun on a cloudy day. What makes it tougher is it's totally unpredictable."

"She's okay at school?"

"Most of the time. She's seeing a therapist."

He made a wry face. "You sure that's the answer?"

"I don't know what the answer is, Dave. I only wish I did. I'm willing to give anything a try."

"I worry about you, Kathryn. No, not just over Emma. You don't eat properly, you don't get enough sleep. You're on call for every rape, every homicide. You're in the middle of a murder trial. You can't handle it all alone."

"I've handled everything else that ever came along."

"I know you have," he rasped. "But I never saw it grinding you down like this. Hurting you."

"You think I don't know what it's doing to me?" she shot back hotly. "I'm just getting through it, Dave, a day at a time. And you know what it's like? It's like I'm a cat sliding down a plate-glass window. All I've got is my claws. I don't know if I can hold on. But I'm trying."

"Aw, shit, I'm sorry, Kathryn," he said. "It's just . . . look, I only want what's best for you. For both of you. Tell me how I can help."

"If you really want to help, give me time, give me room," she said. "I need it, and I know Emma does too."

Granz held up his hands in surrender. "If that's what you want, that's what you've got."

"Thanks, Dave," she said, "for being a good friend."

"Not quite what I had in mind," he muttered, and she wondered what he meant, but something in his eyes told her this wasn't the moment to ask.

13

He was angry with himself. Furious. He hammered his fist on the steering wheel. Stupid, stupid, stupid. How could he have been so stupid? Everything had been perfect, everything. And then he had blown it. Something about her, something about the little pig had set off an explosion, a clamoring urgency inside him that fired a disregard for the consequences.

He knew it was a bad mistake, knew it the second, the moment he did it, exultant with the salt taste of blood on his lips, but then it was already too late. He had broken his own cardinal rule again. Stupid, stupid, stupid.

The little pig lived in a ranch-style house on Tamarisk Drive at La Loma Beach, about a mile southeast of Laguna del Mar, an upper-income area where houses sold for between three and four hundred thousand dollars. He preferred to find his victims in neighborhoods like this. It was easier; they all had that confidence that comes from the comfort of money, the conviction that nothing bad could ever happen to them here.

Her name was Stacie Percell. He found her in the weddings and engagements section of the local paper. Everything he needed to know. Even a photograph. She had short blonde hair and a wide generous mouth. He liked women with full lips. The item in the newspaper said she was a manager at the Men's Store in Laguna del Mar. He went in a few times and shopped. She was a tall girl, slender without being skinny, soft-spoken, with an air of vulnerability that excited him.

And so the stalking began. The building excitement of it, watching her come and go from work, establishing the pattern of her days, identifying her parents, her friends. The first penetration, entering the house, touching her possessions, smelling her clothes.

He wanted to stretch it out longer but when her parents went on vacation it seemed like too good a chance to miss; maybe that had been why it went wrong. Maybe he was too hasty. Maybe he should have just filed it for later. But he wanted her. The more he watched her, the more he wanted to do it. So he went in.

He'd been as careful as he always was, everything checked, everything worked out. The phones unplugged, the escape route open and waiting. He put his hand over her mouth and she woke up with a muffled grunt, arching her body upwards.

"Hello, little pig," he said. He let her see the combat knife. She went very still, her whole body trembling. Lust raged through him like water. She made a sound beneath his hand.

"Be quiet," he told her, making his voice harsh. "If you promise to be quiet and cooperate, I won't hurt you. Nod your head if you understand."

Her eyes were huge in the semi-darkness. He could see what she was thinking. You could always see what they were thinking. She nodded her head.

"I'm going to take my hand away. If you scream, I'll kill you. I just got out of prison two weeks ago. Don't make any trouble because I've killed other girls I did this with."

She nodded her head again. He took his hand away and she drew in a long, deep, quavering breath.

"Don't hurt me," she managed. "Please. I'll give you money . . ."

"Shut up," he said. "I'm not in the mood for talking."

"Please," she said again.

He laid the knife blade along her cheek. "Do as I say, little pig," he said. "Take everything off."

She took off her nightgown and panties, shivering. The clothing made soft sounds against her body. Her breasts gleamed in the darkness. Her skin was faintly damp with perspiration. He could smell it.

"Spread your legs," he said.

"No," she whimpered. "Oh, please, no."

"Do it, or I'll hurt you bad," he threatened.

She parted her legs and he heard the familiar thunder inside his head. As he was about to enter her, she tried to twist her head away and anger surged up inside him. Her hair brushed his mouth and he thought, Bitch! He heard her scream as his teeth met and he felt warm wetness on his lips and face. He clamped a hand over her mouth before she could

*scream again, jamming her head back hard into the
bloody pillow. She was crying now, but he ignored that.
They all cried.*

*"Spread, spread!" he growled. "Come on, piggy,
shove your ass!"*

*He was angry, angry with her, angry with himself.
She had made him do that. It was an error, and she
had made him make it. She contorted with pain as he
jammed himself into her, feeling her soft roughness
envelop him. She was nobody now, nothing. He was
alone, king, conqueror. It was like going up a mountain, always the same, never ever the same. He hurt her
and he was glad.*

*"You made me do that," he said when it was over.
"It was your own fault."*

*He slid off her, still angry. In the darkness he saw she
was lying on her back, rigid, staring at the ceiling,
holding the side of her head with bloodstained fingers.
Tears coursed down her face.*

"You said . . . you said . . ." she sobbed.

"I lied," he said and left her there.

County Communications called at a little after 3
A.M. They gave Kathryn the address where the rape
had occurred. Kathryn asked the dispatcher to notify
Inspector Gaines and have him meet her there. Next
she called her neighbor, Ruth Draper, who lived on
the floor below, to come up and stay with Emma.

That done she took a quick shower and got dressed:
Guess jeans and a chambray shirt. She took time to
apply a light touch of color to her eyes and cheeks, ran
a comb through her long dark hair. By the time she
was ready to leave, Ruth arrived, half asleep, a quilted
robe wrapped around her chunky body. A little more

than fifteen minutes after receiving County Comm's call, Kathryn was on her way.

Tamarisk Drive was a steeply curving road running between Loma Prieta Boulevard and Shoreside Drive, about half a mile east of Marina Village. Its residents would be shocked. Rape wasn't supposed to happen on tranquil, affluent streets like Tamarisk Drive. But it did.

Crime scenes always had a certain sameness about them: the yellow-taped cordon, the carelessly-parked patrol cars, the background squawking of police radios, the weary cop telling curious neighbors to keep moving, the crime-scene van outside the house. Kathryn parked her car behind one of the several patrol cars and got out. As she started up the path she saw Michael Gaines's car pull to a stop behind her little red Mazda. He hurried over to join her.

They showed ID to the reserve at the door of the house logging the names of everyone who entered. His nameplate said PETERSEN.

"Morning," Kathryn said. "Who's in charge?"

"Jack Burrows," Petersen said.

"Bad one?" she asked. Petersen tipped back his hat with a stubby forefinger and shook his head.

"Bad enough," he said resignedly. "Go on in."

Inside the house, investigator Charles Yamamoto was photographing the crime scene.

"Hey, Charlie," she said.

"Kathryn," Charlie nodded. He was a short man with lank jet-black hair and the build of a jockey. He always looked harassed, but his work was impeccable.

"When you get through photographing, could you video the scene from the victim's account?" she asked.

Charlie pointed a finger and thumb at her like a pistol. "You got it," he said, and pulled the trigger.

The routine never varied. The crime scene was photographed, measured and diagrammed. Investigators dusted for patent and latent impressions; others collected trace evidence. A search was conducted for shoetrack and footwear evidence. If any were found, tire impressions from vehicles were made. Nobody hurried, nobody took short cuts. There were no second chances at a crime scene.

The I/O—investigating officer in charge at the scene—was Jack Burrows, a sergeant in the Sheriff's Office. He was a short, stubby, balding man with a brusque manner. They had both worked with him many times.

"She live alone?" Gaines asked, looking around.

"With her folks," Burrows replied. "They're away on vacation. Antigua, someplace in the Caribbean. I got someone trying to locate them."

"How about a description?"

"She did the best she could. Medium to tall, strong build, a long face."

"Forced entry?" Gaines asked.

"Cut out a pane of glass, let himself in," Jack said, "unplugged the phones."

"Any prints?" Gaines asked.

"Looks like he wore gloves."

"Anybody see or hear anything?"

"We're going door-to-door now."

"Have you thought about bringing in search dogs?" Kathryn asked.

"Might be worth a try. But he probably had a car parked somewhere close."

"Any shoetracks?"

"Some indentations. It's a gravel path."

"You take her to County General?" Gaines asked.

Burrows nodded. "She was bleeding pretty bad. The bastard bit half her ear off."

"He what?"

"Go look at the bed."

"Jack, radio your detective at the hospital," Kathryn said urgently. "Tell him to make sure no one touches the area of the bite with their bare hands. And have him tell the nurse examiner to put a protective cover over the bite to prevent abrasion or contamination."

She turned to face Gaines. "Michael, arrange for a forensic dentist and a photographer to meet us at the hospital. And make a note to confirm the SANE swabbed the bite for saliva."

Bites could yield a great deal of information about a rapist: not only was it possible to determine the biter's blood type from traces of saliva on the bitten skin, but once the suspect was apprehended, his teeth could then be compared to the bite mark, placing him at the scene.

"Yamamoto can take one-to-one photos of the bite mark," Burrows said. Michael made a notation.

"Who took the victim's statement?"

"Woods," Burrows said. "SO deputy who responded to the 9-1-1. You want to talk to him?"

"Where is he?"

"Should be back about now. I told him to go get some coffee."

They went outside; Woods was standing next to his patrol car sipping coffee from a paper cup. He was on the thin side, with straight, black hair and deep-set dark eyes. He looked young and inexperienced; Kathryn could feel his hand shake as she introduced herself. It wasn't just the victim who got hurt in a rape.

"What time did you take the call?" Gaines asked him.

"Three minutes after two," the deputy replied. "I was over on Lighthouse. Took me a couple of minutes to get here. It was foggy. Then all at once I see her in the headlights. She was naked. Looked like she was covered with blood. I stopped, jumped out of the car. She ran right into me. She was hysterical. There was so much blood, I thought she'd been knifed."

"Did she give you a description of the rapist?"

"She wasn't making a lot of sense at first. But I got her calmed down a little. He was a big guy, she said. Above medium height, well built. Middle thirties, dark hair and dark staring eyes. She said he was strong."

"Go on."

"She said she was asleep. When she woke up he was sitting on her, you know, astraddle. She said he had a knife. He said, 'Hello, little pig.'"

"He said *what?*" Gaines voice was thick with disbelief.

"He said, 'Hello, little pig.' He told her if she was quiet and cooperated he wouldn't hurt her."

"Did he tie her up? Gag her?"

"He had a hand over her mouth. He told her he just got out of prison two weeks ago and he'd killed other girls he'd raped."

"And she believed him."

"She said she was scared, but she was trying to think of a way, you know, to hold him off. She said she tried to talk to him, but he said he wasn't in the mood to talk. He put the knife against her face and told her to take off her clothes."

"What was she wearing?" Kathryn asked.

"Nightgown, panties."

"Make sure they seize them, Michael."

Gaines nodded. "She tell you anything else he said?"

"She was falling apart, shivering. The bastard bit off her ear, did you know that?"

"We know," Kathryn said. "You radioed for an ambulance?"

"First thing I did. She wouldn't go back in the house. I talked to her in the car. See the blood?"

"Did she tell you what else he did to her?"

"He told her to spread her legs. Shove her ass."

"Exactly those words?" Gaines asked.

Woods nodded. "Yeah, 'Shove your ass.' That bastard. She said he hurt her. I guess they can tell you more at the hospital."

"Anything else we ought to know?" Kathryn asked.

"Yeah. He told her it was her fault. She made him do it."

"Do what? Rape her? Or bite her ear off?"

Woods made an angry sound. "Who knows what the fuck the asshole meant?"

"Take it easy, Woods," Gaines told him. "No use getting mad."

"Sure," the deputy said, looking at the blood on the seat of the patrol car. "Sure. Take it easy."

14

When Kathryn got to the hospital, the rape kit examination of Stacie Percell was about halfway done. Nurse examiner Jane Ostheimer had attempted recovery of saliva from the bite mark, using swabs wetted with distilled water. She had also sampled the adjacent area as a control for later forensic examination.

Kathryn caught Jane's eye through the window, raised her eyebrows questioningly and pointed at her watch. The nurse opened and closed her hand four times. Twenty minutes: almost finished. Kathryn nodded and made can-I-come-in? signals. Jane beckoned and Kathryn entered the examining room, standing at the foot of the examining table out of the way but where she could watch.

"Stacie," Jane said, "this is Kathryn Mackay from the District Attorney's office. She's the prosecutor who is going to help you and she would like to watch the examination. Would that be okay with you?"

Stacie Percell nodded. Her skin was as white as the sheet on the examining table; there were dark shadows like bruises beneath her eyes. "I don't mind," she said, her voice not much more than a whisper. "I'm glad you're here, Ms. Mackay. I've read about you in the newspaper."

"Please, Stacie, call me Kathryn. I just want to be sure we don't miss anything. Jane, sorry to hold things up."

"No problem," Jane said. "I was just getting to the toluidine blue."

"Isn't that the dye that highlights lacerations?" Kathryn asked.

"That's the one," Jane said, more for Stacie's benefit than Kathryn's. "Toluidine blue is a nuclear dye. It discolors and stains skin-cell nuclei."

Normal vulvar skin cells contain no nuclei, she told them, so the dye did not affect undamaged tissue. However, injuries caused by forced intercourse exposed deeper layers of the epidermis where the cells *are* nucleated and therefore susceptible to the stain in the dye. So lacerations retained the dye and showed up stained a deep royal blue.

Lacerations of genital tissue were significant evidence that a rape had occurred, Kathryn knew; such damage was exceedingly rare in consensual intercourse. Using this new technique would greatly enhance the examiner's visual scrutiny for signs of genital injuries, often so tiny they could easily be missed.

"Now, Stacie, this won't hurt a bit," the nurse said, applying a small amount of one per cent aqueous solution of toluidine blue to a cotton-tip applicator. "I'm just going to swab a little bit of your skin with dye. It will turn dark blue where there are small lacerations and I will take photographs to show the injuries. This will help Ms. Mackay to prove what happened when they catch the man who did this."

Jane swabbed the fourchette with the dye, let the area dry for a few seconds, then wiped it gently with a cotton ball impregnated with lubricating jelly until there was no further recovery of the dye.

"Two things we have to be concerned about," she explained to Kathryn, "tiny skin crevices need to be wiped carefully so they don't show up as lacerations in the photographs. Second, we must clean the test area very carefully because both the dye and the lubricating jelly are spermicides, and any incursion of either into the vagina might preclude recovery of motile sperm in subsequent forensic tests."

"Then why not do the toluidine blue exam after the internal examination?" Kathryn asked.

"Well, you'd think that would be better, but it isn't. Sometimes insertion of the speculum, especially if it isn't done carefully, can create small lacerations not dissimilar to those caused by the forced intercourse."

Kathryn nodded her understanding. "And there goes the evidence."

"Right. So we do the blue dye first. Look. Positive. See those tiny dark blue jagged lines? Lacerations."

The 35mm tripod-mounted Pentax camera clicked off half a dozen frames as Jane pressed the remote shutter release cable.

"Won't be able to argue with those pictures. Just a few more minutes, Stacie, and we'll be all done. Are you okay?"

"I'm okay, but I'll be glad when this is over."

"I know," Kathryn said gently and squeezed her hand. "Just hang on. It won't be much longer."

Jane Ostheimer touched her shoulder and nodded in the direction of the office. Kathryn understood.

"Stacie, I need to leave for a minute and meet the inspector from our office. I'll be right outside, and we'll come in to talk with you as soon as Jane is finished. Will that be okay?

"Anything will be better than this," the young woman said softly.

Kathryn went back to the office. It seemed like a long time until Jane came out of the examination room, snapping off the surgical gloves and tossing them into a bin. She was a short, plump, motherly-looking woman with a ready smile. She flopped into a chair and let her breath out with a grateful sigh.

"I'd kill for a cup of coffee," she said, as Michael Gaines came in through the outer door.

"I'll get you one," he offered. "How do you take it?"

"Thanks, Michael, maybe later. I don't want to leave Stacie alone. She's been through too much already."

"Kathryn?"

Kathryn shook her head. "If I drink any more coffee I'll ricochet off the walls," she said. "Can we talk to Stacie now, Jane?"

"I ought to put her to bed," Jane said. "She was trembling like a leaf."

"I noticed that. It's hardly surprising."

"How has she been?" Michael asked.

Jane looked at him. "How do you think?"

"She didn't talk about it at all?"

"Only, you know, answering questions while I examined her."

"No anger?"

"Not yet. It'll come."

"By the way, Jane, I don't remember seeing that camera equipment before," Kathryn remarked. "How did you talk the County into springing the dollars?"

"I didn't." She smiled; probably the first time she had smiled all day, Kathryn thought. "A friend donated it to us—camera, flash, tripod, motor drive, remote cable—even threw in a roll of film."

"Some friend. How did he know you needed it?"

"Oh, I guess he just got sick of me complaining about the lack of equipment and the lack of money to buy it," Jane said, "and my bellyaching about having to borrow Polaroids from the cops who bring in the victims."

Kathryn smiled at the picture Jane painted. Everyone in law enforcement knew about having to improvise on the spot.

"Hey, could you introduce me to this friend of yours?" she said. "We could use a few more computers in the DA's office."

"Sorry, Kathryn, he's my private resource."

"I was afraid you'd feel like that. Well . . . let's go in, Michael," Kathryn said. "And thanks, Jane."

"Sure," the nurse examiner said, watching them dispassionately as they went into the examination room. The young woman sitting on the bed looked up and Kathryn saw in her eyes the pain she had seen in the eyes of so many rape victims, the ineradicable realization that every certainty in her life was gone forever.

"Stacie, this is Michael Gaines, the inspector I

mentioned. He was at your house after they brought you to the hospital. We'd like to talk to you if you're not too tired."

"Hello, Stacie," Michael said. "Is there anything we can get you?"

Stacie Percell started to shake her head, then winced with pain, a hand moving involuntarily toward the padded dressing covering her left ear.

"How long do I have to stay here?" she asked.

"The doctors decide that, not us," Kathryn said. "Do you feel like talking?"

"I already talked with Jane."

"This isn't part of the exam," Kathryn said. "We need to know what you saw, what you heard. What your senses told you."

Stacie Percell shuddered. "Isn't it enough I had to live through it?"

"Stacie, we're here because we want to catch the person who did this to you. Anything you can tell us is important," Michael said. "There are probably things about this man you don't even realize you know."

Stacie frowned. "How can that be?"

"Think," Michael said urgently. "Think back. Close your eyes. You're in your room, asleep. What's the first thing you remember?"

Stacie closed her eyes. She was silent for a moment, then spoke in a rush. "I thought it was a dream. I was under something, in the dark. It was on my chest, heavy. Then I woke up."

"What could you see?"

"Someone was there. Him. He was there, on me, on me, sitting on my stomach . . . a shape. His hand was over my face. Like this." Stacie clasped her hand over her nose and mouth, pushing her head back to demonstrate.

"Gloves?" Michael asked. "Was he wearing gloves?"

"Rubber," she said. "Yes. Surgical gloves."

"Could you see his face?"

"Eyes," Stacie said and shuddered again. "Glaring eyes. He wore a mask. Like a ski mask. Black. Rough. When he . . ." Her hand moved toward the side of her head. "I felt it on my face. Wool, maybe. Or something rough like that."

"Clothes," Kathryn said. "Could you see them?"

"Sweats, I think."

"What color?"

"Black," Stacie said. "No, blue. Navy blue sweatshirt and sweatpants."

"Are you sure, did you touch them?"

"No. Yes. I must have."

"What was the first thing he said?"

"He said, 'Hello, little pig.'"

"You're sure?" Again Kathryn heard the tension in Michael's voice.

"I'm sure. He had a knife in his hand. I could see it."

They could see her remembering the fear, remembering the helplessness, terrors scurrying in her mind like rats in a cage. They waited.

"I must have made a noise, because he said, "If you promise to be quiet I won't hurt you." He told me to nod my head if I understood."

"Did you?"

Stacie nodded. "He said he was going to take away

his hand and that if I screamed he'd kill me. He said he'd only just come out of prison and—"

"Were those his exact words, 'I've only just come out of prison'?"

Stacie hesitated, frowned. " 'I just got out of prison two weeks ago,' is what he said. He said he'd killed other girls who made trouble."

"Stacie, try to remember exactly what the man said," Kathryn told her. "I know it's painful, but it's very important."

"He said, 'Don't make any trouble.' I wanted to scream, but he had the knife . . . I said I would give him money, only not to hurt me. And he told me to shut up."

"He said that, 'Shut up'?"

"No. He said, "Be quiet." Like he was angry. *'Be quiet.'* "

"And then?"

"He said, 'I don't want to talk,' or 'I don't feel like talking,' something like that. Then he . . . he put the knife on my face and he . . . he . . ."

"It's all right, Stacie," Kathryn said soothingly. "You're under no pressure here. Do you want to stop for a while?"

"Yes. No. It's . . . I'm okay. Just . . . what happened. What he did."

"Would you like something to drink? Some tea?"

"No. I want to finish this. I want it to be over." She said it with a faint trace of anger. That was good, Kathryn thought. She was fighting back.

"All right. He put the knife against your face. Where?"

She touched her left cheek. "Here."

"Go on."

"He told me to take off my clothes. I tried to . . . I said, something, 'no,' 'please,' I don't remember. He said, 'Do as I say, little pig.' It . . . he . . . he . . . I could hear him breathing. Like someone who's run upstairs. Angry. Then he . . . then he said, 'Spread your legs.'"

"Did you take off your clothes before he said that, or after?"

"Oh, my clothes, I forgot, yes, I took them off. When he told me."

"Why?" Kathryn asked, gently. "Why did you do that?"

Stacie Percell's eyes widened. "I had to. I had to."

"I know you did, Stacie. But why?"

"I was afraid he would kill me if I didn't," Stacie said.

"I want you to remember that," Kathryn told her. "Keep on telling yourself. You didn't do anything willingly. You didn't have any choice. The only reason this happened was because you were afraid he would kill you. You have nothing to be ashamed of."

"He said, 'Do it, or I'll hurt you.' He had his hand flat on my chest, pushing me down on the bed, and I was afraid he was going to cut me with the knife. His voice was mean, and he said, 'Shove your ass, piggy, come on, spread, spread.' Then he . . . then he . . . did it."

Tears coursed down her face, but she made no sound, her eyes staring past them. There was nothing they could do. They sat and waited. It was painful and it was sad, but they had no choice.

There was a great deal more they still needed to know. Knowing the rapist's words and actions after the rape was as important as knowing what he had said and done during the attack. After that they would need to question Stacie about her life over the past month or so; whether she had received any hang-up phone calls, or noticed anyone watching her, or following her. Whether there had been any indication of a break-in at her home, whether any of her clothes were missing or rearranged in her dresser drawers, whether anything else unusual had happened.

The questioning was like a dance, following a form they had hammered out in the course of hundreds of interviews like this. Neither had to think about the other, knowing that every cue would be taken, every nuance heard. Even so, it was only the beginning. Next came the investigation; to oversee these for the DA's office, Kathryn relied on Michael Gaines and he always delivered. At what cost to himself, she did not know, but that it was high she did not doubt.

Rape victims were extremely emotional and drew greedily on the investigating officer's every resource. There was no give and take; it was all give and give. But Michael seemed to be able to handle it. He gave no sign of the shell so many investigators developed—the detached attitude, the cool indifference, the sick jokes that masked the reality of what they saw every day.

She remembered a conversation she had with Michael soon after he was assigned to work rapes. She had asked how he worked off the inevitable stress of his job.

"I've talked it over with Doc Nelson," he said.

"He says you've just got to find a way to deal with it; work some of it out and learn to live with what's left over."

There were only four ways to handle stress, Doc had told him. You could bury it in your subconscious, prefer not to remember, the way some rape victims repressed every detail of what had happened to them. That'll get you a heart attack by the time you're forty-five. You could blame others, project your own shortcomings on to something or someone else. That'll lose you what few friends you have, plus get you a heart attack by the time you're forty-five. You could rationalize what you were doing; why you became a cop, why you work sex crimes, why rapes happen. That'll get you crazy because you can't rationalize that stuff no matter how hard you try. Or you could try to displace the bad feelings by substituting more acceptable ones.

"That's what works for me," he said. "When I get bummed, I work out. I like to play basketball, punch a bag in the gym, lift weights; anything that makes me sweat. Half an hour, forty-five minutes. Like when I was a kid in Texas. Get mad, then go shoot some hoops in the driveway or go a few rounds with the heavy bag in the garage. Something real satisfying about punching a bag that can't punch back."

"Maybe I ought to try it," Kathryn said.

"You come round any time," he grinned. "You can punch mine."

She found herself wondering whether a few rounds with the bag was still working for him as she looked up at the wall clock. Thank God, tomorrow was a Friday: the courts were dark. Monday she would begin her closing argument in the Riker trial. She put that out of her mind and refocused her attention on Stacie Percell. Monday was a long way away. This was now.

"Just a few more questions, Stacie," she said. "It won't take much longer."

Michael's eyes met hers and she knew what he was thinking. They were only just beginning.

15

At the end of a trial the adrenaline ran out of you like water through a sieve, followed by an inevitable feeling of anticlimax. The weeks of preparation, the continuous parade of witnesses, the day-to-day confrontations with the defense attorney; they all took their toll. The trial took over your life. Everything else was relegated to the background. Only the courtroom was real. Then all at once, it was over; the jury was out and you were in an emotional vacuum.

This was the part Kathryn hated most of all; waiting. Now, uncertainties rushed in to fill the void created when the jury retired to deliberate. Had she selected the right jury or had she left someone on who was likely to hang them up? Juries were unpredictable at best. Even though perhaps she should not, Kathryn always internalized the outcome of a trial. There was no middle ground: it was either a personal victory or it was a personal defeat.

She looked up as the door of her office opened and Dave Granz poked his head round it.

"Kathryn, I need to talk to you," he said. "Now."

"Come in," she said, shaking off her preoccupation. "Have a seat."

Dave plopped in his favorite spot on her leather sofa. "You remember we discussed the Bosendorf autoerotic death?"

"Yes, go on."

"There were bloodstains on the sheets under the body. Nelson typed them. Bosendorf was type A. The stains are type O. The blood wasn't his."

"So, someone who had type O blood shared the bed with him before he died," Kathryn said. "Why is that significant?"

"People who play autoerotic sex games play them alone," Granz said. "And they don't invite spectators. Remember the other autoerotic death Doc mentioned?"

"Of course," Kathryn replied. "Paul Croma. He had the tape marks on his wrists, too."

"I ran his rap," Dave told her. "I also had the SO and the police departments pull their FI cards on any reports in which Croma was listed as a suspect or a witness."

"I thought we agreed the adhesive was probably just coincidence."

"We did until Bosendorf came along. The Espanola PD investigated Croma for rape about two months ago. They never had enough evidence to submit it to our office for filing, so he was never charged."

"Wait a minute," Kathryn said. "What are you saying?"

"Three autoerotic deaths. All three investigated for rape but not charged. All three had traces of adhesive on their arms or wrist. Blood typing puts someone else with Bosendorf at the time he is supposed to have died alone. The question is, did they fall or were they pushed?"

"Are you telling me that someone is killing these men and dressing up the death scenes to look like autoerotic accidents?"

"I've done some checking, Kathryn. Piselli had an on-again-off-again girlfriend name of Susie. Susan Fletcher. She claims he wasn't into autoerotic sex games."

"What about Croma?"

"Friends and family claim he wasn't into it either," Dave replied.

"From my understanding of autoerotic practices, his friends and family would be about the last people on earth to know," Kathryn observed.

"Maybe, but you'd think they'd know if the guy was into anything kinky and according to everyone I've talked to, none of them was."

The phone rang before Kathryn could say anything more. It was Marcia, Kathryn's secretary, reminding her of tomorrow's management meeting at 11. She put the phone down with a sigh.

"Nervous about the Riker jury?" Dave asked.

"Yes. They've been out too long," Kathryn replied. "Maybe Bradley won them over."

In his closing argument Paul Bradley had told the jury that Karl Riker had not murdered Bradley Jasen. That he had shot him was not in doubt. But it was not murder. Karl Riker, he said, had acted in the heat of passion; a passion that clouded his mind, took over his reason and made it impossible to control his behavior. Incensed at learning Bradley Jasen was his wife's lover he had acted rashly, without deliberation and reflection. But out of passion, not judgment.

"Justice is what we are talking about here. Justice is what we are asking. Justice requires that you convict Karl Riker of voluntary manslaughter," Bradley had concluded.

When she got up to speak, Kathryn attacked his conclusion head-on. "Karl Riker isn't seeking justice," she said in rebuttal, "he's looking to make a deal and he wants you to cut it for him. Don't do it. Your job as jurors is to hold him accountable for his actions.

"Passion is what a man experiences when he catches his wife having sex with another man and he picks up the first thing he spots—a lamp beside the bed, for instance—and kills his wife's lover. No rational thought, no deliberation, no planning. That's manslaughter. But when he finds out about his wife's infidelity and then decides and plans to kill her lover, that is murder.

"Karl Riker made choices. Conscious, deliberate

choices. To buy a gun; to load that gun; to confront his wife's lover; to use the gun. In other words, he chose deliberately to kill Bradley Jasen. There was no passion involved. And after he killed Bradley Jasen, he made more choices. He chose to remove the dead body from the scene. He chose to dismember the victim's body by severing the arms and legs from the torso. He even chose to cut off the victim's head in the hope of avoiding detection. Karl Riker made a lot of choices and now you, too, must make a choice. Make the right one. Convict Karl Riker of the murder of Bradley Towne Jasen."

"Revenge killing might explain one murder dressed up as an accident," said Dave bringing her out of her reverie and back to the present, "but three?"

"What, then?"

"How about a vigilante?"

Kathryn stared at him wide-eyed. "A vigilante?"

"A vigilante killing rapists who have so far got away with it."

"And how does this vigilante track down these rapists?" Kathryn asked.

"All she or he would have to do is read the newspaper. I called the librarian at the *Gazette;* she located articles on all three. Photos of the rapists ran alongside the account of the rapes."

Kathryn frowned. "I hope you're wrong about this, Dave," she said. "Some people perceive vigilantes as good guys, that killing a criminal is justified if the legal system fails to stop him. You remember the case where the father shot the man who raped his daughter? There were crowds outside the court where he was being tried for murder holding banners that said 'Justice and law are not the same.'"

"A lot of people thought he was right."

"Maybe. But a lot more people believe that if law and order means anything in this country, you don't take the law into your own hands. You don't kill another human being. You let the justice system work."

"You know that and I know that, Kathryn," Dave said. "But a vigilante doesn't think like you and me."

"All right, let's suppose you're right. Where do we go from here? Do you want me to get a court order to exhume the bodies so Morgan can re-examine them?"

"I already talked to Doc, Kathryn. We're too late. They've been cremated."

Kathryn thought for a moment. "Okay, then let's focus on Bosendorf. Search his home and car. If he had a desk or locker at work, search it. Seize his personal telephone and address book. Check the contents of his telephone answering machine and review his telephone bills for toll and long distance calls. We can use the numbers to locate friends and relatives he may have in common with Croma and Piselli on the off-chance there is a connection among the three of them. Seize notes, cards, letters, snapshots, slides, home videos, photo albums, undeveloped film, negatives. Take his checkbook, receipts, correspondence, magazines. Run his credit history. Do the same with Croma and Piselli. See what that gives us."

"Tall order," Dave observed.

"You can do it. Whatever you're able to seize, I'll help you search. Maybe we'll get lucky."

"Maybe," Dave said. "Where would we be without that word?"

Diane Parker had to be in her middle to late thirties, Kathryn thought, but she looked younger. About five four or five, she had nice brown eyes, a firm, well-shaped mouth, short, cropped reddish-brown hair and a fresh complexion. Her simple dark blue suit and understated white silk shirt, like the steel-rimmed half glasses tucked in the jacket pocket, seemed almost like props, carefully selected to make her look older, graver.

"It's good of you to spend so much time with Emma," Kathryn said. "I have to confess that at first I wasn't sure therapy was the answer."

"Some people prefer to think of it as support, rather than therapy," Diane Parker said. "Counseling, if you like."

"I'm not concerned about the label we attach to the therapy," Kathryn said. "But I am concerned with helping Emma."

"I'm glad to have this chance to talk," the therapist answered. "To get a different perspective on the problem."

Kathryn nodded, sensing she was having difficulty knowing how to begin. "You want to ask me some questions," she volunteered. Maybe that would make it easier for her.

Diane nodded, not letting anything show, and leaned back in her chair. "Grief is an overwhelming emotion," she began, "especially to a child."

"You don't have to tell me that."

"Emma is . . . confused. With her father gone, the person she needs is the surviving care taker. But she's having a problem with that. With you."

"Why?"

"Let me ask you something. How did you handle your feelings?"

"About Jack's death? I think I just buried them in my work. Never let it get to me."

Diane Parker squinched up her eyes a fraction; it made her look a little older. "A lot of people take that route. Did it work?"

"It kept me . . . calm. I was able to be objective about it."

"That was important to you?"

"Yes. I had to be. I was in the middle of a murder trial."

"I see. And that took priority?"

"No, of course not. But I had to do a sort of . . . balancing act. I always do."

"Would I be right in saying you weren't very close to your ex-husband?"

"I was still very fond of him. But . . . nothing more. We weren't exactly strangers, you understand, but we weren't close friends either. Does that make sense?"

"May I ask how long . . . ?"

"Six years. Seven."

Parker nodded, encouraging her to continue.

"People drift apart. The bond . . . withers. Then death, so suddenly. You feel you ought to be grieving, but you're not."

"Is that what happened?"

"Something like that. I remember walking through the funeral as if it was a dream I didn't belong in."

"And how did that make you feel?"

"Odd. It was like, what's wrong with me? I ought to grieve."

"You felt guilty because there was no anguish."

"I don't know that I felt guilty. Surprised, I think. Confused. I expected to feel more. To hurt more."

"And Emma?"

"You've seen how she is."

"Adults rationalize. It's much harder for children to come to terms with loss. Do you think Emma knows how you feel about . . . Jack's death?"

"We haven't discussed it. But I think she might have sensed my feelings."

"Do you think she would understand them?"

Kathryn shook her head. "I can't see how."

Diane Parker leaned back in her leather chair. Her office was cool and comfortable, with bookshelves lining two walls and a second-floor window looking out on to Mercado Street, the pedestrianized Old Town shopping center.

"So how do you think Emma would react?" she asked. "Try to put yourself into her place. Think as she thinks."

"I'm not sure I can."

"Try."

"I—she—might be thinking, why isn't she hurting the way I am? Why doesn't it seem to matter to her the way it matters to me?"

Parker nodded again. "Very good. Let's say that might well be the cause of her problem. What we're trying to isolate is the effect."

"Anger? Is that what it is? Is that what's going on inside her head?"

"Probably. Kathryn, your daughter loves you. You know that. You're her heroine, her role model."

Kathryn shook her head in contradiction. "She doesn't want to be a lawyer. She's always been very positive about that."

"Perhaps," Diane Parker said. "Nevertheless, she knows you do it well and she admires you."

"Do I detect a 'but' in there?"

"She loved her father, too. Admired him. In a different way and for different reasons. But because she sees—or perhaps only feels—that you didn't, subconsciously, or even consciously, she wants you punished. At the same time she's terrified that her thoughts might make something bad happen. That's the dichotomy inside her, her anger at war with her love."

"The love will win," Kathryn said.

"I don't doubt it for a second," Parker told her. "But it's not going to happen overnight. Emma has to recognize her anger for what it is and come to terms with her feelings. Until then she is going to be a very unhappy little girl."

"How long are we talking about?" Kathryn asked. "Weeks, months?"

Parker shook her head. "I'm afraid I can't answer that."

"I see."

"Do I detect a certain impatience?" she asked.

"Possibly," Kathryn said.

"It'll come, Kathryn," Diane Parker said gently. "Give it time."

Their eyes met and for the first time Kathryn felt

the other woman's strength, her confidence. She wondered why it should come as a surprise. Diane Parker was clearly very capable. "What can I do to help?" she said.

"Be patient. Try to avoid confrontations, but when they occur, be firm. Explain. Share your feelings. Tell her what you expect and why."

"I feel better," Kathryn said, "knowing what we're fighting."

Diane Parker stood up and walked around her desk. "I'm glad," she said. Her handshake was firm and cool. "And you're right. Love will win."

16

"*H*ello, Mother," he said. "How are you?"

"*I've been wondering when you'd get around to calling.*" Her voice was reproachful. So what else is new? he thought.

"*I've been working, Mother.*"

"*Too busy to call your poor old mother.*"

He let that one go as well. "*You're not old,*" he said "*Sixty-five isn't old these days.*"

"*What time is it out there?*"

"*Seven thirty. I was about to go out and get some breakfast.*"

"*You should get married, Dicky. Eating out all the time can't be good for you. And the money you'd save.*"

"*A wife would be cheaper, right?*"

"*It's time you settled down, had a family.*"

"*Don't start that again. What's your weather like?*"

"*Thundery. It was in the high eighties yesterday. I hate it when it's humid like this.*"

"*You should come out here for a couple of weeks.*"

"*Oh, yes. And sit at home all day while you go play with your computers.*"

"*I don't play at it, Mother,*" he said patiently.

"*Well,*" she said, the way she always did when she wanted you to know she had her own opinion. "*I don't pretend to understand them.*"

Like, you tried, he thought. "*Have you heard from Sylvia?*"

"*She wants to come for the weekend with the children.*"

"*That'll be nice. You'll enjoy that.*"

"*And all the hard work.*"

"*Come on, Mother, you know you love having your grandchildren over.*"

"*It will be George's birthday on the fourth of next month,*" she said. "*He would have been forty this year.*"

For the first sixteen years of his life, the star of the Hoffman family had been his older brother. George was the handsome one. George was the clever one. George was the one who was going to have a brilliant career.

"*Mark my words,*" his father used to say. "*He'll go far, that boy.*"

Until Justice Is Done

*His father wanted George to become a professional:
a doctor or a lawyer. In retrospect it was easy to see
that he hoped George would realize all the dreams and
ambitions he had not.*

*His father took a sort of perverse pride in having
been "a child of the Depression" who had never gone
to college. Then the war came; when he got out of
the Navy, he had gone to work for the State Power Authority. Security, he always told them, that was the
thing to aim for. A nice home with the mortgage
paid off, savings in the bank. Security came to the
man who offered probity, reliability. Nobody would
trust a man without any bottom to him. What he
never said was that it was his wife's trust fund that
paid off the mortgage, not his middle management
salary.*

*George was named for his father, as his father had
been before him. Richard was named for his maternal
grandfather, investment banker Richard Charles Bak-
er. Everyone called him Dicky. Sweet child, they used
to say, never any trouble. Then when George was seven
and Dicky was four, Sylvia came along; from that day
on, she was her mother's total preoccupation, as if
Claire Hoffman had been waiting only for her arrival
so she could show the world how doting a mother she
could be.*

*"You'll spoil that child silly, Claire," his father used
to say. "Mark my words."*

*The in-between kid, that was Dicky. George got all
the admiration, Sylvia got all the love. Just do well at
school, son, his father would tell him. Be like your
brother. You'll find everything will come right as long
as you work hard and tell the truth. At first, he worked*

at being liked, especially by the older boys: his brother's friends Jim Adams, Sam Watmough. He ran errands for them, helped them with their homework, gave them his pocket money. But it didn't make them like him. Nothing he did made them like him. The rejection made him determined: I'll show them. I'll learn and learn and learn. I'll be smarter than any of them. And he was. And he could remember anything he read, anything.

As he got older, when kids his own age made fun of him, he'd fight them. Eventually all the boys his own age were scared of him. They left him alone. When his brother's friends made fun of him, he took them on too. And he almost always won because he simply ignored whatever pain they might inflict; he never let anybody see they could hurt him.

When he got to high school he discovered his true gift. Anything to do with numbers—geometry, algebra, trigonometry—was a breeze. He was always first in his class. He was never able to understand why his classmates found math difficult. He did his brother George's math homework. George would take it to class and let his buddies copy the answers. His teachers could never figure out why George always did so well in school and so badly in exams.

When George graduated from high school, his parents gave him a sports car, an Alfa Romeo Spyder. It was beautiful.

"All the girls will want to go for a ride with you," his father told George. "Mark my words."

Secretly, his mother was pleased about the car. She liked her friends and the neighbors seeing that they could afford to give their son a European sports car as a graduation present. To her husband, however, she complained.

"All that money," she would say.

"Can't keep it all in the bank, dear," Dad told her. "No good just sitting there."

And Mom would say, "Well," which always meant the same thing. You can say what you like, George Hoffman, but I have my own opinion. She disapproved of just about anything that was fun for its own sake.

Well, that time she was right. Five weeks after he got the car, George ran it off the road up near Irondequoit Bay; it took the "jaws of life" nearly four hours to cut his dead body out of the wreckage.

After that, his father never really took much interest in anything. It was like something inside him died with George. He got suddenly old; his hair turned grey in what seemed like a matter of weeks. He took early retirement at fifty-five, the same year Richard got his bachelor of science degree from MIT in Boston. He died the following year while Richard was working on his master's.

After his father died, his mother lavished all her time and money on Sylvia. She continued to receive income from the trust fund supplemented by the life insurance and her husband's pension. But it was the money Richard gave her that made it possible for her to keep up the appearances that were so important to her.

It was like she thought she was entitled. When he received his doctorate, she was impressed not by his achievement but because he got his name and picture in the local paper. She was not interested in his work. She never even tried to understand what he did.

Nothing he did impressed her, no matter how hard he tried.

He was headhunted for a job in Atlanta that paid him twice what he made in Rochester. He bought her a new silver Olds Cutlass Supreme before he moved. But all she did was complain to him over the phone about how lonely she was. Even now, despite all the money and gifts, she still complained. She still somehow managed to make him feel inadequate. Nothing was ever enough. Nothing ever would be. She had a poison mind. All women were the same. The trick was to give it to them before they got the chance to give it to you.

It was all about power. Strength. Power. That was what women respected. He had long ago recognized the dark urge inside him for what it was. It was always there, controlled, like a chained beast he released whenever the mood took him. Like a wolf. His alter ego. He knew all the psychobabble. It never ceased to amuse him that the words "therapist" and "the rapist" were to all intents and purposes identical.

"Well," his mother said into what he realized had been a silence.

"I better get going or I'll be late," he said. "Did you receive my check?"

"Last Friday." No thanks, of course. She took it for granted. She always had. He wondered if she had any idea how much he hated her.

"I have to go, Mother," he said. "I'll call again soon."

"You always say that," she said.

He didn't tell her to take care, she didn't tell him to

look after himself. There had never been any affection between them. He was still angry in an unfocused way as he got into his car. An hour later he stopped off at a coffee shop in Mountain View, up in the hills above Santa Rita, and read the social pages of the local paper while he waited for his breakfast.

Jennifer Camara had married Stephen Skelton on June 15 at Catalina's First Baptist Church. The groom, a golf pro at the Cathedral Heights golf course, was just a face with a mustache; but the bride was movie-star beautiful, with blond hair and a wide smile.

He read on. After an eight-day honeymoon in Mauna Kea, Hawaii, the bride, a graduate of Fresno State U., would return to work as a programmer with Maximedia Technology in Highland Valley. Another little piggy in her straw house, waiting for it, asking for it. And only a few miles away, he thought.

He smiled and folded up the paper.

The Riker jury was still out. What was bothering them? she wondered. She looked out of her office window. Below in the parking lot, county workers were leaving for lunch. Over on the Pacific Street side, she saw Judge Spencer get into his Lexus. The telephone rang and she picked it up. It was Dave Granz.

"We've got another one, Kathryn," he said. "Another autoerotic death."

"Damn. Do you know who it is yet?"

"Yeah," he said quietly. "It's Johnny Bitzer."

"Where are you?"

"With the body," he said. "Memorial Avenue in Liberty. I called Doc."

"I'll be right there," she said.

Liberty was about fourteen miles south of Santa Rita, a largely Hispanic community surrounded by featureless vegetable- and fruit-growing fields, halfway between the ocean and the foothills of Mount Madonna.

Memorial Avenue was a non-residential two-lane road above Palomino Lake, a couple of miles north of Catalina Municipal Airport. It took her about twenty minutes to get there. The coroner's van was parked by the roadside alongside a white Ford pickup.

As Kathryn parked her car one of the deputy coroners came over. His nameplate said CAREY. His shoes were dusty and he looked hot.

"Who found the body?" she asked.

"Highway Patrol," he said.

"What do we know so far?"

"Apparently Bitzer worked part-time as a delivery driver for a furniture store in Catalina," Carey told her. "He went out yesterday afternoon to make a delivery about two miles from here: he never showed. When he didn't come back that evening, the store manager called the cops, thought Bitzer had split with the furniture. CHP found the pickup and the body. The chippy checked for signs of life, found none and called the coroner. Inspector Granz is already down there."

"What about Dr. Nelson?"

"Not here yet," Carey told her.

"You want to direct me to the body?" Kathryn asked. The deputy looked at her shoes and she grinned. "It's okay, Carey, I've done this before."

She took them off and tossed them into the back of

the car, fished out the Reeboks she always carried and slipped them on.

"This way," Carey grunted. Kathryn looked up to see Dave Granz coming to meet them.

"Thanks, Jeff," Granz said to the deputy. "Kathryn, come take a look, tell me what you think."

The dead man was hunched over in a kneeling position, face down, with the upper portion of his body resting on his forearms. A rope secured by a slip knot ran from his neck to the branch of a tree about six feet overhead. On the ground immediately to the left of the body were several porno magazines. The man wore a cheap checkered woolen shirt. His pants were undone and his briefs had been moved down sufficiently to expose his sexual organs.

"Nice, huh?" Granz said.

Kathryn bent down to get a closer look at the contorted face. Frothy mucus streaked with blood had oozed from both nose and mouth. The rough half-inch rope of the noose had bitten deeply into the skin of the dead man's neck, leaving an ugly red welt.

"Asphyxiation?" she offered.

"Looks like it," Granz confirmed. "And to save you looking, there's ejaculate on his briefs."

"What do you think happened, Dave?" she asked quietly.

Granz shrugged. "Looks like he was playing auto-erotic games. Half-hanging himself. Pulled a little too hard on his noose, constricted the carotid arteries and—zap."

"You said 'looks like.'"

"Yeah. My gut instinct tells me it's another homicide, dressed up to look like accidental death," he said, speaking almost in a whisper.

"You think it's your vigilante again?" Kathryn asked in a hushed voice.

Granz said nothing.

"Anything at all to support it? Contusions, bruising, anything?"

Granz shook his head. "Nothing I can see."

"Any sign of a struggle?"

"No."

"How long has he been dead?"

"He was last seen alive at four-thirty yesterday. That was when he left to make his delivery."

Kathryn looked at her watch. "So we're talking less than twenty-four hours. Doc will pin it down when he gets here."

"He may be a while. He was in the middle of an autopsy when I talked to him."

"Don't let anyone move the body until he gets here," she said as she looked back toward the road trying to envisage a scenario that fitted together with what they had found.

Contrary to popular belief, it was extremely difficult to strangle a man without leaving some sign of a struggle and there was no sign of a struggle here. Did that mean he had been killed someplace else? Again, almost impossible without leaving some sign, drag marks, shoetracks.

If it was a homicide, Dave's vigilante at work, how did he do it? Which led back to the earlier, still unanswered question: why?

Her pager sounded, making her jump. Dave Granz handed her his cellular phone and she dialed County Communications.

"Superior Court bailiff Jorgensen called, Ms. Mackay," the dispatcher's neutral voice announced. "The Riker jury has got a verdict."

"Call the bailiff, tell him I'll be there in fifteen minutes," Kathryn said. "The Riker jury is coming in," she told Granz as she handed back his phone.

"You want me to go back with you?"

"I'd rather you stayed here until Doc arrives. I'll call you with the verdict."

Kathryn took one last look around the death scene to fix it in her mind and then headed back to her car. It took her exactly fourteen minutes to get to the courthouse. Her heart was hammering with tension as she walked into the courtroom.

The bailiff saw her come in. He picked up his phone and spoke into it. Kathryn glanced around. Riker and his attorney, Paul Bradley, were already in their places at the defense table. District Attorney Hal Benton was sitting in the front row of the spectator section. This was an important verdict for Hal.

The jury room door opened and the jury filed in to take their seats. Their faces were composed, showing nothing. Kathryn waited tensely, wishing Dave were sitting next to her. Arnie Jorgensen, the deputy acting as bailiff, snapped out his command and everyone stood as Judge Spencer came in.

"Be seated, please," he said, then turned to the jury. "Ladies and gentlemen, have you arrived at a verdict?"

The foreman stood. He was a gangling, gray-haired man of about sixty-five, with shrewd eyes and a thin, uncompromising slit of a mouth. His prominent Adam's apple moved up and down as he replied.

"We have, Your Honor."

Deputy Jorgensen walked over to the jury box, took the verdict forms from the foreman and handed them up to the judge. Spencer read them impassively then passed them down to the court clerk.

"The clerk will read the verdict," he said.

"On the charge of murder, guilty," the clerk intoned. Kathryn felt a huge rush of relief as she heard her say the word guilty; she looked over her shoulder. Hal Benton gave her a thumbs-up sign.

Judge Spencer asked Bradley if he wished to have the jury polled; when Bradley said no, the judge thanked the jury and dismissed them. After they filed out, he told the defendant to rise.

"Karl Riker, you have been found guilty of murder," he said. "Sentencing is set for six weeks from today, that's August 24." He looked around his courtroom and nodded, as if he was satisfied with the way things had come out. "Court's dismissed."

Paul Bradley watched sourly as the judge got up and went into chambers; he touched his client on the shoulder as Jorgensen came over to escort Riker out. As he passed Kathryn, Riker glared at her, his eyes were full of animosity. It never ceased to surprise her how defendants somehow convinced themselves that it was the prosecutor who was responsible for their conviction and not the terrible acts they had committed.

17

The little pig's car was parked on a side street a block away from the building where she worked. He could hear the traffic going by on the Valley Springs Road. It was pleasant and warm in the deep shadow cast by the squat and unlovely warehouse buildings on both sides of the street. He heard footsteps and saw her coming. He ducked behind the flatbed truck that was parked directly behind her car and waited. She reached the car; when he heard the jingle of her keys he stepped swiftly behind her, taking her neck in the crook of his arm and putting the pistol to her temple. It was only a toy, but it was a realistic one.

"Not a sound," he hissed. "Not a sound or I'll blow your fucking head off."

She moved her head, signifying understanding. He wrenched the rear door open and shoved her inside. She put up her hands in front of her as if to ward him off.

"No, no," she wailed. "Leave me alone, leave me alone."

"Shut up," he snarled, enjoying her fear. "Just do what I tell you and you won't get hurt."

He shoved the barrel of the gun hard into her breast and she cried out with pain. There, bitch. He reached up under her skirt and pulled down her panties.

"Come on, lie back and spread 'em, spread your legs."

She shook her head dumbly and he let the anger show.

"Do what I tell you!" he snapped. "Do it or I'll kill you."

"Please," she whimpered, "please don't hurt me."

It was amazing how many of them said that, or something like it. Like they could stop him by saying "please."

"Take off your shirt," he said. "Come on, take it off."

"I can't," she whimpered. "I can't."

He made an impatient sound and ripped her shirt open. She didn't wear a bra: that was one of the things he had noticed when he was watching her. Her nipples were dark and roseate; he licked one of them, waiting for it to spring erect. As it did he bit it. Jennifer Skelton screamed and he laughed out loud.

"No, please, don't," she moaned. "Please, no. How can you laugh when I'm bleeding?"

"Blood makes me laugh."

To Kathryn's surprise, the door buzzer sounded; she rarely had callers after eight. The voice on the intercom was that of Dave Granz. When she opened the door, he stood on the threshold with a thoughtful look on his face. "May I come in?" he asked almost shyly.

"Of course," Kathryn replied.

They went into the living room. The lights of Espanola twinkled through the sliding glass doors that led to the balcony. Dave went across to the wine rack and picked up a bottle.

"Robert Mondavi Woodbridge, 1990," he said. "Cabernet Sauvignon. Very nice."

"Open it," Kathryn said. "Pour us each a glass."

He got two glasses from the cabinet above the wine rack, stripped the foil from the neck and extracted the cork. The wine made a comforting glucking sound as he poured.

"So," she said, as they sat down facing each other on the armchairs flanking the window. "What brings you here tonight?"

"How's Emma's therapy going?"

"Slowly," she said. "Diane told me it would. She said people always expect miracles, but there aren't any. It's a long-term process. Now, what brings you up here at this time of night?"

"I wanted to talk to you."

"About what?"

"About marriage."

Kathryn stared at him dumbstruck. "What?"

"You heard. I asked you to marry me."

She shook her head. "We don't work, Dave. We just don't work."

"That's not true, Kathryn," Dave said. "We always worked fine. The trouble was we both wanted to be boss at the same time."

She remembered watching Dave walk up the steps holding Emma's hand. Was he right and she wrong? Could she have been that wrong?

"We still would."

"No," Dave said. He looked straight into her eyes. "I'm not the same man I was then. When I got . . . hurt, I did a lot of thinking."

"I remember, we talked about it."

And you said, "Yesterday's gone, tomorrow never comes. Seize the day."

"Listen, Kathryn," he said. "Just listen. Right now you need someone. So does Emma."

"Dave, Emma isn't your responsibility, she's mine."

"I would like her to be. And besides, Emma is only a part of it," he said. "This is about you and me. I'm ready to make the commitment, do whatever it takes. The question is, are you?"

"It's too big a question."

"You don't have to answer it right away. Just promise me you'll think about it. You can be more than a mother and a prosecutor. You can be my wife too."

"Oh, Dave," she sighed. "Part of me wants to say yes."

"But part of you doesn't."

She spread her hands. "That's how I feel. I won't lie to you. It's just . . . I don't know, Dave. I'm not sure."

He made a wry face and finished his wine. "I can wait," he said. "I just wanted you to know. I love you, Kathryn. I think I always have."

She kissed him and felt the strength of his arms around her. Maybe it would be nice to let go, she thought. Let someone help her slay the dragons. Then the phone rang.

"Damn," Granz said and let go of her as Kathryn picked up and heard the familiar voice of Michael Gaines.

"Kathryn, I'm sorry to disturb you," he said. "Is it okay?"

"Sure, go ahead."

"We've got another rape."

"Run every detail you have by me."

"A twenty-four-year-old woman named Jennifer Skelton was walking to her car after work when a man grabbed her throat and told her to be quiet or he'd blow her head off. He forced her into the back seat of her car. He pulled her panties off and told her to spread her legs. When she refused, he threatened her until she complied. He performed oral sex on her. He told her to take off her shirt. When she refused, he ripped it off. He started licking her breasts, then he bit her. Next he raped her and tried to sodomize her. When she objected, he raped her again. This time he ejaculated."

"Was she able to get a good look at him?" asked Kathryn.

"She said it was too dark to see and he was careful not to raise himself above her where she might be able to get a better look at him."

"How long did the assault take?" asked Kathryn.

"She guessed about fifteen minutes. After he ejaculated, he asked her "if this little pig was going to call the cops." She told him no. He had four strips of cloth with him. When he used one of them to blindfold her she noticed he was wearing gloves. Then he tied her hands behind her back and bound her ankles together. With the last strip, he wiped her vagina. Then the car moved and she heard the door open and close. She waited a few minutes before she began to work the strips loose. She managed to get the blindfold off first. It took her about half an hour to untie herself. She climbed into the front seat, drove to the nearest gas station and asked the attendant to summon help."

"Where is she now?" Kathryn asked.

"Here with me and her husband at the hospital. They've only been married three weeks. He's ready to go get a gun and hit the streets looking for the bastard."

"I'll be right there."

"No hurry," Michael said. "It'll be two A.M. before the rape kit is done. We can wait and talk to her then."

Kathryn thought about it and decided Michael was probably right. "All right," she said. "You got a description of the rapist?"

"Like I told you, she didn't see much. She said he sounded like he was in his thirties, big, strong. She described him as speaking in soft to normal tones and that he seemed very articulate."

Kathryn made a face. That description would fit half the men in Santa Rita.

"Call me just before the exam is done and I'll meet you at the hospital."

As she hung up the phone, she turned to Dave. "Dave, I'm sorry, it was—"

"I heard," he said. "Another rape. When do you have to leave?"

"Later."

He put his arms around her waist and held her, leaning back so he could look into her eyes. Kathryn reached up and ran her finger along the faint white traces of the scars than ran diagonally from his left ear to below the jawbone.

"I wanted to make love to you," she said.

"I know," he said, very softly. "Don't worry, I'll stay with Emma."

Kathryn laid her head against his chest, wishing

just for once she didn't have to face what was waiting for her out there, the naked pain, the grinding anguish, the inescapable tragedy of another young life devastated. Then she stepped out of the strong safe circle of Dave's arms, kissed him on the lips and got ready to do what she had to do.

18

Jennifer Skelton lived in a neat little three bedroom home on El Camino, a quiet street in Valley Springs. Gaines parked his dark blue Thunderbird at the curb. As they got out of the car, Kathryn saw the downstairs drapes were still drawn, as they had been ever since Jennifer came home from the hospital.

As they walked up the path, they saw a drape move; but they gave no sign of having noticed. Gaines rang the doorbell; the Westminster chimes sounded very loud in the silence of the afternoon. After a while, they heard a movement and the rattle of a security chain.

"Jennifer, it's Michael and Kathryn," he said. "Michael Gaines and Kathryn Mackay."

The door opened. Jennifer Skelton was a tall, slender woman with long blond hair which she usually wore tied back with a bright strip of ribbon. Today it hung untidily around her shoulders. Her eyes were dull and her skin was sallow. She looked at Kathryn and Michael apathetically.

"How are you, Jennifer?" Kathryn asked.

"Hello," she said wearily. "Come in."

It was cool and dark inside. They followed her into the living room. The drapes were drawn across the sliding glass doors that looked out on to the patio and a small back yard. Apart from a baby grand piano with wedding photographs in silver frames which dominated it, the room had a distinctly southwestern flavor; saddle stools, Navajo rugs, Zuni pottery, a framed print of a Charles M. Russell painting on the wall above the fireplace. Jennifer Skelton's husband Steve came from the same part of west Texas as Gaines; he had introduced a little of its ambience into their California home.

"I've always liked that picture," Michael said. "Where did you get it?"

"That museum in Fort Worth," she said vaguely. "Amos Carter?"

"Amos Carter," he said. "My dad used to take me there when I was a kid. He was from Dallas. Dallas people always used to call Fort Worth 'Cow Town.'"

"Would you like some coffee?"

"Thanks. How are you feeling?" Kathryn asked.

"I'm managing," she said, spooning instant coffee into three stoneware mugs behind the breakfast bar. It was like she needed a barrier between them, Kathryn thought.

"Have you been out ... anywhere?" Michael asked.

She shook her head. "I can't," she said. "I can't face

it, Michael. I can't leave the house without . . . seeing him."

His eyes narrowed. Sometimes the bastards did come back.

"Have you noticed anyone near your house?"

"No," she said dully. "He's in my head, Michael. I can't get him out of there."

"We've asked the deputies who patrol your neighborhood to drive by your home several times a day," Kathryn said. "We want you to feel safe."

"That's what Steve says. But I can't walk down the street, I can't go into a store, any place there are people. I keep expecting him . . . someone, to grab me."

"We know. And we know you can't make the fear go away. You just have to take it a day at a time."

"How many days, Kathryn? How many days?"

Her voice was wretched. Kathryn didn't answer her question; there was no answer to it. Rape destroyed two essential beliefs: the victim's sense of self-worth and her sense of control over her own life. Some eventually got it back; some did not.

"Have you . . . is there any news? Is that why you came?"

Michael shook his head. "The lab got traces of semen on the swabs that were used during the . . . when you were examined at the hospital."

"What good will that do?"

"Semen contains DNA," Kathryn told her. "Once we have a suspect in custody we can run tests to see if we have a match."

Jennifer frowned and shook her head. "Match for what?"

"There was a very famous murder case in England," Kathryn said. "Two sexual assault-murders committed three years apart, one in 1983 and the second in 1986. A suspect was arrested and the police had DNA tests made on semen specimens recovered from the victims in both rapes. The tests not only established that both had belonged to the same man but that they did not belong to the suspect they were holding. Eventually their investigations led to another man. When samples of his blood were compared to the semen samples recovered from the victims, they were found to match. There was no possibility of error. The suspect pleaded guilty and was sent to prison. That's how DNA testing works."

Jennifer nodded her head, as if she was too weary to understand or care.

"Steve wanted me to ask about the car—how much longer do you need to keep it?"

"It's in the sheriff's warehouse," Kathryn told her. "They needed to search your car for hairs or clothing fibers the man who attacked you might have left behind."

"What they do is they vacuum and use oblique and ultraviolet lights," Michael explained, "but it's too soon yet to know whether they recovered any evidence that will help us. Steve can call me and I'll arrange to have the car released to him."

"Did you talk to people in my office to see if anyone saw or heard anything?" Jennifer asked.

"Yes, we did," Kathryn told her. "Detectives contacted everyone in your building. No one saw or heard anything. They put up notices asking anyone who might have seen anything suspicious in the parking lot to contact the sheriff's department. They received a lot of calls, but none of the interviews has led anywhere yet. How about you—did you think of anything you haven't already told us?"

"I tried. I can't go on . . . reliving it."

"How's Steve?"

She shook her head again, the long blond hair moving across her face and then back. "He . . . this is hard for him."

"Is he still having problems?"

"He . . . tries to understand. But . . ."

"Tell us."

"He keeps saying the same thing. Different ways, but basically the same thing: what I can't understand is why you weren't beaten. Like the rape wasn't enough, like he thinks, he thinks I—oh, dammit, like he thinks I didn't fight back, that I should have resisted more."

Tears glinted in her eyes. She brushed them away angrily with the back of her hand.

"That happens sometimes," Michael said. "He's having to deal with a lot of conflicting feelings. Remember how he was the night it happened."

"Yes. He was angry the right way, then. He wanted to kill him, the man who did it. But now . . . it's me he's angry with."

"Why do you think that?" Kathryn asked.

Jennifer Skelton walked across to the piano, picked up one of the photographs. "This was taken at Mauna Kea," she said. "On our honeymoon."

Kathryn and Michael remained silent, waiting.

"After we got back it was still . . . a honeymoon. Until . . . that night. Now he doesn't . . . I think he's ashamed. Of what happened to me. It's as if he . . . he doesn't want to believe it, but it's like a worm in his brain, asking the same question, over and over and over, would the man have raped me if I'd resisted more?"

"Jennifer, you did what you had to do to stay alive," Kathryn said. "Don't put yourself through that kind of guilt."

"I never knew there were so many different kinds to choose from."

"Do you want me to talk to Steve?" asked Michael.

It always helped if the couple could discuss the rape, identify the issues that were upsetting them, gain control over their feelings and lessen their painful memories. Unfortunately, avoidance was more often the norm.

Jennifer Skelton's answer was another shake of the head. "He's . . . so remote. I don't think you could reach him, Michael. I can't."

"You've tried?"

"If you only knew."

"Tell me."

"He won't . . . he said he couldn't touch me. He cried, he said he wanted to, but . . ."

"He blames you for what happened?"

"No, not blame. It's not blame. He didn't . . . I think he can't bear it. That I . . . I . . . had sex with another man."

"Is that how you think he sees it?"

"I don't know. I think maybe, yes."

"It's hard to understand, Jennifer," Gaines said. "But he has pain too."

"Ah," she said very quietly. "His pain."

She picked up the empty coffee mugs and went back behind the breakfast bar. "More coffee, anyone?"

"No, thanks," Kathryn said. "Are you going to be all right?"

Jennifer wrapped her arms around herself, tight. "He's still out there," she said. It was nearer an accusation than a question.

"We're working on it," Kathryn said. "We're doing everything we can, but these investigations take time."

"Time," she said fiercely. "That's what he wants, isn't it? That . . . that bastard. So he can defile someone else."

"You're not defiled, Jennifer. You mustn't think like that. It wasn't your fault."

"You don't know. You don't know what it's like. I keep thinking, if only I hadn't said I'd work late, it would never have happened."

"We'll stop by and see you again in a few days," Kathryn said and opened the door.

"Is there anything else we can do?" Michael asked.

"Yes," she said fiercely. "Stop him. Stop him, Michael!"

"I will," Michael said. "I promise you."

"I want to believe you. But he's in control."

"I'll catch him, Jennifer."

"How?"

"I don't know. Not yet. But I will."

Her face betrayed her thoughts. *No, you won't.* The door closed and they heard the locks turn and the chain being slotted into its housing. They walked down the walkway to the car and drove away in silence.

19

"Why do I have to go to school anyway?" Emma said. "Why can't I just come to the office with you?"

No, Emma, Kathryn thought. Please, sweetheart, not this morning.

"Sweetheart, you know that isn't possible," she said. "You just know it isn't."

"We've done it lots of times," Emma said. "When they've called you. Remember when we took my Barbie dolls to the Sheriff's Office, and I played in their lunchroom while you talked to the detectives?"

"That was an emergency, Em," Kathryn said. "Just a couple of hours. You can't sit in my office all day and play with your dolls."

"Sure I can," Emma said stubbornly. "I could take Sam with me."

"No, Em," Kathryn said, not allowing it to develop. "You're going to school."

"I just hate it there. The way everyone is being so *nice* all the time."

"They know how upset you are."

"They think they do. But they don't. Nobody does."

"Eat your breakfast, or we'll be late."

"I don't want it," Emma said, kicking the side of the cabinet beneath the breakfast island.

"I thought you liked Honey-Nut Cheerios."

"I'm not hungry."

"You've got to eat, Emma."

"No I don't. Nobody can make me eat if I don't want to."

Don't get into an argument, Diane Parker had told her. Be fair, but firm. "I just don't want you to get sick, honey."

"And I *wish* you'd stop calling me honey. I wish you'd leave me alone. I wish everyone would just leave me alone!" Emma said, her eyes swimming in tears. "Especially that Dr. Parker, that Dr. Nosy Parker!"

"Dr. Parker is trying to help you, Emma."

"I want her to stop asking me things. I want you to tell her to stop."

"Do you want to talk about it? Tell me why?"

"She just keeps asking me and asking me," Emma sniffled. "Who I'm angry with. Why."

"And do you know?"

"You don't care!" Emma shouted. "You don't care about anything except work. Work, work, work!"

"That's not true, Emma," Kathryn said, dismayed. She tried to put her arms around her daughter, but Emma pushed her away.

"It is, it is. You don't care. You don't care what happened to Daddy, you just go to work and I, I have to, I have to—"

Kathryn stood stricken as the tears flooded down, watching her daughter sobbing. Me, she thought dully. She blames me. After a while the sobs lessened and then stopped.

"Sweetheart, listen—" Kathryn began.

"I don't love you any more," Emma interrupted. Her eyes were angry, defiant. The words went like a dagger into Kathryn's heart and she turned away so that Emma would not see her face.

"I see," she managed.

"I thought you'd be angry."

"No," Kathryn said, picking her words with enormous care. "I'm not angry, because I think I know how you feel. One day you'll be grown up, too, Em, and maybe you'll have a daughter and something like this will happen to you. You won't get angry either, because you'll understand, the way I do now."

She looked at Emma out of the corner of her eye. Her daughter was standing with her head down, the long dark hair concealing her face.

"I just feel so . . . mixed up," Emma said. "I'm afraid you'll stop loving me, Mommy. That's what you did with Daddy."

Kathryn shook her head. "You're my daughter, Em. I'll never stop loving you."

"Are you sure?"

"I'm not sure about a lot of things, Em," Kathryn said. "But I'm sure about that."

Emma was silent for what seemed like many moments. Then she drew in a deep, deep breath. "We'd better go," she said. "Or we'll be late for the bus."

Was it a victory? Kathryn wondered as they drove up the hill. Or merely a postponement? She was no nearer an answer when she got to her office and the unforgiving demands of the day enveloped her.

* * *

"Heeeeeeere's Johnny," Morgan Nelson said, as he wheeled in the gurney bearing the body of Johnny Bitzer.

It had arrived via the staging room, where it had first been put on a gurney and weighed, then meticulously photographed before being brought down to the small autopsy suite.

Dressed in surgical greens, Nelson maneuvered the trolley alongside the stainless steel table and with practiced strength lifted it in two movements on to it. Then he adjusted the rake of the table so the naked body lay tilted feet-down toward the stainless steel sinks and constantly flowing water.

"You know, Doc, there's something I don't understand," Dave said, as Nelson adjusted his face mask. "Tell me, how does almost choking oneself to death give someone a sexual kick?"

"The prevention of a basic life drive such as breathing excites some men," Nelson replied. "Another might need pain or humiliation. Or he might be experimenting—trying for something new and different that turns out new and dangerous. The point to be made is, no autoeroticist deliberately sets out to kill himself. But for some of them that's part of it, flirting with death. Other times the guy can be unaware of how dangerous what he's doing is, until it's too late. Either way, he's just as dead."

He hitched a thigh on to the gurney next to the body and looked at Kathryn and Dave expectantly.

"Okay," Nelson said. "I take it what we want to know is, did our friend here slip, or was he pushed, right? First question: was anything found near the body other than the porno magazines?"

"Nothing," Granz said.

Nelson nodded. "Let's get right to it, then. Something's been bothering me ever since I first saw the body at the scene. You know what this is?" He pointed at the ragged welt on the dead man's neck.

"Sure, that's the mark the rope made when he hanged himself," Kathryn said. "What's bothering you about it?"

"It's atypical," Nelson said. "There was no buffer between the rope and the neck."

"How's that again, Doc?" Dave queried. "Buffer?"

"Either of you know anything about roping?" Nelson asked. He saw their puzzled frowns and grinned. "Rock climbing?"

"Come on, Doc," Dave said. "What are you getting at?"

"You're going to half-hang yourself, right? You're using a length of cheap half-inch rope. You've done it before. You know, you can't help but know, the way ropers and climbers know, rope running hard against your skin burns like a red hot poker. You need something between it and you, a scarf, a strip of plastic foam. That was why I asked you whether anything else was found at the death scene."

"So maybe this time our vigilante slipped up," Granz murmured.

"Let's not jump the gun," Kathryn cautioned. "Morgan, what we need to know is whether Bitzer strangled himself or someone else did it. Will your examination establish that?"

"It's pretty difficult to conceal a manual strangulation, although it's not impossible," Morgan said. "I'll get to that in due course. I have to see if anything inside has been fractured."

"And how long will that take?" Dave asked.

"Three, maybe four hours," Nelson said cheerfully. "Look, if you're going to be here half the night you might as well make yourselves useful. Take this clipboard, Dave, and write down what I tell you."

"You better just hope my union doesn't find out about this," Granz told him as Nelson swiftly made the Y incision that opened up the torso and set to work.

At 11 P.M. it was over, the brain and other vital organs weighed and sectioned, specimens of each placed in labelled bottles of formaldehyde. After sewing up the emptied throat, replacing the cranium and reworking the scalp back over the top of the skull, Morgan Nelson wheeled the body into the cold storage room and closed the door. "That's it," he said, tiredly. His voice was hoarse, his shoulders sloped with fatigue. Heaving an inanimate corpse around was hard, punishing physical work.

"So, do we have an accident or a murder?" Kathryn asked.

Nelson sighed. "The external injuries to the throat are consistent with the victim's having been strangled by a noose, as in an autoerotic accident. However, the internal injuries paint a different picture. As I had you note, Dave, there were hemorrhages in the soft tissue overlying the laryngeal cartilages and in the connective tissue and strap muscles around the inferior margins of the thyroid gland. There was a further hemorrhage at the superior margin of the right anterior wing of the thyroid cartilage and various other contusions which basically add up to one thing. This man didn't hang himself: he was strangled manually."

"We have a murder," Dave told nobody in particular.

"Show me, Morgan," Kathryn said. "I want to know how he did it."

"Dave, come here," Doc said. Standing behind the inspector, he cupped his left hand behind Granz's neck, then placed his right arm around in front so Dave's chin was in the crook of his powerful forearm. "I push hard with my left hand, and at the same time, tighten up my right."

"Wouldn't he struggle?" Kathryn asked. "Wouldn't he fight back?"

"If the killer was a strong man, there might be a brief struggle, followed by abrupt unconsciousness and collapse. Ten, fifteen seconds is all it would take. Less, if the victim was either asleep or unconscious. Either way he wouldn't have a lot of time to react. And there would be no external signs of injury. Which of course is what our killer was banking on."

"So what you're saying is, when he staged the death scene, the killer expected you to make a preliminary determination it was another autoerotic accident and leave it at that."

"And if he hadn't forgotten to put a buffer on the body, that's what very well might have happened," Nelson said. "I would have had no real reason to open up the neck. Yes, Johnny Bitzer was strangled, and the autoerotic death scene was staged *post mortem.*"

"I guess that makes it official, then," Dave said. "We've got ourselves a vigilante."

"I hope you didn't mind my asking to see you again so soon," Kathryn said, as she finished telling Diane Parker about Emma's outburst the preceding day.

"Not at all," the therapist replied. "I'm glad you told me about it."

She leaned back in her chair, left leg crossed over the right. She had on a light-blue silk shirt and navy blue linen pants. The late afternoon sun coming through the leaves of the potted fern in the bay window laid a random leaf pattern on the wall behind her.

"Emma's going through something she's never experienced before," Diane Parker said. "A sort of 'if only' thing. If only you hadn't divorced, if only things had been different, maybe what happened wouldn't ever have happened. She doesn't quite know how to handle it."

"That," Kathryn said, "makes two of us."

"Would you mind if I asked you a few personal questions?"

"Why?"

"The quality of your relationship with your daughter is central to my counselling. I'd like to hear about it from your viewpoint as well as from hers."

"What do you want to know?" Kathryn said.

Diane Parker smiled. "Thanks to Emma, I already know quite a lot about you. I know you were born in Kansas City, that your mother remarried after your father died and still lives there. I know you have a brother named Paul and a sister named Teresa."

"She's a chatterbox."

"She told me you once worked in the public defender's office. Why did you change to prosecution?"

"It's a long story."

"We've got time."

"I was seventeen and I knew it all. One night I was with some kids in a bar for over twenty-ones, using a phoney ID. The police arrived, and the next thing I knew I was on my way to juvenile hall. My stepfather wouldn't come down to the hall and he wouldn't let my mother go either. So there I was, very scared and all alone. Then this woman from the public defender's office came to see me. Her name was Melinda Gray; she'd been assigned my case. She got me released and placed on informal probation. She gave me the support my parents wouldn't. I can't tell you how important that was to me then."

"Is that where you got the idea of becoming a lawyer?"

"I guess . . . I wanted to be like her. After college I enrolled in law school. When I graduated, I went to work for the Public Defender."

"And now you're a prosecutor. Why did you change?"

"I started out an idealist. Public defenders were the last line of defense. I found out real quick there wasn't much room for idealism in a PD's office. The name of the game was survival. Don't get me justice lady, get me off."

"But surely, not everyone—"

"There was no time for fine distinctions. It was like I was on a production line that kept on bringing me an endless procession of wife-beaters, child molesters and rapists, so-called 'clients' who stank so badly of guilt it made me want to spray my office with Lysol after they left.

"They said I'd learn," she added. "And they were right. I learned how to use the law, bend the law, twist it on behalf of clients whose cases I took on because I had no choice, people I knew were guilty the minute I laid eyes on them. I learned to carry packs of gum to damp down the liquor breath of the hung-over flotsam the system washed into my office. I learned never to be alone with certain men or women. I learned never to wear jewelry or have anything valuable in sight. I learned how to cut a deal, how to discredit a witness, how to play a jury for sympathy. I learned how to spot a flaw in a hastily prepared prosecution, how to sense the uncertainty of a prosecution expert, how to cast doubt into a juror's mind. And here's what's funny—you know what it took me longest to learn? That I was in the wrong place. I stuck it out for a long time before I was willing to admit I had made a mistake."

Diane Parker shook her head wonderingly. "And do you prosecute with the same intensity I just heard?"

Kathryn nodded. "I sometimes wish I didn't care about it so much, but I do."

"And you get so deep into it—"

"When I'm in trial I forget everything else. Everyone."

"Including Emma. Which makes you feel guilty."

"Of course it does. I'm torn when it comes to school holidays and vacation days because I still have work to do. I can't be all hers the way she wants me to be."

"Do you ever wonder deep down inside whether you ought to get out, do something else?"

"Sometimes," Kathryn admitted. "The longer you play the part the more it becomes you, the more you carry that hard edge into your personal life. You find yourself cross-examining the people you love and hating yourself because you can do it so well."

"Do you do that with Emma?"

"Not often. I usually catch myself in time."

"That's good. You need to ease off on her, especially now."

"I'm aware of it."

"I'm glad you came by. It's been very helpful."

To whom? Kathryn wondered as she got into the car with Emma and started for home.

"You were a long time," Emma said. "Were you talking about me?"

Kathryn shook her head. "Not really. More about us. How we tick. You know what I mean?"

"I know," Emma said reproachfully. "I'm nearly eight years old, Mom."

"How was school today?"

"We're studying about the planets. The solo system."

"Solar, sweetheart."

"Right. We had to draw pictures with crayons. Mars is red. Earth is blue. Jupiter is green. I think. We're going to the planetarium."

"Sounds like fun."

"It's really neat when we have lots to do. You don't need to think so much about . . . everything."

"That's good," Kathryn said gravely. "Did you enjoy talking with Dr. Parker today?"

"It was okay," Emma said. "She's not as bad as I thought she was at first. But she asks an awful lot of questions."

"What do you talk about?"

"Oh, you know, feelings. Being sad. Being angry. Trying not to."

"It's hard, isn't it?"

Emma sighed. "I'm hungry, Mom. Could we get some frozen yogurt?"

"Why not?" Kathryn smiled. "And hey, what do you say we go out to dinner this weekend, just the two of us?"

"You know what I'd really like?" Emma said. "If Dave could come too. Could he, Mom? I'd really like that."

I'm ready to make the commitment. The question is, are you?

"I'll call and ask him," she told Emma. "As soon as we get home."

20

Michael Gaines sat alone in his small office, staring at the instructions for the VICAP forms. They were similar to the Scantron answer sheets college instructors use to grade student exams, requiring virtually no human involvement, and by definition little subjective interpretation. If filled out accurately, however, the VICAP forms provided extremely reliable results.

Like most cops, Gaines hated paperwork; but the more involved he became with the rapes he was investigating, the more convinced he became that if he submitted them, VICAP would locate similar rapes in their national database.

He blew out a gusty breath of impatience. This was going to take time, and time was always the enemy. There were still leads to follow up in connection with the Jennifer Skelton rape. But he wanted this bastard, and if filling in forms meant the difference between catching him and not catching him he would sit at a desk for a week.

The first job was to get the Crime Analysis Reports—CARs—to the FBI-funded VICAP, which received and analyzed such reports from law enforcement agencies all over the United States, as well as Canada and other countries. Its purpose was to document, and wherever possible link, violent crimes committed by repeat violent offenders.

He forced himself to concentrate. The CAR form comprised several pages divided into sections. Section I contained only check-box responses; Section II, only fill-in questions; while Section III had space for a short narrative response.

Questions were Yes–No, or multiple-choice; only one response box could be blacked out. They elicited specific information about the victim: age, sex, physical characteristics, occupation, residence, by geographic region, by style of dress, by ethnic background.

If a weapon was involved, further questions identified the type of weapon and the manner in which it had been used. If physical force had been used, the questions solicited the nature of the attack: whether, for example, the victim had been struck with an open hand, fists, or an inanimate object; and where; face, head, chest, back, belly, buttocks, thighs, or other parts of the victim's anatomy.

Facial disguises or masks, if any, were classified as either partial or full. It was considered especially significant if the perpetrator removed the disguise during the crime.

Because violent criminals almost always achieved a comfort level with certain types of physical surroundings, the VICAP report requested the location of the offense; remote, isolated, or public place; a description of the topography such as beach, orchard, mountains, residence, vehicle. In addition, it was crucial to specify the time of day at which the offense occurred: early morning, midday, afternoon, evening, nighttime; the day of the week, month and year . . . and so on.

He wondered who the man was. Tall, casually styled blond hair, middle to late thirties, fit-looking; he wondered where the scars on his face had come from. An automobile accident, perhaps. He watched as they got into Kathryn Mackay's little red Mazda. Colleagues, he decided. A detective or someone who worked in the DA's office. It didn't really matter. He wasn't interested in the man right now.

He had read about Kathryn Mackay in the Gazette *and the photograph had piqued his interest. Long, dark hair, a pert, alert face with wide-set eyes and a confident smile. RIKER GUILTY OF MURDER. Kathryn Mackay, head of the Rape/Homicide unit of the District Attorney's office. She was accomplished. That was good: proficient women used their brains. It was the stupid ones who screamed.*

Like those of most law enforcement people, Kathryn Mackay's address and phone were unlisted, but that was no problem. At the end of a working day he had waited outside the County Building until he saw her come down the steps and get into a little red Mazda sports car; it was easy to follow, the more so because she had no idea anyone was following her.

Using a No. 2 pencil, as specified in the CAR instructions—the electronic scanner at Quantico which picked up the metallic content of the lead could read nothing else—Gaines painstakingly blackened out his responses. Every answer, every detail, every fact, brought back the memory of a victim, the look in her eyes, her voice, her degradation, her pain.

He worked on, reliving and remembering. Lisa Hernandez with her broken face, the glint of dark eyes between slitted, swollen lids; Stacie Percell shaking her head, then wincing with pain; Jennifer Skelton, afraid to get into a car or walk down the street.

Section II was mostly fill-in questions like, *"If the response to Question 15 in Section I is Yes, (Does the perpetrator use any unusual words, phrases or terminology while in the presence of the victim(s)), describe the key words or phrases."* Section III solicited any additional relevant information not obtained in Sections I or II.

When the forms reached VICAP, at the FBI Academy in Quantico, Virginia, the check-box responses would be scanned and electronically analyzed by five veteran FBI employees—a program manager, two crime analysts and two former homicide investigators who served as major case specialists. Employing a judicious mix of their own experience they would compare and assess violent crimes reported on VICAP forms with the database of existing cases. When a correlation was identified, VICAP would notify the investigative agencies involved so they could coordinate their investigations and pool their resources with a view to expeditiously identifying and apprehending the offender.

Gaines put down the pencil and went out into the corridor, flexing his cramped fingers. He got a cup of coffee from the machine and sipped it, making a face at the bitter taste. Back home they said you knew it was good coffee when you threw in a horseshoe and it didn't sink. The inspectors claimed the office coffee was so bad because the machine was connected directly to the sewage plant.

He went back to his desk and sat staring out of the window, reflecting on the information he was providing VICAP. There were quite a few anomalies. Lisa Hernandez had been kidnapped while walking to her car, then driven to a canyon, beaten and raped. Stacie Percell had been raped at knifepoint in her parents' home in a nice residential area. In the case of Jennifer Skelton the rapist had employed another, totally different MO.

Serial rapists rarely, if ever, varied their core behavior, but in each of the three rapes he was submitting to VICAP, it had varied significantly. The manner of controlling his victims and the force he had used varied; his reaction to the victim's resistance was different each time. In one of the rapes, he hadn't even taken any precautionary measures to protect his identity; in another he wore a ski mask and gloves.

Gaines knew many rapists experienced sexual dysfunctions; failure to achieve or sustain an erection, premature ejaculation, or difficulty or failure to ejaculate during intercourse. Yet in all three cases he was submitting, the perpetrator had ejaculated: it was one of three factors they had in common.

Kathryn Mackay's car headed north on Pacific, turning east on to the Alvarado Highway. He followed, keeping two or three cars between them at all times, taking the off ramp at Laguna del Mar behind her car and turning down on to Lagunita Drive.

He knew this area well. One of the little pigs had lived near here, on Tamarisk Drive, six blocks away. It had been foggy that night. Stacie. The one who made him angry.

They all made him angry.

Heaving an audible sigh, Gaines started on another CAR, muttering to himself as he checked the box indicating presence of bites, the second factor each of the rapes had in common. Stacie Percell's rapist had bitten off her ear lobe. Lisa Hernandez's rapist had bitten—or rather, torn—a strip of skin from the inside of her thigh. The man who raped Jennifer Skelton had bitten her breast. "Compulsive?" Gaines wondered aloud. "Whatever, this is one weird fucker."

The third common factor was the words and phrases the rapist had used. He had called each of his victims "little pig" or "little piggy." Not like, You pig! but almost affectionately, as if the victim were a small child. In all three rapes he had used the words "Shove your ass."

* * *

Until Justice Is Done

He followed the Mazda down East Laguna Drive, across the iron bridge spanning the Laguna del Mar yacht harbor, and then along the ocean front to Espanola. He could see the stone finger of the lighthouse on Shelter Island on its bluff across the inlet, sandhills shelving steeply down to the beach. Kathryn Mackay's car turned right on Lighthouse, then left into Seaview Heights. The buildings were named after capital cities. She lived in London House. Well, well, he thought. A condo, probably with an ocean view, very nice. He smiled in satisfaction; everything else he needed to know, he could find out when he came back. He looked up at the lighted windows.

"See you soon, little pig," he said.

Maybe VICAP could make something of all of it, Gaines thought. He was damned if he could. Although a serial rapist's victims could number from two to more than a hundred, his careful and comprehensive computer search had turned up no other rapes in Santa Rita County where the perp had bitten his victims or called them a "little pig."

Nevertheless, experience, judgment and gut instinct told Gaines this bastard had done this before, somewhere else: another county, another state. If VICAP could backtrack him, if his route from wherever he had started out could be determined, Gaines was willing to bet they'd find a trail of rapes in his wake. He was counting on the VICAP database to draw the road map.

Despite the electronic wizardry at its disposal, VICAP stipulated that input forms be mailed rather than faxed, and the original form was required;

photocopies were not acceptable. Before folding the forms and putting them in the preprinted envelope for mailing, Gaines made a call to his old friend Paul Northrop at FBI headquarters in Quantico. It was time to call in some favors and Paul owed him more than a few. After extracting Paul's promise that he would do everything he could to prioritize the processing of Gaines's VICAP requests, Michael added a memo emphasizing the confidential nature of the submission and requesting that all responses from VICAP and inquiries from other agencies be forwarded for his eyes only.

He went across to the window and looked out. "I know you're out there someplace, you bastard," he said out loud to no one but himself. "I know you are. But not for much fucking longer."

21

At first George Zabrowski thought he was paralyzed. Panic swept through him. Then, as consciousness fully returned, he realized he was in the back of a car, face up on the floor between the front and rear seats, his hands in front of his chest. He couldn't move. Lights flicked past. A jackhammer was pounding inside his head. His tongue felt like a rolled-up sweat sock and tasted worse. He tried to sit up and nausea rose in his throat. He gagged and groaned.

"Throw up back there, I'll make you fucking eat it."

The voice was harsh and unfamiliar. Zabrowski struggled to move. No use. His hands were bound with wide surgical tape, his legs and feet in some sort of bag cinched tight around his thighs. What was this? What the fuck was going on?

"What the fuck is going on?" he screamed. It came out a croak. If he heard it, the driver of the car took no notice. Zabrowski tried to turn over, but the nausea surged upward again, so he quit. A dull thud of pain beat like a metronome above his right ear in perfect sync with his own heartbeat. The vibration of the moving wheels hurt his head. What the fuck was happening?

Then he remembered. Through the pain-induced fog in his head, he recalled walking out of La Paloma Cantina and half-seeing, half-sensing the dark shape of a big man coming at him fast and low from behind a parked car. And then something exploded in his head and there was nothing.

He tried to sit up in the back seat. The jackhammer inside his head started up again and he winced. The sound of the engine and the drone of the tires was long and even. They must be out on a highway someplace, Zabrowski thought. As if he had overheard the thought, the driver slowed, turned left and came to a stop in the darkness beneath some overhanging trees.

He got out and came around the car, jerked open

the door and dragged Zabrowski out by his hair, spilling him on to the ground screaming obscenities. With quick, deft movements the man untied the rope cinching the canvas mail sack to Zabrowski's thighs and hoisted him to his feet, left arm thrusting him against the bodywork of the car. His legs had gone to sleep; it was all he could do to stand.

For the first time he noticed that his captor was wearing a three-quarter-length plasticized rain jacket and tight black leather gloves. He knew in his gut he was in deep shit; deeper than he had ever been before. He knew what and he knew why, but he didn't know what to do about it. The clouds moved away from the moon and he saw the man's face for the first time.

"Oh, shit, no," he said. "Oh, Christ, no."

His captor stepped back and for a fraction of a second Zabrowski thought of making a run for it, but then he saw the gun. It was a 9mm Walther PPK/S. His blood ran cold; nobody could outrun a seven shot semi-automatic.

"Stay on your feet, asshole," the man said. He hauled George upright and half-carried, half-ran him, feet dragging, along a scrub-lined path. Way off in the dark a lighthouse blinked. Wind buffeted them. George heard the ocean surging against the rocks below and his stomach lurched as he realized he was standing on the edge of a high cliff. Jesus fucking Christ, it was Lover's Leap!

"Jesus, man, what is this, what the fuck you doing?" he screeched, trying to propel himself backwards away from the edge. He might as well have pushed against a brick wall. The man grabbed his hair and jerked his head back. His eyes were only a couple of inches from George's; it seemed to him they were red with anger.

"Francesca Jaramillo," he grated. "Name mean anything to you, asshole?"

Zabrowski's jaw went slack. "What?"

"Remember how scared she was?" his captor said relentlessly. "Remember how she begged and pleaded with you not to hurt her? So what did you do, asshole? You beat the shit out of her and then you raped her. Just a hooker, right, asshole? Just another dumb whore with no rights. You can do whatever the fuck you want to her and nobody'll give a shit, right?"

"It wasn't me, man," George screeched. "The fuckin' grand jury didn't even believe her. It wasn't me, I swear!"

"Sure," the big man said conversationally. "It never happened. She just had a bad dream." His voice hardened. "And now you're having one, asshole. Where did you hit her first? In the face, right?"

George never even saw the man's hand move. The impact felt like a bomb, a bright flash of white pain. The next thing he knew he was on his knees, head hanging down, senses reeling. His entire face was numb. The left cheekbone felt smashed, loose. He moved his jaw and heard bone grate. Blood was falling out of his face like rain.

"Then the belly, right?"

The man hauled him upright as easily as if he were a child. Swaying, a blood red mist in front of his eyes, George tried to turn away from the blow he knew was coming, but he was way too slow. It was as if someone had struck his body with a sledgehammer. He doubled over, groaning and retching as his paralyzed body tried to function, scrabbling on the ground, trying to crawl away, but it was no use.

The man grabbed him by the collar of his shirt and dragged him like an unwieldy suitcase to the very edge of the cliff. Emptiness yawned below. George screamed.

"You scared now, Georgie?" the man said. His voice was flat with rage. "Go ahead. Cry. Beg, the way Frankie Jaramillo did."

"Listen, man, for Chrissake, listen." George Zabrowski's voice was thin, high, threaded with terror. He got up so he was on his knees and clasped his hands together as if he was praying. "You can't do this. Don't, Jesus, I'm beggin' you. Don't—no more. I never done nothin'."

The man reached down and a fist like a rock bunched George's shirt under his chin, hauling him upright for the third time and taking him back close to the edge of the cliff.

"I'm going to count three," he said. Cold as ice. "Then either you jump or I shoot you in the balls."

"Aw, Jesus, man, you fuckin crazy?" George Zabrowski's voice became an hysterical shriek. "Jesus, don't, don't, you can't!"

"Wrong," the man said. He cocked the gun and jammed it into George's crotch. "One."

"FaChrissakeslistentome!" George screeched.

"Two," the man said.

Without warning he released his grip and at the same time fired the gun past George's ear. Zabrowski's reflex backward step took him over the edge of the cliff. He screamed once as he disappeared.

"Three," the man said.

* * *

It was like a family outing. Kathryn loved watching her daughter laugh at Dave Granz's silly jokes. He always knew how to make Emma laugh, she thought. Me, too. Two peas in a pod; the thought made her feel warm inside. Sometimes she felt Emma was even closer to Dave than to her and that he understood her daughter better than she did.

La Comida Carmelita was Dave and Emma's favorite restaurant. Kathryn liked Mexican food too, but not red-hot and spicy the way Dave and her daughter preferred it. She did like guacamole, though, so Dave ordered a big bowl and some chips with extra salsa. He liked to sprinkle salt on his chips, then dip them into the salsa, which made his mouth burn. He doused the fire with a sip of cold Corona beer; Emma did the same thing, but with Diet Coke.

"You're both going to end up burning holes in your stomachs," Kathryn warned, and smiled at their scornful laughter. Neither of them could speak because their mouths were full of food. She knew anyway what Dave's answer would be: if that were true, he'd have had a stomach full of holes by the time he was ten years old.

The guacamole and chips were almost gone when their dinners arrived. For Dave, a big combination plate of tamale, enchilada, chile relleno, rice and beans, a cheese enchilada for Kathryn and a plain quesadilla for Emma. The usual.

Kathryn settled for a cup of decaffeinated coffee by way of dessert; Dave and Emma shared a chocolate sundae. She marvelled that they could eat so much and stay slim. While Dave polished off the last of the ice cream, Emma wandered over to look at the colorful piñata which hung from the ceiling next to the door leading into the kitchen.

"It's good to see her smiling," Kathryn said. "Thanks, Dave."

"You don't need to thank me," he said. "Emma's a very special person in my life. Sort of the daughter I never had. But, if you really need to thank me, you can pay for dinner."

Kathryn laughed out loud. "I'm not that grateful." On the other hand, she thought, maybe she was.

"You want to go straight home?" Dave said. "It's still early. We could take a stroll along the beach."

"Let's do," Kathryn said. "It's beautiful out and besides, I need to stop at the bakery for a chocolate chip cookie."

It felt good to put aside the stresses of the day, even though, as always, she had work to do at home. She didn't take the opportunity to relax often enough and besides, Emma loved to walk on the beach. And she very much wanted to spend more time with Dave.

"Em, you want to go for a walk on the beach?" Kathryn said when Emma came back to the table.

"Which beach?" Emma asked.

"You decide."

"Not Espanola," she said. "It reminds me too much of Daddy."

"Okay," Kathryn said smoothly. "What about La Loma?"

"Oh, we go down there all the time from school, Mom," Emma said.

"How about let's go over to Seal Point Park," Dave suggested. "See what the seals are up to."

A light breeze came in off the ocean as they walked

along the clifftop. Trees growing along the cliffs leaned dramatically, sculpted by the wind. Down below they could see the seals sleeping on the rocky spur that gave the park its name; every so often one would shuffle to the edge and flop into the water, metamorphosing instantly from comic to beautifully graceful.

Further up the coast two die-hard surfers in their neck-to-ankle black wet suits were catching the last waves of the day before it got dark. The water off the Santa Rita coast was always cold, fifty-six degrees, winter or summer. Surfers always wore wet suits, which made them look exactly like seals or sea lions riding the waves. That probably explained the two or three shark attacks on surfers each year: seals and sea lions are the Great White's favorite snack.

"You're very quiet," Dave said.

"No need to talk," she replied.

"You know, I love this," Dave said. "You're like my family, the two of you; I feel like I'm home."

"Me too."

"Have you thought any more about what I said? I asked you to marry me, Kathryn."

"I know."

"You still haven't answered."

"I know that, too. I'm not ignoring you. I wouldn't do that. But Dave, it's such an important step, and I've been so busy with work I haven't really had time to think. Can't we . . . isn't what we have now enough?"

"If I thought it was, I wouldn't want to make it permanent," he said, but he was smiling.

"Dave, come here," Emma shouted imperiously, her timing, as always, impeccable. He looked at Kathryn with an understanding shrug and ambled over to the rail where she was looking down at the seals. Kathryn could see Emma giggling at whatever Dave was saying, but the surf drowned the sound of his words. My two favorite people, she thought; it ought to be easy to make a decision. But it wasn't, and she didn't know why.

After a while, Dave and Emma wandered back, apparently as bored with the seals as the seals were with them. Emma tugged at Kathryn's hand.

"I'll bet Sam's hungry, Mom. Let's go home so I can feed him," she suggested.

They drove back to Espanola in silence, Dave and Kathryn holding hands across the front seat. When they got back to the condo, Dave got himself a glass of wine and turned on the television to watch a nature program about the African cheetah, while Kathryn busied herself getting Emma's things ready for school. After a while Emma came in from the shower wearing her white terrycloth robe, long dark hair tumbled down in back like a mermaid. "G'night, Dave," she said, kissing him on the cheek. "Thanks for dinner. We sure ate lots of chips."

"Sleep tight, tootsie," he said. He turned off the TV and went out on the balcony. He was still there, looking out across the darkening ocean, when Kathryn came back.

"What is it, Dave?" she asked, softly. "What's bothering you?"

He made no reply and she slipped her arm around his waist. "You can't fool me," she said softly. "What's wrong? Can I help?"

"No, it's work. You know, I'm always telling you to leave it behind when you go home but I can't do it either. I can't get those damned murders off my mind. There's something really wrong in there someplace, more than just wrong. Something weird. I can't figure it."

"Well, why not let's take your advice and forget it for a while? That was a nice dinner. And the walk afterwards. I had a wonderful time."

"I enjoyed it, too. I'd have enjoyed it more if I hadn't been thinking about this damned vigilante the whole time."

"So that's what it was."

"I mean it, it's really getting to me," he said. "What kind of a person are we dealing with anyway, Kathryn? I sit there and stare at autopsy photos and I wonder what the hell is he doing this for? Why did he go to the trouble of staging phoney autoerotic deaths? Why not just buy an eighty-dollar MP-25 and stick it in the guy's ear?"

"It was a way of committing murder without getting caught. Or so he thought."

"He may have been right," Dave said. "He's done it and he ain't caught."

"It's early yet, Dave," she said. "He's had a head start on us. We'll catch up."

Dave put the glass down on the table and took her upper arms in his hands, turning her to face him. There was a rueful expression on his face. She put her arms around his neck and held him tight, but it was like he wasn't really with her, physically present, emotionally elsewhere.

Before she could speak again his pager sounded. He looked at the number on the display. "County Comm," he said.

Damn, she thought, my turn this time. She stood aside as he went into the kitchen, picked up the portable telephone and dialed. She heard him give his name, then he said yes, three times.

"Got it," he said and hung up. He turned to face Kathryn. "I asked to be notified immediately in the event of any suicide or accidental death," he told her. "It's a suicide. At Lover's Leap."

Lover's Leap was a well-known beauty spot near Northport on Highway One. There was a legend that in years gone by a young Spanish couple, refused permission to marry by her parents, had joined hands on the top of the 150-foot-high clifftop and jumped to their death. Kathryn waited, feeling the cold caress of her own premonition. "Tell me the rest," she said.

"He's been ID'd," Granz told her. "It's George Zabrowski."

"Zabrowski?" she whispered. "When did it happen?"

"The body was found about half an hour ago," Dave told her. "Coroner's deputies are up there now."

"You think it's another one, don't you?" she said. "The vigilante."

He shrugged. "Only one way to find out," he said.

22

"This is an unexpected pleasure," Morgan Nelson said, with grave mock-formality. "Tell me, what brings you two down here to the Hellhole?"

He had once referred to his underground kingdom by that name; the description was so apposite it had immediately stuck.

"We were hoping you could spare us a few minutes, Doc," Dave Granz said. They were sitting in Nelson's cluttered office, Morgan in his battered old swivel chair, Kathryn and Dave on the beaten-up shell chairs Morgan kept for visitors. "But if you've got something urgent . . . ?"

"I ought to be in the cutting room," Morgan Nelson smiled, sipping his coffee. "It needs to be done, but urgent it ain't. What can I do for you?"

"We need a favor, Morgan," Kathryn said. "That's really why we came up here."

"Name it."

"To begin with, run your findings on the Zabrowski death by me," Kathryn said. "Dave's briefed me generally on the ride over."

"That's easy enough," Morgan said, reaching for a file. He opened it up and began to read. "George William Zabrowski. Time of death estimated between nine P.M. and four A.M., July 23. The body was found lodged between rocks below the cliffs at Northport."

"I was at the scene," Dave said. "Deputy coroner said if his leg hadn't got snagged between the rocks, he'd probably have washed ashore in Hawaii."

"He was a mess," Morgan said, "in spite of the fact that the body had been in the water less than twenty-four hours. He sustained multiple fractures to the skull. The spine was broken in two places and he suffered massive internal injuries. Death was probably instantaneous."

"I searched the cliffs directly above where the body was found," Dave interposed. "I saw no signs of a struggle; no blood, no shoetracks, no tiretracks, nothing."

"Why do you think it's the vigilante?" Kathryn asked. "It's not his MO. We have no physical evidence to suggest a murder. And if I understand what Morgan is telling us, his injuries are consistent with a fall from a cliff."

"I don't disagree with what you're saying," Dave said. "The problem is if Zabrowski had been beaten to death with an iron bar, it wouldn't show after he fell a hundred and fifty feet on to rocks, right, Doc?"

"That's right, Dave," Morgan said.

"To top it off, the psychology is all wrong," Dave pointed out. "I interviewed his friends; people who worked with him. They all said the same thing: he never gave any sign of being suicidal. In fact, they all said how pleased he was with himself for walking on the Frankie Jaramillo rape. It made him a Little Big Man with some of his friends."

"So you're saying what? The vigilante picked him

up and tossed him over the cliff?" Kathryn asked. "Why has he changed his MO?"

"Hell, Kathryn, I don't know," Granz said wearily. "The more I look at this thing, the more I wonder, is this just one guy? Vigilantes often act in concert. More than one. Being part of a group bolsters their confidence."

"And disperses the guilt," Morgan observed. "In the old days, every member of a vigilante group laid his hands on the rope so no one person could ever be said to have done the deed. You may be on to something there, Dave."

"Are you serious?" Kathryn asked.

"You've heard of the Ku Klux Klan?"

"In California?"

"Look, I'm groping around in the dark here," Dave said. "There's a lot of strong feeling on the street that far too many rapists walk. It's not outside the bound of possibility that some people got together to do something about it, that's all I'm saying."

"Other than your gut reaction, do you have anything, anything at all that indicates murder?" Morgan asked.

"Not a damned thing, Doc," Granz said flatly. "That's why we came up here. We thought you could come up with something."

"For instance?"

"How difficult would it be to go back over your protocols on Croma, Piselli, Bosendorf, Bitzer and Zabrowski?"

"With what in mind?"

"What we're hoping is maybe there's something in there that links them, something other than the fact that they all walked on rape charges," Kathryn said.

"Such as?"

"Hell, Doc, we don't know. I've just got this gut feeling there's something there and we're hoping maybe you could help us find it."

"There doesn't need to be anything else, Dave, you know that. If there is a vigilante out there—or a vigilante group—the fact they were rapists could be enough. It's not inconceivable that a vigilante would target rapists."

"Let's move on from motive, Morgan," Kathryn said, "to method, opportunity and timing. Let's start with method. How much medical knowledge would he—or they, if you prefer—need to have?"

Morgan drew in a long breath, considering. "Quite a lot. Piselli, Bosendorf and Bitzer might have been rendered unconscious and then killed. But how do you explain the presence of ejaculate? Unconscious men don't ejaculate—that is, unless someone inserts a finger into the rectum and massages the prostate."

"A doctor?" Dave asked.

"Perhaps, or someone with a fairly detailed knowledge of autoerotic practices. He, they, take your pick, could get most of it from S&M tabloids, porno magazines, even detective magazines. God knows, there are enough of them around. What else can I tell you? He'd need to be strong—which is why I say it isn't a woman—and he'd need to have a job that allowed him a lot of freedom of movement. Of course both lines of reasoning go out the window if we're talking about more than one person."

Dave made an exasperated sound. "It's like this whole thing is the side of a building and I'm a blind man feeling my way along it, knowing there has to be a window, a door, a way through."

"You want a layman's opinion?"

"You're not a layman, Morgan," Kathryn said.

"I'm not a detective, either, Katie," Morgan smiled. "But I'll tell you this much, you're not going to catch whoever is doing this using conventional police methods. I'll be frank with you, I don't think going through the autopsy protocols is going to cut it, either—although I'll do it for you."

"If that's supposed to be encouraging, I've got to tell you, it ain't getting there, Doc," Granz said wryly.

Nelson smiled. "Just back up a little. You said something interesting, Kathryn, what was it? Something about method, opportunity, timing?"

"And?"

"You want my opinion, that's where the answers are," Nelson said. "In fact I'd bet on it."

Method, opportunity, timing. Granz found himself saying the words over and over to himself like a mantra as they drove back to the office. When he got to his desk, he wrote each word on a Post-it and stuck them on the side of his computer monitor, one above the other.

Method.

Opportunity.

Timing.

Okay, start with method. Like Doc had said, Piselli, Bosendorf and Bitzer might have been knocked out first and then killed. The killer—one of the killers?—would have had to digitally manipulate the prostate via the rectum to cause an ejaculation. It was difficult to envision but not impossible. If didn't have to be a doctor. A nurse, a medical student would have the know-how. As for Zabrowski, he could very easily have been knocked unconscious and simply tossed off the cliffs at Lover's Leap. So what you were left with was that the victims were taken from behind, probably with the crook-of-the-arm technique Doc had demonstrated. It was doubtful if any of them would have known what hit them. Or who. And it still didn't answer the question, one man or several?

Follow through.

Was it possible the victims knew their killer and that was why he rendered them unconscious first? Granz let out another exasperated sigh and shook his head. An assumption, not warranted by the facts established during the psychological autopsies. The simplest, most obvious explanation was it was done because an unconscious victim made rigging the phony autoerotic death scene easier. And it still left the solo-or-group killer question unanswered.

Okay, move on: opportunity.

Where did the killer strike? How did he locate, isolate and attack his victims? He would have to know their movements, their habits. He would have to gauge their strength, the amount of resistance they might offer. Then do it, silent, swift and deadly, without being seen. This was where the vigilante group theory started to become more seductive. With several men acting in concert, strictures like these were much less inhibiting. The same went for the actual killings.

In three of them, Croma, Zabrowski, and Bitzer, it was possible—probable—each of the victims had been attacked in some secluded place and then taken unconscious to where he was found dead, because it was highly unlikely any of them would have gone there without some kind of struggle. If more than one vigilante was involved, the whole scenario became much easier to imagine. But what about Piselli and Bosendorf? Would either have let a posse of potential killers into their homes unless . . .

They knew him?

All of them? Or just one of them? Either way, it wasn't possible. He had been all the way down that road, cross-checking every name, every lead, every fact against every other name, lead and fact. And come up with zilch.

He swung around in his swivel chair, facing the window that looked out on the downtown area beyond. Whoever did this is out there, he thought. In plain sight. But invisible.

In plain sight, but invisible.

Am I looking in the wrong place? he wondered. No, it wasn't possible. Or was it?

23

VICAP faxed Michael Gaines a list of eight rapes similar to the ones he had submitted. They had been committed in three different states: two in New York between 1984 and 1986; three in Georgia between 1987 and 1989; and three more in New Mexico between 1990 and 1993.

The name of the law enforcement agency, the case

numbers, the officer contact and the telephone number were included along with a short description of each rape.

Both New York rapes had occurred in Rochester. Anita Templeton, age twenty-two, was raped the evening of May 14, 1984. She lived alone. The rapist entered her apartment through a rear door. He disconnected her phone. In the course of the rape, he had called her "little piggy" and bitten her left breast.

The second Rochester rape was in February 1985. The victim, twenty-year-old Myra Penfield, was a student nurse at the community college. The rapist broke into her parents' home while they were away. During the rape, he bit off the tip of her little finger and used the words "a little pig."

The contact officer on both rapes was Detective Kevin McNulty, Rochester PD (716) 232-3311.

The three Georgia rapes all took place in Atlanta and were spread out over a two year period. The victims were again all young women, two of them married. The first was Sherri Kleck, twenty-seven years old, single, manager of a sporting goods store. She got off work on June 24, 1987 and drove home. Upon entering her ground floor apartment, she was grabbed by a man who raped her. He had used the words "little pig," during the rape; then bitten flesh from her neck.

The second victim, Tammy Confino, age twenty-eight, married, was asleep in her home on March 11, 1988. Her husband was away on business. She was awakened to find a man sitting on her body. He said, "Hello, little pig," then raped her. In the course of the rape he bit off a piece of her left cheek.

On March 12, 1989, Leila Teague, age twenty-five, married, was raped and sodomized in her home while her husband was at work. The inside of her thigh had been bitten; one of the key phrases was used: "little pig." The contact in Atlanta was Detective Maurice Fulton (404) 658-6666.

In New Mexico all three of the rapes had been committed in Albuquerque. In the first, on July 22, 1989, a man broke into the apartment of Carol Scott, age twenty-eight, around 11:30 P.M.; the victim lived alone. He disconnected the phone. He forced her to perform oral sex three times, then he raped her. Over the course of the assault, he called her "little pig" several times. Before he left, he bit her belly.

On March 28, 1991, Julie Corradini, twenty-four, single, an employee of Mountain Bell Telephone at Silver and Seventh, was abducted from the parking lot of her office building by a man who forced her to drive across the river to an isolated place near San Gabriel State Park, where he raped her twice and sodomized her. Afterward he drove her back to the office parking lot. Before he left her, he whispered into her ear "this little pig better not call the cops." Then he bit her ear.

In his mind's eye Michael Gaines saw Jennifer Skelton in the darkened living room of her neat little house in Valley Springs. *Catch him, Michael. Catch him!*

The third rape was committed almost exactly a year after the second; Tracie Soren, twenty-two years old, worked as a waitress at the same restaurant where her husband worked as the night manager. The rapist broke into their home one night while her husband was at work. He called her a "little pig." He raped and sodomized her. Then he bit off a piece of her breast. The contact in Albuquerque was Detective Albert Armijo (505) 982-8521.

Gaines reviewed what he had. There didn't appear to be any pattern: some of the victims were blonde, others brunette, one a redhead. Their ages ranged from early twenties to thirty. A number were married, some were single, one was divorced. Some of the victims had been living with their husbands in single family homes; others lived by themselves in apartments. No arrests had been made in connection with any of the rapes.

Slightly more promising, but only slightly, was the fact that each of the victims had described the rapist as thirtyish, medium height, well-built, strong or muscular. The down side was that the description fitted far too many men to be useful.

Gaines read through the fax again twice, glaring at the pages as if somehow his anger would make them tell him what he wanted to know. He could feel the tension in his body, the added electricity he always felt when an investigation started to break. Whether you liked it or not, it was an excitement you shared with every hunter. Including the one you were hunting.

He looked at the stack of files that contained his investigation notes on the Lisa Hernandez, Stacie Percell and Jennifer Skelton rapes, all the hours wasted chasing phantoms. Well, not any more. Although he did not yet know what it was, he knew there was a lead someplace in the information before him. I am going to find it, he vowed silently. However long it takes, however hard the road, I am going to find it.

And then, you perverted fucking imitation of a human being, I'm going to find you.

"Hey," Dave said softly. He leaned over and kissed Kathryn's bare shoulder. "It's been a long time since we did this."

"Too long," Kathryn murmured, stretching her toes under the sheets. "You want something to drink?"

"It can wait," he said. "Let me just revel in the fact we're finally in bed together."

Kathryn sat up and reached for the morning's paper at the foot of the bed. A headline halfway down the page caught her eye: SEATTLE COP SLAYS SUSPECT.

"Did you know about this?" she said, holding it up where he could see it.

Dave shook his head. "But some of the inspectors were talking about it today. What does it say?"

"'At about three P.M. yesterday,'" Kathryn read aloud, "'Seattle detective Robert Barron, thirty-eight, walked into an interview room at police headquarters and shot to death Eugene Kaplan, twenty-two, a suspect being interviewed in connection with a rape investigation. A spokesman confirmed Barron is under arrest pending psychiatric examination.'"

"I'll bet you I know what happened," Dave said. "The poor bastard snapped, just like Sam Perry."

"Sam who?"

"Sam Perry. He was my partner when I was in the SO a long time ago."

"What did you mean, he snapped?"

Dave drew in a long breath. "You sure you want to hear this?"

"Of course I do. There's such a lot I want to know about you."

"I first met Sam when we were both new deputies with the SO. He had a sister, Moira, who was married to a deputy named Nick Provencio. One day he's on patrol. He saw a fight, looked like two drunks. He decides to try and break it up without calling in for backup. One of the drunks pulls a knife and stabs Nick to death. Moira is six months pregnant when Nick is killed, so Sam moves her in with him, he's all the family she's got. After the baby is born, Sam takes on the role of Dad as well."

"That can't have been easy," Kathryn observed.

"Damn right it wasn't, but that was the kind of guy Sam was. Anyway, one day, it's like three years later, Sam and I are partners assigned to 'crimes against persons' in the detective division. I remember it was a real hot day, the way this summer has been. County Comm notified us of a 187, homicide, a young woman stabbed to death in Cabrillo Park. We get up there and . . ."

"Not his sister?"

"His sister. She's lying in this clump of bushes, some maniac cut her to ribbons, thirty-four knife wounds in her body. Her little boy, he's three, he's hugging her body, screaming, covered in her blood. Dozens of people in the park, but nobody saw or heard a thing."

"What was it?" Kathryn asked. "Rape?"

"Looked like. I got Sam out of there, told him to leave it to CSI. Then he and I hit the streets. Every cop in the county was out there looking for Moira's killer. This guy, if he'd gone to Guatemala we would have found him. By ten o'clock that night someone snitched him off. Parolee by the name of Johnny Roibal, twenty-eight years old, recently paroled having done three years on a rape. His parole officer told detectives where to pick him up and they brought him in for questioning. When they searched his place they found the bloody knife with his prints still on it."

"But?"

"Sam asked if he could sit in on the interrogation. The lieutenant told him no, on account of the personal involvement. Sam looked him straight in the eye and says, 'Come on, Lieutenant, this bastard killed my sister, I need to hear what he has to say. That's all.'"

"Was that Walt Earheart?"

"Before his time," Dave said. "Barney Arrowsmith was lieutenant in charge of detectives then."

"And he okayed it?" Kathryn asked, letting her surprise show.

"You didn't know Sam Perry," Granz said. "He was strong, solid as a rock. If he gave his word, that was it. And I guess the lieutenant figured he owed him that much. So Sam goes down to the interrogation room. There's three of them in there, two SO detectives and Roibal. Sam walks in, smiling, pulls out his gun and blows Roibal's brains all over the wall."

"You'd think they'd have known better," Kathryn said. "You'd think they'd have seen it coming."

"Listen, he was my partner and I'm telling you, if he'd asked me if he could sit in, I'd have okayed it."

"What happened to him?"

"The jury found he was insane at the time of the crime. The judge placed him on out-patient status for six months," Granz told her. "He was finished as a cop, of course. Last I heard he was running a sporting goods store in Burlingame. Adopted his sister's kid. Little Sam must be about fifteen now."

"What a waste," Kathryn sighed. "What a terrible waste. Not just Sam Perry. This other cop too. The one in Seattle. It's like history repeating itself, the same thing all over again."

To her surprise he was silent for a long moment, as if he was thinking about what she had just said.

She thought for a moment she saw something in his eyes, but then it was gone. He got up and walked across to the window, a frown creasing his forehead. Then almost inaudibly she heard him whisper a single word.

"Jesus," he said.

"What?" she said, sensing whatever had just been said was suddenly greatly troubling him. "Dave, what is it?"

"Nothing," he muttered, lifting his hand in a sort of "stop" gesture, without turning around. "It's nothing."

And more he would not say.

24

The phone rang on Dave's desk and he picked it up to hear Morgan Nelson say, "Dave, I'm glad I caught you. I tried Kathryn's office, but apparently she's already gone. I was afraid I wouldn't reach either of you."

"You can always reach me, Doc. I thought you knew, I live here."

"I know, I know, and right now I'm glad you do. I was wondering, could you get here right away?"

"Sure," Dave said. "But what's the big hurry, Doc?"

"It was something you said the other day, when you called me about your vigilante. You said, what if it was history repeating itself."

Not just Sam Perry. This other cop too. The one in Seattle. It's like history repeating itself, the same thing all over again.

"You found something?"

"I think maybe I have."

"Jesus, Doc, don't keep me in suspense."

"I'd rather go over it with you in person. I think it's important."

"Give me fifteen minutes."

He made it to the morgue in twelve.

Morgan Nelson looked up in surprise as Granz stalked in. "My God," he said, "that was fast."

"I hurried," Granz said, the tension showing. "What have you got?"

Morgan gestured toward a stack of files on the table. "Sit down, Dave," he said benignly. "Take it easy."

"Tell me how," Granz said, but he scraped one of Doc's battered old shell chairs over to the table and sat down facing the pathologist.

"I can't believe I didn't make the connection myself," Nelson began almost apologetically. "But it wasn't until you told me about your conversation with Katie that it hit me, my brain finally got into gear and I remembered."

"What?" Dave said impatiently. "What, for Chrissake?"

"Let me just explain. Out of every hundred suspicious deaths, it's rare if more than one or two are autoerotic accidents. They're usually pretty sad affairs and they tend to get blurred out by the murders and the more spectacular accident cases. Until you tripped the switch, I'd completely forgotten that about five or six years ago we had a series of accidental autoerotic deaths over about a two-and-a-half-year period. I went back into the files and damned if they weren't identical, or almost identical, to the four you're investigating. Those were accidents, though, no question about it. So I pulled the autopsy protocols and coroner reports on each. Take a look at them."

He shoved the files across the table. The smell of old paper and dust came off them. Dave opened the one on top. The tab read HUBLITZ, PHILIP. Hublitz had been in his mid-twenties; he had been found dead as a result of an autoerotic accident, electrocuted by a faulty floor buffer. He speed-read the first page which contained the factual information pertaining to the death, followed by the name of the physician performing the autopsy. The pathologist, Morgan Nelson, MD, FACS, was listed as coroner in each case, although technically the sheriff was the coroner under California law. Beneath Nelson's name was that of the assistant coroner, who attended the autopsy as the sheriff's representative. The cover sheet was signed by both.

Dave opened the next file labeled ALTEN, ARTHUR JAMES. The man had been found dead in his bedroom, a sanitary pad lodged in his throat. Cause of death, asphyxiation. The factual entries were as before, the names of the pathologist and coroner were the same.

So were those for SELKIRK, ALEXANDER, age twenty-nine, found naked in a manure silo, cause of death exposure, and FUENTE, DESIDERIO, who had accidentally hanged himself while engaged in autoerotic activities in secluded woodland at Pinos Altos.

Each case was a paradigm for the vigilante killings: Piselli electrocuted, Bosendorf asphyxiated by a sanitary pad, Croma in the silo, Bitzer hanged. He looked up and met Morgan's gaze.

"You see what I mean about history repeating itself," Nelson said. "Except for one thing."

Dave nodded. "I got it. The Alten case. There were no bloodstains on the sheets."

Nelson nodded. "You sound as if it isn't a surprise."

"Not altogether," Dave said without elaborating. "There's something else, Doc."

"Something else?"

"Answer me this: could the same assistant coroner have been in attendance at every one of these autopsies? Is that possible?"

Nelson scanned the reports and protocols, then let out a long, low whistle. "Are you thinking what I'm thinking?" he said.

"What do you think I'm thinking?" Dave said harshly. "Come on, Doc. Is there any possibility at all someone made a mistake here?"

Morgan Nelson shook his head. "None," he said. His voice was soft. "None at all."

Dave angrily pushed the autopsy files away from

him. "Shit," he said bitterly. "I had to know, didn't I?"

"It's not proof, Dave," Morgan said. "Suspicious, yes, but not proof."

"I know that," Granz said harshly. "But it sure as hell spreads coincidence pretty thin."

"Let's assume for the moment it is him; why, Dave, why?"

Dave heard his own voice, speaking to Kathryn. *Because he hates them.* He wasn't aware he had said the words aloud until Morgan repeated his question.

"Yes, but why?"

He stuck out his lower lip, considering Morgan's question. "They must have hurt him. Somehow, they must have hurt him real bad. But how? By what they did, or by what they represent? Collectively or individually? All of them the same way, or all of them in a different way?"

"You're asking the wrong questions," Morgan said. "You said that they hurt him, but he isn't hurt. Not physically. So they must represent the hurt: a psychic wound."

The drums sounding in the psychic male forest. Revenge. Revenge.

Someone he loves.

Of course.

25

Michael Gaines made three unsuccessful calls to Rochester before connecting with Kevin McNulty. The detective had a hoarse, tired voice; he sounded like he just yelled his way through a football game.

"Sorry I missed you," he said apologetically. "This urgent?"

"We've got a serial rapist out here," Gaines told him. "VICAP faxed me two cases listing you as the contact."

"Right. Give me the victims' names, dates and case numbers," McNulty said.

"Anita Templeton, May 14, 1984, and Myra Penfield, February 18, 1985," Gaines dictated. Then he gave McNulty the case numbers slowly, so the detective could jot them down.

"You got a suspect?"

"Not yet."

"Leave it with me, I'll get right back to you," McNulty said.

"When?"

"If they're on microfilm, right away. If not, I'll have to order them from the warehouse."

"Thanks, Detective."

"No problem," McNulty said and hung up. An hour and a half later the phone rang. Gaines picked up and gave his name.

"Hey, Gaines. What's your weather like out there?"

There was no mistaking the hoarse voice; it was McNulty.

"Same as always," he said. "Sunny and hot."

"Hot I could deal with," McNulty told him. "It's like a fucking sauna on the streets here. Thought maybe you needed the reports delivered in person."

"Nice try," Gaines smiled. "But Federal Express will do."

"Figured," McNulty said. "Okay, I retrieved the files you asked for. Both investigations are still open."

"Did you submit them to VICAP?"

"Yeah. No hits, though. What makes you think your serial rapist did our rapes?"

"He bites and he calls them little pigs."

McNulty drew in a breath. "What do you need to know?"

"Everything you can tell me," said Gaines.

"The Templeton rape was a real nasty one. He beat her up pretty bad. Forced oral cop, multiple rapes. Took a two-inch strip out of her breast during the assault."

"Bite or tear?"

"Tore it away."

"Did you find the flesh?"

"Negative. We figured he took it with him, some kind of psycho souvenir. That what your guy is doing?"

"He bites, but not the same place each time," Gaines said.

"Is his MO the same?" asked McNulty.

"The MO in the Templeton rape is similar to one of our rapes, but not the other two."

"Maybe he varies his MO," offered McNulty.

"That would be pretty unusual."

"Listen, if you're right and it's the same guy, here, Atlanta, New Mexico, now California, this isn't some greenhorn you're dealing with," McNulty said harshly. "He's been doing this, what, at least nine years. And getting away with it."

"Do you remember anything special about the investigation of the Templeton rape?" Michael asked.

"We called in a forensic odontologist," McNulty told him. "He took photos of the bite mark. Our lab recovered semen on the vaginal swab."

"Was the MO the same in the Penfield rape?" asked Michael.

"Apart from the fact he called her 'little pig' and bit her, no, everything else was different."

"Did either victim give you a description of the rapist?" asked Michael.

"Yeah, both women described him as young, dark hair, thin face. Templeton said he had 'staring eyes.' Penfield told us he was 'well-spoken.'"

"Can you overnight express me copies of your files?" asked Gaines.

"It's already done," said McNulty.

"Figured," Gaines said and McNulty laughed.

He put down the phone and stared at it for a few minutes. Then he picked it up again, this time dialing Atlanta, where he asked for Detective-Sergeant Maurice Fulton.

"This is Inspector Michael Gaines," he said when

he was connected, "District Attorney's office, Santa Rita, California. I need some information about three rapes your agency investigated between 1987 and 1989."

"Who did you say this was?" The voice sounded cautious. Gaines repeated his identification.

"What's the number there?" Fulton asked.

Gaines told him.

"I'll get right back to you," Fulton said and hung up. Gaines sat and watched the clock impatiently. Five minutes. Ten minutes. Come on, damn you. The phone rang.

"Gaines, DA's office," he said.

"This is Fulton, Atlanta PD. Sorry for the delay. I called your sheriff's department, made sure you were who you said you were."

"So now you know," Gaines said impatiently. Then he caught himself. "Sorry if I sounded rude. It's just I . . . we've got a serial rapist. And I want him. Real bad."

"I know the feeling," Fulton said. "How can I help?"

Gaines gave the Atlanta detective a brief summary of the rapes and the facts contained in the VICAP hits.

"If it's the same bastard we had down here, I wish you luck. And you're going to need it. Our investigations never turned up any suspects. It was like hunting a ghost."

"This is no ghost, believe me."

"Newspapers here called him the Wolf Man," Fulton said, a soft Southern drawl surfacing.

"Wolf Man? Why?"

"One of the victims, Sherri Kleck, said he told her

he was the Wolf Man. One of the detectives leaked it to the press. Next thing you know it was on every front page in the state."

"Did you work the Kleck rape?" asked Gaines.

"Yeah, and I'm here to tell you it was one of the worst. Poor kid had to have plastic surgery on her neck where the sonofabitch bit a piece out of it."

"And they didn't find the bitten flesh, right?"

"How'd you know?" Fulton said, sounding surprised.

"Am I right?"

"Yup. General consensus was he took it with him."

"But you didn't think so?" asked Gaines.

Fulton sighed. "Hell, Gaines, I'm betting you know damned well what I thought. The psycho bastard ate it."

"What about the Confino rape? VICAP says she was bitten, too."

"Yeah. With her it was her cheek. Tore a piece right off the left side."

"And did they . . . ?"

"No. Same as the Kleck rape."

"What about Leila Teague?"

"She lived near Hartsfield International airport. The husband was a sanitation engineer there; he was working nights. She left a key for him under the doormat. The guy let himself in, raped and sodomized her, then bit her inside thigh. And before you ask, no, the piece of skin was never recovered."

"Can I get copies of the lab reports on all this?" Gaines asked.

"Our computer people can probably let you have whatever you need on disc," he said. "Or they can send it via modem."

Gaines gave him the address, thanked him and hung up, a thoughtful expression on his face.

Wolf Man, he thought. Maybe in her terrorized state, Sherri Kleck had heard it wrong. What if he had said he was the Big Bad Wolf, not Wolf Man. Then it all started to make a mad kind of sense: the references to little pigs, the wolf, the grotesque perversion of a children's fable.

Hello, little pig, may I come in? Not by the hair on my chinny-chin-chin. Then I'll huff and I'll puff and I'll blow your house down.

The Big Bad Wolf. A figure moving through the fog. A shape darker than the darkness. The face you never saw in the nightmare that shocked you awake. But real. Deadly real.

Gaines flipped the page of his notepad over and got ready to make his third call. Albuquerque should be easier than Rochester or Atlanta. It was smaller, more accessible.

"Police Department, Detective Armijo."

Gaines gave his name and the reason for his call. Armijo promised to call back as soon as possible and was as good as his word. The phone rang after precisely seven minutes.

"Okay, what can I do for you?" Armijo said. He sounded brisk and efficient. Gaines explained and outlined his earlier conversations with McNulty and Fulton. Armijo listened without interrupting except for an occasional checkback.

"We ran our rapes through VICAP at the time," he said, when Gaines finished speaking. "How come they never came up with the Rochester or Atlanta rapes?"

"Rochester submitted their rapes to VICAP," Gaines explained. "A few months later, there was some sort of computer failure and the Rochester rapes were lost. Atlanta didn't submit theirs at all. So the data bank didn't come up with any hits."

"Shit," Armijo said. "If this is the same rapist, we might have been able to stop the bastard before he ever got anywhere near Santa Rita."

"Maybe we can do it now," Gaines said. "Were you the I/O in any of the investigations?"

"Yeah, I was in charge of the Scott rape," Armijo said.

"Do you have a few minutes to run it by me?"

"Scott was single. Lived alone in an apartment building on Marquette. Just a few blocks along from the police department, believe it or not. We figured her attacker broke into her place prior to the rape because he was able to bypass a panic-button alarm. Cut the phone lines. Forced oral cop. Rape. Bit her. Damn near ripped off her navel."

"And he called her 'little pig,' right?"

"Yeah. And the same with Corradini and Soren."

"What about a description?" Gaines asked.

"The descriptions all three women gave us were close: big guy, thirty or so, dark eyes. But in one rape he wore a jogging suit, another a ski mask and tennis shoes. The third he wore a business suit, shirt and tie. Never the same outfit twice."

"That's what's bothering me," Gaines said. "If the bastard can change his MO for each rape, there's no telling how many other rapes he's responsible for that VICAP didn't match."

"Let's hope you're wrong. If it helps, I remember

one of the victims described the rapist as well-spoken and said he had manicured hands. She thought he might be some kind of professional man."

"He's certainly not stupid, that's for sure," said Gaines. "He obviously knows that all the semen and saliva in the world doesn't mean shit without a sample of his blood."

"A lot of them do these days," Armijo replied. "Even the morons watch TV."

"What time of day or night did the rapes occur?" asked Gaines.

"Different times in each case. Morning, afternoon, night-time. There was no pattern. You want my opinion, the fact there's no pattern is the pattern. Maybe you should be looking for a guy who makes his own hours. He can take time off mornings or afternoons and not have to answer to anyone."

"Like a salesman?" offered Michael.

"A place to start," replied Armijo. "Meanwhile, I'll fax you the reports. Call me if you need anything else."

"Thanks, Armijo."

"De nada."

"You speak Spanish?"

"Nah," Armijo said and he sounded like he was smiling. "It's not compulsory. Yet."

26

"Talk to me, you son of a bitch," Michael Gaines muttered under his breath, but loud enough that if someone else had been with him in his office they would have heard. Not that he gave a damn one way or the other. The VICAP reports were spread out on his desk, arrayed in a fan shape like a fistful of cards in a poker hand. The investigating officers he had spoken to in Rochester, Atlanta and Albuquerque had been cooperative, but offered little beyond the original VICAP hits. He felt sure—no, he *knew*—that buried somewhere in the rapist's movements from city to city lay the secret to his identity. He just needed to ferret it out.

From his upper right-hand desk drawer Gaines pulled out a well-used AAA road map of the United States and unfolded it flat on his desktop. It was one he always kept handy for both business and personal purposes, most frequently for planning vacation trips that never materialized. Using a red felt-tip marker he drew a circle around the cities of Rochester, Atlanta, Albuquerque and Santa Rita. Then, using a ruler, he connected the circles with straight lines.

The earliest rapes had occurred in Rochester in May 1984 and February 1985. Next, chronologically, were the three Atlanta assaults in June 1987, March 1988 and March 1989. The rapes in Albuquerque had begun in July 1990, with another in March 1991 and the last one in March of the following year.

He drew in arrows on the connecting lines pointing in the direction of travel; they made a sort of reverse dog leg from Rochester to Santa Rita. What was the connection? Whatever it was, it sure as hell was no accident.

He reflected on what he knew about the man. First, the sonofabitch was smart. Real smart. Articulate, well spoken, maybe a professional man some of the victims had said. Not the kind of man who simply moved around the United States at random. Whatever it was, he had a reason for moving from one place to another. Find the reason and he would be halfway there.

Gaines checked the yellow pages, picked up his desk phone and punched in a number. The phone answered on the second ring.

"Good morning, Santa Rita Realtors' Association. This is Sharon. How may I direct your call?"

"Actually, I just need some information," Gaines answered.

"I'll be happy to help if I can, sir. Are you a member of the Association?"

Although he knew it probably didn't matter, Gaines decided not to reveal his identity.

"No I'm not," he began. "I'm doing a research paper on the mobility of American society. I know once I saw some data on how often people move from community to community—you know, where they move, why they move, the troubles they encounter in relocating and so forth. I thought you might know where I could locate information like that."

"Why, I sure can," Sharon replied. "As a matter of fact, our National Board of Realtors keeps that information and I'm sure I can get it for you. Meanwhile, I'll send you a packet of helpful tips and information for new residents moving to Santa Rita—sort of a 'Welcome Wagon' package, y'know? There's a little section in one of the brochures that discusses the information you've asked about."

"Would it be okay if I drove down and picked it up? My paper is due tomorrow and I'm in big trouble if I don't turn it in on time," Gaines lied.

"Sure, I'll have it out for you. Ask for Sharon."

When Gaines got back to his office with Sharon's package, he threw away everything except one of the brochures and the list of helpful hints. The brochure was printed on high-gloss paper, triple-folded so it opened out full page, with a giant photo of Santa Rita Beach in the center. To the left of the photo was a block of type that said:

"Welcome to Santa Rita. We hope your move here will be a pleasant experience. Did you know that the average American family moves to a new city or state every five years, usually in connection with a new job or business?"

Gaines read no further. There was the answer, staring him in the face. The rapist had moved from state to state, from New York to Georgia to New Mexico and finally to California, because he was starting a new job, or because he had been transferred by his employer to another facility. What he needed to do now was figure out which employer.

Okay, follow through. People usually remained employed in the same line of work, especially highly intelligent, well-educated people. And he had no doubt the rapist was both. Proceeding on that assumption, what sort of work would have brought him to Santa Rita?

He retrieved a coffee-stained yellow legal pad from a desk drawer and listed Santa Rita's major employers and industries: agriculture and food processing; tourism; education; government; computer software development and peripherals; construction. Nothing unusual there. Education, government and construction were common everywhere, and hardly likely to tempt workers to move from one area to another. That left as unique to the area the agricultural and food processing, tourism and computer/high tech industries.

Now, he thought to himself, smiling when he realized that for once, he had not spoken out loud to an empty room, if this guy stays in the same line of work each time he moves or is transferred by his employer to a branch operation, then Rochester, Atlanta and Albuquerque should have at least one of the same industries.

For no particular reason he decided to begin with the Albuquerque Chamber of Commerce. Cindy, the young woman he spoke to, was extremely helpful: she promised to send him a list of the area's major industries and employers. Pre-eminent among them were the giant Sandia Labs, doing solar and nuclear research, a hundred firms engaged in electronics manufacturing and research and development, as many more producing durable goods, clothing, business machines. Albuquerque was also proud of its small but lucrative agricultural and food processing industry, she said, which grew and packaged almost all the country's chili peppers.

"Electronics?" Gaines said. "You mean computers?"

"Yeah," Cindy bubbled. "Computers. Quite a few large hardware and software manufacturers have located near the city. Some of the stuff they produce is so hush-hush nobody really knows what they do because they have defense contracts. I bet some day our Silicon Valley will be bigger than yours."

Michael acknowledged that if taxes weren't brought under control soon, New Mexico might have all of California's business. He thanked her and hung up. One down; two to go.

The Chamber of Commerce in Atlanta connected him with its business development department and in response to his questions a lady named Gayle Ormsby went to considerable lengths to emphasize the fact that Atlanta's economic base included every facet of industry, Coca-Cola, Holiday Inns and the CNN network for openers. Furthermore, she proudly pointed out, the city was home to computer and software development companies, including large IBM and Apple Computer facilities.

"Atlanta," she told him in conclusion, "is one of America's fastest-growing, best-managed, most liveable cities." Yes, ma'am, he thought, putting down the phone. Just like in the advertisements.

At the Rochester Chamber of Commerce he spoke with someone called Helene, in Public Relations, whose officious voice made it sound as if she was reluctant to let anyone know what a wonderful place Rochester was. The economy, she told him, was manufacturing-oriented and included some of the biggest names in the imaging industry: Xerox, Kodak and IBM. And while the city's computer and software industry was smaller, a lot of highly secret government contracts were carried out in the area. Gaines thanked her and hung up.

He knew where he was going now. Rochester, Atlanta, Albuquerque and Santa Rita had something in common and that something was the computer industry. It was there, he felt certain now, he would find the man he was looking for. Nor would he stop until he did.

A memory from his childhood threaded its way through his mind, his mother sitting on a wicker chair beside the bed, the moon outside the window, the soft cadences of her Texas accent as she read to them from a book, a poem whose name he no longer remembered with words he had never forgotten.

> *For I have promises to keep.*
> *And miles to go before I sleep.*

27

The late morning sun slanting in through the window painted everything in the office a glowing gold. For most of the people working in the County Building it was just another day; but not for Michael Gaines. Fierce elation ran through him like electricity: he knew where he was going and why he was going there. He had dates, he had places. He had somewhere to look.

First, he had got back on the phone to Detective Maurice Fulton in Atlanta and asked him to check Georgia State Department of Motor Vehicles records for anyone who had surrendered a New York driver's license and/or applied for a Georgia license between February 1985, the date of the last rape in Rochester and 24 June 1987, the date of the first in Atlanta.

Then he had called Detective Armijo in Albuquerque and asked him to check New Mexico DMV records for anyone who surrendered a Georgia license for a New Mexico license anywhere between the date of the last rape in Atlanta, March 12, 1989, and the first in Albuquerque, July 22, 1989. Then, while he waited for their replies, he contacted California DMV in Sacramento and asked for a check for anyone who

237

had surrendered a New Mexico license between March 1992 and June 1993.

The Atlanta PD faxed Gaines a list of thirty-four names who had turned in New York State driver's licenses and applied for Georgia replacements. In the relevant three years, Albuquerque DMV had processed nineteen surrenders from Georgia. Sacramento gave him eight names. Sixty names in all. Only eight were common to all three lists.

Three of these were women; he threw those out immediately. That left five men. Two of them had the same names as women on the list and had supplied identical old and new addresses. Both men were in their late fifties; he set them aside also. Three suspects left.

He ran through the DMV license details. One of the three men was over sixty years old; discard. Two left now. The first was Samuel Wortley, born Genesee, New York, April 2, 1950. Wortley was five feet eight tall, weighed one hundred fifty-two pounds, had dark hair and gray eyes. The DMV records indicated he wore glasses. The address he had given, 238 Jade Street, was in South Alameda, a low-income residential area on the "wrong" side of Alameda Creek.

Gray eyes, glasses, low income; it didn't fit the profile Gaines had of the rapist, but Gaines determined to check it out anyway. By means of a series of calls on Samuel Wortley's Jade Street neighbors he learned Wortley was an inoffensive sort who enjoyed a couple of beers on Saturday night but otherwise kept himself to himself. His car was a beat-up old Chevy.

In the course of his interviews Gaines also quickly identified and located the local "window detective," an elderly woman named Amelia Church who lived in a house that smelled strongly of cats, directly across the street from Wortley.

She told him Wortley was from Roswell, New Mexico, where his wife had died in a car accident a year earlier; there were no children. He worked as a stock clerk at the Safeway market across the street from the Linda Vista Mall.

"What's he done?" she asked, her rat eyes glittering. "What's he done?"

"Does he go out much?" Gaines asked, ignoring the question.

"Him? Not likely," the old lady snapped. "Comes home from work, plonks himself down in front of the TV drinking beer. That's the kind we get around here nowadays. When I was young—"

"You'd know if he went out?"

The old woman drew herself up in outrage. "Do you think I spend my entire life watching my neighbors, young man?" she snapped. "I've got better things to do, I can tell you."

"I'm sure you have, Mrs. Church," Gaines said placatingly. "I just thought an intelligent, observant person like yourself would probably notice such things."

"Hmph," Mrs. Church said, mollified. "That old clunker he drives, I should say so."

"Noisy, is it?"

"Noisy? Darn muffler sounds like it's got more holes in it than Swiss cheese. If you policemen were doing your job properly he wouldn't be allowed to drive it."

"But surely he could leave the house on foot without your knowing, Mrs. Church?"

"Not that one," the old lady said. "His ankle was crushed in the car smash. Wears one of those things on his leg, the poor thing." There was not an iota of sympathy in her voice.

"You mean a caliper?"

"That's it, a caliper. He can't walk more than a few hundred yards at a time."

And then there was one.

"Richard Charles Hoffman, born February 12, 1955," he read aloud from the printout. "Brown hair, brown eyes, five feet ten inches tall, one hundred and seventy two pounds, address 48 Montecito Drive, Valley Springs."

The driver's license photo showed a long-jawed, thin-lipped face with a jutting forehead and slightly receding hairline. Was this the Big Bad Wolf?

"If you are, you're sharkbait, you sonofabitch," he said to the photo.

In the period since he had received the information from DMV, Gaines had also checked with NCIC, the National Crime Information Center, who informed him they had no file on Hoffman; the man had no criminal history of any kind.

It was hard to believe; it was a rare rapist indeed who didn't have priors. Prowlings, burgs, assaults, something. Of course, the absence of a criminal record didn't mean he had never committed a crime; only that he never got caught.

Over the next few days, further investigation revealed that Hoffman was a computer software engineer specializing in UI toolkits, X11, C++ and Windows imaging. In Rochester he had worked for a company called Cassandra Communications; for

Syntacticon Systems in Atlanta; and Zia Technology in Albuquerque.

He had not married. He lived alone in a condominium in Valley Springs. He was presently a software design and development engineer with Hypernet Graphics, a billion-dollar corporation whose new, hi-tech headquarters had been built just a year ago on the site of an old roller-skating rink at Highland Valley, in the foothills about fifteen miles above Santa Rita.

"Accomplished," Gaines noted. "High IQ. No dependants." You're looking good, Hoffman.

Gaines picked up his desk phone and punched in the number for Hypernet Graphics in Highland Valley. After a brief argument with the receptionist who wanted to connect him to the payroll clerk, he was put through to the director of personnel, Tom Schroeder.

"Mr. Schroeder," he said. "My name is Michael Gaines, and I'm an inspector with the Santa Rita District Attorney's office."

"What can I do for you, Inspector?" Schroeder asked, in that wary, guarded tone people always used when they got an unexpected call from someone in law enforcement.

"I need to speak with you right away," said Gaines.

"Why not now?" asked Schroeder.

"What we need to talk about is extremely confidential and can't be discussed over the telephone," said Gaines.

Without giving Schroeder a chance to say anything, Gaines told him he would be at his office in twenty minutes. Five minutes later, he was in his car headed north up Highway Seventeen.

Silicon Glen, as they were calling Highland Valley's burgeoning sprawl of computer-oriented industry, was a self-contained, purpose-built community. New housing tracts and condominium complexes were springing up in nearby Valley Springs and further north in Culloden.

Gaines took the exit ramp off Seventeen, stopping to check his directions on a large map standing near the entrance to the industrial park. Gates Drive, the road he was on, ran roughly north, paralleled by the older Valley Springs Road. Between them ran five numbered avenues, intersected by East Road and West Road.

The modernistic glass and steel buildings shimmering in the sun looked like the set for a science-fiction movie; you half expected to see Luke Skywalker come around a corner. The names on the signs were a futuristic litany: Omnidigital, SynchroGrafx, Datalex, Questor. Gaines recalled reading somewhere that the headquarters of one of the larger software companies up here boasted its own interior campus, streams, waterfalls, jogging paths lined with fledgling redwoods and a full-service twenty-four-hour fitness center for the use of its employees. On the corner of Second Avenue opposite its main entrance was a cafeteria and a bistro; further along there was a convenience store and even a video rental shop.

The Hypernet Graphics headquarters was a rectangular three-story building faced with black reflective glass; it took up most of the block south of Second Avenue at East Road. Gaines parked his car in one of the slots marked "Visitors" and went into the air-conditioned chill of the foyer, an atrium-like open area just a little too small for a football game. The receptionist handed him a numbered lapel tag similar to the kind worn by airline personnel, with the word VISITOR prominently displayed.

"Please wear your interactive tag at all times, sir," she said. "If you take it off, you will trip the alarms."

Tom Schroeder turned out to be a tall, well-built blond haired man of perhaps forty-five, wearing a white short-sleeve shirt, dark pants and tasseled loafers. An ID tag similar to the one Gaines had been given was clipped to his shirt pocket.

"Is all this security necessary?" Gaines asked.

"We spend something like a half a million dollars a quarter on research, Mr. Gaines," Schroeder smiled. "A single document or product development plan can be worth hundreds of thousands of dollars to one of our competitors. We need to be sure none of it walks out the door, accidentally or otherwise. Let's go up to my office, shall we?"

His office on the third floor was uncluttered and airy, with a large desk and executive chair and the usual electronic accessories: PC, laptop, laser printer, fax, conference phone, desktop copier.

"I didn't expect it to be so busy up here," Gaines said as they sat down.

"It is unusual," Schroeder conceded. "In the past, most of our employees vacationed in August, resting up for the rush after Labor Day. But business is booming right now. We can't afford to take time off."

"Coming out of the recession, huh?"

"Slowly," Schroeder smiled. "The defense business has been shrinking, but that's been offset by an upsurge in venture capital investments. There's a synergy, a convergence of computers, communications and entertainment going on out there. We're working around the clock to capitalize on it."

As Schroeder talked on, something about forty percent of all the available venture capital being channeled into the biotechnology and medical-products industries in the Bay Area, Gaines nodded sagely, trying to gauge the man's personality.

"On top of that there are the environmental technologies," Schroeder was saying. "Flat panel screen industries are just around the corner. Oh, we've lost a few battles, like DRAMs—dynamic random access memories—but we've more than held our own in most of the others. It's a tough racket, especially if you're small like us, but we're hangin' in there."

"This is small?" Gaines said.

"We're new kids on the block," Schroeder told him. "Only a billion turnover. The really big players are IBM, Microsoft, Borland. Hewlett-Packard in Palo Alto turns over seventeen billion dollars a year; Apple in Cupertino, seven billion; Intel in Santa Clara, six. There's a couple of dozen companies in the two, three-billion bracket: Sun Micro, Seagate, Amdahl."

"How long has Hypernet been around?" Gaines asked. It wasn't that he wanted to know. The idea was to get Tom Schroeder relaxed. Let him trot out his spiel.

"The company was founded in 1987 by two guys who were working for Bill Gates at Microsoft and decided to try it on their own," Schroeder said. "Paul Gammond and Anthony Lombardino." He paused. "The names don't mean anything to you, do they?"

Gaines smiled apologetically. "I'm a cop, Mr. Schroeder."

"Sure, sure. Well, both of them are shaping up to appear in next year's *Fortune* five hundred," Schroeder told him. "They've built this business up on a simple philosophy. Hire the best, buy the best, sell the best, be the best."

"Looks like it's working," Gaines said. "This is a very impressive set-up. Which brings me to the reason I came up here."

"I was just about to ask you," Schroeder said.

"You have a software engineer working here, Richard Hoffman."

"We employ a great many software engineers, Inspector. Some of them work here full time, others work from their homes. We give them everything they need, a desktop, laptop, fax, modem, cellular phone. They interact with our systems electronically, just as they would if they drove in every day. The County Transportation Commission will require large employers to have a certain percentage of its staff telecommuting by the year 2000. We're way ahead of them. What did you say the name was again?"

"Hoffman. Richard Charles Hoffman. He may be one of your engineers that works from his home."

Schroeder nodded and punched a few keys on his PC. The screen blinked a few times as he manipulated the mouse, then he nodded.

"There he is," he said. "Dick Hoffman. You were right, he's based out of his home. What's your interest in him?"

"Let me ask you something first," Gaines said. "You're obviously security minded here at Hypernet. So how do you screen prospective engineers?"

"We have a very strict hiring policy," Schroeder

said. "It's a condition of employment that every prospective engineer agrees to a rigorous security clearance investigation."

"How rigorous?"

Schroeder looked faintly surprised at the question. "We conduct a series of interviews, and every reference is checked, all the way back, college records, previous employers, marital history, credit agencies . . ."

"Medical tests?"

"Of course. Every prospective engineer submits to a blood test for the purpose of detecting substance abuse. Two samples of blood are taken in case the findings are positive and the employee wishes to contest the results."

"Do you have your own facility for conducting these tests?"

Schroeder shook his head. "It's easier and cheaper to sub-contract it. We've got a first-aid station staffed with a registered nurse but for employment examinations and blood tests, we use Caduceus Medical Services in Santa Rita. It saves us the capital investment in storage freezers and all the other paraphernalia." He stopped to look shrewdly at Gaines. "But would you mind telling me what this is about, Inspector?"

"I'm afraid all I can tell you is that I am investigating a criminal matter," Gaines replied. "The name of Richard Hoffman has come up and I need to eliminate him from our investigation."

"Inspector, you'll understand I have to ask you this—does your investigation involve Hypernet in any way?"

"No, sir, nothing like that. All I need is a copy of Hoffman's personnel file," Gaines said. "I'll also need to look at his test results at Caduceus and seize any remaining blood samples. And before you ask, yes, I do have a search warrant."

He took the warrant he had prepared that morning out of his inside pocket and unfolded it, laying it on the desk in front of Schroeder. Schroeder picked it up, read through it quickly and nodded, pushing a button on his intercom.

"I need a copy of a Richard Charles Hoffman's personnel file, Mary-Beth," he said into the intercom. "Right away, please."

The box squawked an answer and he flicked the off switch. "It'll take a few minutes," he told Gaines.

"Would you mind telling me who you deal with at Caduceus, Mr. Schroeder?"

"Sure. His name is Ralph Fresquez," Schroeder said. He wrote something on the pad on his desk, tore off the page and pushed it across to Gaines. The heading read *From the desk of Thomas Schroeder* and featured the Hypernet logo, a hand holding a bolt of lightning. Below it he had printed the name Gaines had asked for. As Gaines folded it and put it in his wallet, Schroeder's administrative assistant came in with a folder. She was a good looking woman of around thirty, dressed in a neat suit and white shirt-style blouse.

"Thank you, Mary-Beth," Schroeder said. He handed the file to Gaines. The photocopies inside it were still warm from the machine.

"Hoffman's file," he said. "Is there anything else you need, Inspector?"

"Just the search warrant," Gaines said, reaching across to pick it up. "I'll need that to show to Fresquez."

Schroeder hesitated a moment, then shrugged. "Okay. If you're all set, I'll come down with you."

They rode down in the elevator without speaking. As they shook hands in the foyer, Schroeder asked one last question. "Has this . . . what you're working on, you're quite sure it hasn't got anything to do with the company?"

Gaines put on a serious face. "I'm sorry, Mr. Schroeder. I've already said more than I should."

"You understand my concern, Inspector."

"Of course. Look, I really don't think you need worry."

Schroeder looked relieved. "If you say so."

"One last thing, Mr. Schroeder," Gaines said. "I'd be grateful if you could keep my visit confidential."

"From Hoffman you mean?" Schroeder said. "No problem at all."

"I appreciate it," Gaines said. "And I know my people downtown will, too."

He kept his expression grave until he got back to his car in the parking lot out of sight of the reception area. But by the time he took the ramp on to Seventeen and headed for Santa Rita he was smiling. Two hours later he seized the extra sample of Richard Hoffman's blood from Caduceus.

28

SO property officer Lee Carson ran his fiefdom in the basement of the County Building as if it was NASA. It took him only minutes to locate the Hernandez, Percell and Skelton rape kits. Each was filed by its case number and the relevant section of the Penal Code, together with the date and the scene number from which it had been seized.

Carson confirmed that each kit had recently been returned from the regional crime lab, where samples collected by the SANE from each of the victims had been examined for the presence of elevated acid phosphatase, indicative of the presence of semen. The reports attached to each kit indicated the presence of sperm in semen extracted from each of the swabs.

Carson had Gaines sign for each of the three rape kits. Gaines returned with the rape kits to his office. Once there with the door shut he picked up the phone and dialed Benchmark Diagnostics, in Lakewood, Ohio; when he was connected, he asked to speak to the Laboratory Director.

"Greg West."

"Mr. West, my name is Gaines. I'm an inspector with the DA's office in Santa Rita, California, and I'd like to submit some physical evidence to you for DNA analysis."

"What type of DNA analysis?" West asked. "RFLP or PCR?"

"Run them both past me," Gaines said.

"PCR—Polymerase Chain Reaction—works best with smaller or degraded samples. Restriction Fragment Length Polymorphism, RFLP to you, is less sensitive and requires a much larger sample size. The results in population statistics are considered more significant when using RFLP than when using PCR—when enough probes are used."

"How much semen do you need for RFLP testing?"

"Half the cotton swab, or a glass slide with numerous sperm from the rape kit will produce a result. For PCR, a swab with a weak presumptive test or a glass slide with only a few sperm is sufficient."

"Its beginning to sound like I need to go the PCR route," Gaines said. "Are there any disadvantages?"

"The PCR process can include or exclude someone as a suspect, as can RFLP. The difference is PCR cannot definitively identify someone as a suspect the way RFLP can," West explained. "Set against that is the fact that RFLP has a longer analysis time, four to six weeks, against PCR's one or two weeks."

"We need the results yesterday," Gaines said. "PCR it is."

"Do you have a set of Benchmark instructions and forms?" West asked. "If not we can overnight express them—"

"No need," Gaines told him. "We have everything here. I'll get the evidence out to you before the end of the day."

"Okay," Greg West said. "I need a covering letter which lists what you're sending—with identification numbers, please—the subject's race, the name and address of a contact person."

"Thanks, I've done it before. I'll be shipping via UPS overnight. I'll confirm the waybill number to you by telephone as soon as the package is picked up. What's the fee, by the way?"

"On our current fee schedule a PCR analysis runs to $535, Inspector."

"Fine. I'll be in touch."

Gaines put the phone down. With precise, deft movements he took the tube of Hoffman's blood out of his refrigerator and labeled it. Next he removed cloth strips from each of the rape kits. Each cloth strip contained a sample of each victim's blood; he packaged, sealed and labeled each of them individually. Then he removed vaginal swabs from each of the rape kits and followed the same procedure with those. All the physical evidence went into a cardboard box along with the requisite covering letter. The package was ready for the 4 P.M. pickup.

Gaines leaned back in his chair with a satisfied sigh. In a few days' time he would know whether the PCR test excluded Hoffman. If it did not, he would move to the next and final phase.

His first stop today was at an apartment building on Kinsley Drive in Alameda Heights, where Granz spent an hour talking to the manager.

From there he cut across to Pinos Altos, what the realtors called a desirable neighborhood in the hills north of Laguna del Mar. It was a little after three when he pulled up outside a pleasant family home on a residential avenue that curved up the hillside off Salmon River Road.

Three bedrooms, two and a half baths, he guessed; there would be bay views from the upper windows, maybe a patio with a built-in barbecue and a kidney-shaped in-ground pool in the sunny back yard.

He got out of the car and walked up the neat shrub-lined driveway to the roofed porch. His ring was answered by a woman in her early sixties wearing a light-blue cotton dress. Her hair was almost pure white, her face drawn and tired. He knew her name: Ellen Frazer. She looked at him blankly.

"Hello, Mrs. Frazer," he said. "Can you spare a few minutes?"

The woman's features rearranged themselves slowly to look puzzled. "Who . . . ?"

"Oh, I'm sorry," Granz said, flipping open his ID wallet. "My name is Granz. I'm an inspector with the District Attorney's office."

"What's it about?" Ellen Frazer queried.

"As a matter of fact, it's your daughter I'd like to talk to," Granz said. "I stopped at her apartment but there was no one home. I thought she might be over here with you."

"No," the woman said. "I . . . she's on vacation. She went down to San Diego. To stay with my sister-in-law."

"Might I ask you when she'll be back?"

"We . . . not for a while."

"Who is it, Ellen?"

A tall, stooped, narrow-shouldered man appeared, frowning at Granz from beneath bushy gray eyebrows. An unlit briar pipe was clenched in his right hand. George Frazer was perhaps eight or ten years older than his wife. He wore a shapeless grey woolen jacket over a pale-blue woolen shirt. His pants were baggy and flecked with tobacco ash. His feet were in carpet slippers.

"Mr. Frazer?" Granz said. "My name is Granz. I'm an inspector."

"From the District Attorney's office," Ellen Frazer added.

"Yes, yes. And?" her husband barked brusquely.

"I need to talk to your daughter, Mr. Frazer. But your wife tells me she's gone to San Diego."

"La Jolla," Frazer said impatiently. "Not San Diego, La Jolla. What's it about?"

"Do we have to talk out here, Mr. Frazer?" Granz said. "Couldn't I come inside, or is there some reason you don't want to talk to me?"

Frazer looked disconcerted, like a man caught in a lie he didn't know the truth of. Granz waited, letting him wriggle.

"You'd better come in," Frazer said, his mouth like a wound. "Come in, come in. Shut the door, Ellen."

Ellen Frazer led the way through a door to the left into a small living room furnished with an L-shaped sofa, a round dining table and chairs, a corner bar and a large TV fitted into the lower shelves of a bookcase packed with books by popular authors.

"Shall I make some tea?" she said, looking at her husband. Granz thought he saw a signal pass between them, but you could never be sure. People who had lived together a long time were often able to communicate without words.

"Thank you," he said. "I don't want to put you to any trouble."

"It's no trouble," she said. "We always have tea in the afternoon. George's family was English."

She looked at Granz as if expecting a reaction to her remark; when none was forthcoming, she turned and went out into the kitchen.

"Sit down, Mr. Granz," Frazer said. "Sit down. I gather from what you said that you know Jennifer's fiancé, is that right?"

"We work in the same office."

Frazer nodded, as if he had scored a point. "I'm surprised he didn't tell you she was away."

"Maybe he did," Granz said, putting on a rueful grin, "and I just forgot."

"Exactly what is it you want to talk to her about?"

"I'd rather wait until I can talk to her personally, Mr. Frazer," Granz said. "When did she leave, by the way?"

Frazer frowned. "Let me think . . . About the end of May, beginning of June."

"She's been down in La Jolla for two months?" Granz said, surprised.

"She'd been . . . unwell," George Frazer said, the hesitation barely perceptible. "We could see it. She was run down. Studying too hard for her doctorate. Not eating properly. I . . . we told her she needed a break, sent her down to my sister."

"In La Jolla," Granz nodded. "Do you have a number for her there, Mr. Frazer?"

"Look, I think I'd like to know what all this is about before I let you start pestering my daughter," Frazer said.

Ellen Frazer came back into the room carrying a tray on which was a white bone-china teapot, cream jug and sugar basin and three cups and saucers with a delicate floral pattern. As she put it down on the dining table, Granz saw there was also a silver-plated dish of homemade cookies.

"That's Royal Doulton, isn't it?" Granz said.

"We like to do things nicely," she replied primly. "Milk? Sugar?"

"Milk, but no sugar, please," he said.

The little ceremony with the English china seemed to increase the tension rather than disperse it. As Ellen Frazer handed her husband his cup, Granz again got the feeling messages were being exchanged.

"Have you seen Michael lately?" he asked artlessly. Ellen Frazer looked at her husband, who nodded.

"He was here the day before yesterday," he said.

"Tuesday," his wife added.

"Has he been down to La Jolla to see Jenny?"

George Frazer cleared his throat and fumbled in the pocket of his jacket, fishing out a pipe-smoker's penknife and scraping the dottle out of his pipe into an ashtray. "The doctors felt . . . I thought, we all thought Jennifer ought to have complete rest," he said. "Complete rest. Away from everything. We talked it over. Michael understood."

"He thought it was a good idea?"

"It wasn't a question of whether he thought it was a good idea or not," Frazer replied coldly. "Our only concern was what was best for Jennifer."

He could not have made it more clear that he disliked Michael Gaines if he had sprayed it on the wall with a paint can, Granz thought.

"And how is Jenny now?"

"She's . . . improving. Slowly," Frazer said. "But

look, I'll be frank with you, she's not recovering as quickly as we had hoped. Is it absolutely necessary for you to see her just now? I really think . . . from what Connie says . . . she's still . . ." He made a vague gesture with his right hand.

"Connie is your sister?"

"That's correct."

"I can wait a few days," Granz said. "If you think that would be helpful."

"I'm not sure . . . a few days," Ellen Frazer said, her hands fluttering. Granz let the silence lengthen, wishing there were some way he could ease the pain that was apparent in everything they said, in everything they were not saying.

"Was it very bad, Mrs. Frazer?" he asked, softly. "Do you want to talk about it?"

For a moment she froze, her eyes huge, like an animal caught in a spotlight. She turned to her husband, her lips trembling, her hand plucking at the collar of her dress. "George," she murmured, only just managing to say the word.

"See here," the old man said to Granz. "See here, Mr. Granz."

"You've got to tell someone sooner or later, Mr. Frazer," Granz said. "You can't go on acting as if nothing happened."

"I don't know what you mean," Frazer said, but his eyes were evasive and there was no longer any conviction in his voice. "No idea what you're talking about."

"Tell me," Granz urged softly. "Tell me about Jenny. It doesn't have to become official."

"I won't have this!" George Frazer shouted, getting to his feet. "I won't be . . . badgered like this, in my own house! You have no right to do this. I want you out of here, now, you hear me?"

"No, George," Ellen Frazer said, as Granz got to his feet. Her voice was unexpectedly firm and decisive, and all at once everything fell into place for Granz, the reason for George Frazer's pathetic defiance, the pain and regret swimming in his wife's eyes. The old man's fierce bark was as sham as her genteel deference. It was quite obvious which of them was the strong one. "It's time we spoke about it."

"Ellen, for God's sake!" George Frazer said hoarsely, his face slackening. He slumped down into his chair, looking suddenly very old. "For God's sake, no!"

"Sit down, Mr. Granz," Ellen Frazer said. "And we'll tell you what happened."

29

It was a little after 2:30 P.M. as Richard Hoffman cruised down Espanola Drive toward the ocean. He loved California. After the greasy humidity of Atlanta, after the flat desert heat of New Mexico, living in Santa Rita was like being sent on a paid vacation. And the women. It was like they had a special plant someplace to turn them out. Lithe, long-legged, long-haired animals bursting with health and energy, they swam and surfboarded and roller-bladed and volleyballed and danced and laughed as they lived the gilded Californian incarnation of the American Dream.

In Espanola the streets were crowded. Shoppers, vacationers, one-day visitors and cyclists wandering wherever they chose slowed traffic to a snail's pace. The color and movement were in sharp contrast to the way the place had looked the weekend before last, when the heavy, unseasonal rain had cleared the streets as effectively as an air-raid warning. Casual shoppers had stayed home. The pizza parlors and fast food joints in Espanola and Marina Beach Village, normally crowded with tourists, were empty and abandoned looking; the beaches bare except for flocks of despondent-looking gulls.

It amused him; it was as if Santa Ritans thought it was supposed to be the same every day, up around the high seventies by midday, then cool at night and in the early morning. When it wasn't, the shoppers and the tourists and the golden girls all stayed home.

Halfway down Lighthouse he swung into the Linda Vista Mall and parked; it took him perhaps ten minutes to pick up the bouquet of flowers he had ordered by phone; he paid cash, giving a false name. He put the flowers on the back seat, then drove down toward the beach. The fog was already burning off; it looked like it was going to be another fine, sunny day.

He made a right into Seaview Heights and parked on the street fifty yards below the entrance to London House. He left his jacket in the car and got out. He was wearing dark-gray slacks, with a white shirt and ox-blood loafers. All part of his strict routine. The best disguise is no disguise at all. Always look as if you have every right to be where you are, doing what you are doing. It always worked.

He checked the mailboxes until he found her name: MACKAY, K. 22-A. *That would be on the second floor. He walked back down the stairs and down the ramp leading into the underground garage. There were plenty of empty spaces. The residents' elevator was on the far side, with a light over its door and a numerical panel set into the wall. He went across and pressed the call button. Nothing happened. No elevator without the secret number.*

He smiled. Who's afraid of the Big Bad Wolf? Everyone.

He went back to the car, picked up the flowers and his clipboard, and returned to the front entrance, where he pushed one of the call buttons on a mailbox marked P.F. GARRETT. *Nothing. If at first you don't succeed. He pushed another. A woman's voice squawked a who-is-it? at him out of the intercom.*

"Linda Vista Floral Creations, Ms. Winsocki," he said. "I have flowers for you."

Squawk-squawk-from?

"The envelope's sealed, ma'am," he said. "You want me to leave the flowers here by the door?"

Squawk-squawk-up.

He checked her number, 33-C, as the door-release buzzer sounded. He pushed the door open, exulting. In like Flynn. The foyer was small but pleasant, with gilt-and-glass occasional tables and comfortable looking chairs. He called the elevator and got in, pressing 3, noting that the inside control panel had a button below L, marked B for basement. Child's play.

The doors slid open and he stepped out into a carpeted corridor. He already knew there were eight condos on each floor; four facing the ocean, the others with a view of the Pinos Altos foothills. He walked confidently along the corridor carrying the flowers and rang the bell of 33-C. A security chain rattled and the door opened a few inches to reveal a plump, unmade-up, red-cheeked face framed with stringy blond hair.

"Ms. Winsocki?" he said. "Your flowers."

"Who they from?" the woman said, her voice suspicious. She was wearing a shiny nylon robe; she looked like someone had gift-wrapped a sack of potatoes. "Don't expect me to pay for them."

"I don't know who they're from, ma'am," Hoffman said, putting on a winning smile. "I just deliver. And there's nothing to pay."

"Let me have them here," the woman said, grabbing the bouquet with a plump fist. "Wait a minute."

She tore open the envelope and squinted at the card on which Hoffman had printed the words "With all my love, John." Her face furrowed into a childlike frown.

"You sure these're for me?"

"Winsocki, 33-C, London House," he said, pretending to check his clipboard. "That's you, right?"

He watched her eyes as cupidity fought with truth and won. Nobody ever lost a buck underestimating the greed of the average American housewife, he thought.

"Oh!" she said, as if a sudden recollection had come to her. "Of course! They're from John!"

"Yes, ma'am," Hoffman said. "Thank you, ma'am."

"Y'welcome," she snapped, and shut the door with a bang. He walked along the corridor and used the stairs to descend to the floor below. No one came out to ask him how he had gained entry. No one ever did. Too many crazies out there. He grinned his wolf grin.

The lock on Kathryn Mackay's door was a simple one; as soon as he was sure there was no alarm, he was inside the condo in a matter of seconds. His heart leaped as a puppy came scampering across the room toward him carrying a rawhide chew in its mouth, growling and shaking its head. It was clearly harmless, so he ignored it. After a while it went back to its basket in the kitchen.

He looked around. This was exciting. He was standing in a small hallway with closets to the right, a door to the left. He opened it and looked inside. Bright fluorescent lights, mirrors, tiles: a guest bathroom.

To his right was the living room. It was open plan, the kitchen separated from it by an L-shaped breakfast bar with long-legged stools.

Directly ahead were five steps leading down to another door: this was the one he wanted. He felt the tension in his legs, the slight increase in his pulse and breathing rates. It was omnipotence, it was possession, better than drugs, better than anything. Only someone who had done it could know how exciting it was.

He picked up her pillow, turned back the bedspread and smelled the perfume of her body on the sheets. He went into her bathroom and buried his face in her towels. He checked the cabinet and drawers for her cosmetics: eyeshadow, mascara, nail polish, lipstick. Her closet was jammed full of clothes. Lots of suits. Jeans and shirts for casual wear. He smelled them, fondled them, unfastened his pants and rubbed them against his genitals.

On her dressing table were some snapshots in a mini photo album. He picked up the album and flipped through it. Then he put it on the nightstand next to her bed.

The living room had sliding glass doors which opened on to a balcony. On the outside balcony were two white vinyl chairs and a row of terracotta planters. There was a fine view across Shelter Island to the ocean. Two cream-colored leather armchairs flanked the doors inside; a sectional sofa with a glass-topped table behind it. He picked up the spread of magazines and laid them down askew, arranged in a different order.

A media storage unit rose from floor to ceiling, housing a Philips 16-bit CD player, a Sony combination TV/VCR, a Fisher compact stereo system, CDs, audio and video tape storage units and photo albums.

He took one of the photo albums off the shelf and leafed through it. A younger Kathryn Mackay with a thin, smiling man looked out at him. There were no captions. She was carrying a bouquet. A wedding? Others showed smiling older people, glasses raised, frozen in time. There were pictures of an older woman, gray-haired. Mother? Where's the father? Divorced? Dead?

More pictures of Kathryn and the young man. On a beach, tanned, in a restaurant, smiling at the camera. Views. Hawaii, by the look of it. So: she'd been married and got rid of the wimp.

He stayed in the condo for well over an hour, getting to know everything he needed to know: telephones, light switches, locks. Which way doors opened, which way windows slid, what made a noise. He rearranged one or two of her books, not too many, just enough. When he was satisfied, and only then, he let himself out into the carpeted corridor and went down to the underground garage in the elevator.

A late lunch in that Mexican place, Sophia's, in

*Laguna del Mar, he decided; it had been a very
successful day's work. He did not notice the dark blue
two-door T-bird pull out behind him and follow him
down the hill.*

It was odd, Kathryn thought: some of the books on
the shelves seemed to have been rearranged, the small
photo album was resting on her nightstand. In addition, some of her suits which she grouped by color
seemed to have changed position in her closet. It was
always possible Emma or even Dave had moved the
books and photo album but Dave had no reason to go
into her closet and it was off-limits to Emma.

"Emma, did you go in my closet?" she asked her
daughter. Emma looked up wide-eyed from her book,
surprised by the question.

"No, Mom," she said. Curled by her feet, Sam
looked up at the sound of Kathryn's voice and
thumped the floor with his tail. "Is something
wrong?"

"It's nothing," Kathryn said. I must be getting
absentminded in my old age, she told herself.

Later, after Emma had gone to bed, she crossed to
the window and looked out at the darkening ocean,
conscious of the silence. Tomorrow would be a busy
day; when the school summer holidays had begun,
Helen Corcoran had invited Emma to come stay with
Julie at their Tahoe condo. The offer was heaven sent:
for the first time in weeks, Emma had been her old
self, animated and excited about her forthcoming
vacation.

I ought to get started on packing her things,
Kathryn thought. In a moment, she said to herself, as
she went over to the window and looked out at the

shining ocean and the regular yellow blip of the lighthouse on Shelter Island.

Benchmark Corporation outdid themselves. Just three working days after submission of the evidence, they faxed Gaines the results of the PCR test and advised him that their full report would follow by registered mail.

The results were conclusive: the subject could not be excluded as the source of the semen on each of the vaginal swabs submitted. What that meant was that the semen recovered in the rape kit examinations of Jennifer Skelton, Lisa Hernandez and Stacie Percell and the blood Gaines had seized from Caduceus Medical Services all came from the same person.

Richard Charles Hoffman.

While waiting for the results of the PCR test, Gaines used the personnel file he had seized from Hypernet to supplement his investigation. He had made a list and worked methodically down it, ticking off each line as he obtained the information.

High school and college transcripts, past employers, TRW credit rating, phone bills from his condo and for his cellular phone, bank statements, savings account records, a year's credit card charges, e-mail messages. Put them together and they made interesting reading.

Richard Charles Hoffman, born Rochester, N.Y., February 12, 1956, was one of three children of George and Claire Hoffman. The father, who had died in 1979, had been a lifelong employee of the New York State Power Authority; the mother was a home-maker who was still living in that city. His bank records showed she received regular support checks from her son.

Hoffman's older brother, George, had died in an automobile accident in 1971, age eighteen. A younger sister, Sylvia, was married to an architect and lived in Cleveland.

In 1978 Hoffman received his bachelor of science degree from MIT. Then he went on sabbatical for a year traveling throughout Europe. Upon his return to the U.S. in 1979, Hoffman was offered a position with Cassandra Communications, a software company located in downtown Rochester. He worked his way up from an assistant project leader to head of the product design division. Evenings he worked on his graduate studies, receiving his doctorate in 1984. In 1986, Hoffman was head-hunted to the much-larger Syntacticon Systems Corporation in Atlanta, Georgia. He remained in Atlanta until 1990, when he successfully applied for a position with aerospace giant Zia Technology in Albuquerque, specializing in networking, object-oriented design for Booth, Coad and configuration management. In 1993 he joined Hypernet.

Gaines ran him again for any criminal history. Hoffman had none. Detectives in Rochester, Atlanta, Albuquerque confirmed that Hoffman had never even been "FI"d. According to his DMV printout he had never even received a traffic ticket.

Gaines began his stakeout. Hoffman drove a black BMW 530i V8 with an electric sunroof, cruise control and alloy wheels; each time it came up out of the underground garage, he would tuck himself in three cars back, staying on Hoffman's tail wherever he went.

It was obvious the man's job allowed him considerable freedom of movement: the kind of work he did could be done at home as easily as it could in an office. Most days Hoffman worked in his fourth-floor luxury condo on a hillside in Valley Springs. Mondays and Fridays he went over to Silicon Glen, presumably to pick up assignments or turn in whatever he was working on.

He ate out regularly, nearly always alone. He seemed to have no close friends, although he appeared to be on amicable terms with his neighbors. He had a fitness room in his condo where he worked out regularly; on weekends he usually ran an early-morning six or eight miles. On the face of it, he was a successful, highly paid and well-adjusted member of society. He was good at his job, he was kind to his mother.

That was the façade. Behind it lurked the darker self, the multiple rapist. Devious, dangerous and very successful, with a string of rapes that stretched back at least nine years and probably longer.

On the third morning, to Gaines's surprise, Hoffman swung east on the Alvarado Highway instead of heading toward either Silicon Glen or Santa Rita as he usually did. He exited at Alameda and drove up to Altamira, where he parked on a quiet residential street. Gaines watched as the man walked down the hill and then abruptly disappeared from sight between two houses.

What was this about? Coasting down the hill, Gaines determined that the house Hoffman had gone into was either 32 or 34 Joshua Drive. It was perhaps an hour and a half before he reemerged, got into his car and headed for Espanola, stopping off at a florist to pick up a bouquet of flowers.

After inching through the busy streets of the seaside

resort, he parked outside a condo building in Seaview Heights—by an odd coincidence the same one where Kathryn Mackay lived—and walked down into the underground garage. After a few minutes he came out again, returned to his car, took off his jacket and then walked back to the main entrance, carrying the bouquet.

Almost immediately the door opened and he went in. He did not reappear for over an hour; when he did, he drove to Laguna del Mar, ate at a Mexican taqueria and then returned to his condo in Valley Springs.

At around eight he drove to a steak and salad bar on Valley Springs Road, where he ate alone. He was back at his condo before ten; Gaines stayed in position until well after midnight, but Hoffman did not come out again.

Next morning Gaines was again ready and waiting, but Hoffman did not leave home until well after lunchtime. After a stop of about an hour at Hypernet, he returned to his car to head downtown. Gaines followed him and parked some way back along State Street, watching as Hoffman fed a meter and went into the College Bookstore.

Gaines got out of his car and walked along to where the sleek black BMW was parked. He could see Hoffman inside the store, looking at the new fiction. In the window facing the street was a huge blow-up of an article about the bookstore from the Living pages from last week's *Gazette,* featuring a grainy photograph of the smiling staff in a group, with their names below: Morris Bernstein, John Ryan, Madge Collins, Carrie-Jean Wilson and manager Leona Flynn. Above it was tacked a banner that said YOU READ ABOUT US, NOW COME IN AND TALK TO US.

Gaines went back to his car and waited until Hoffman came out and got into the BMW. He glanced at his watch: it was a few minutes before four. After another five minutes Hoffman moved off. He turned right into Juniper Street, then right again on Union, crossing the bridge and heading east on Bonita to pick up Alameda, driving at a leisurely pace.

Gaines quickly realized that Hoffman was following a white two-door Honda Prelude. He noted the license number and contacted County Comm on the radio for a check on the Honda's registration. As he crested the hill above the Alameda Valley, the radio crackled to life. "The car is registered to a Leona Flynn, 34 Joshua Drive, Altamira, Inspector," the dispatcher told him.

It hit Gaines like a rock, the whole thing. The bastard, the bastard, he was stalking her, stalking his prey. That was how he found them—he saw their pictures in the newspaper. Leona Flynn in the bookshop feature. Jennifer Skelton when she got married. Lisa Hernandez when her team won the volleyball championship and Jenny when she got her master's in oceanography. Oh, sweet Jesus Christ, Jenny.

I miss you, Jen.

I'm sorry, Michael. I can't come back. Not yet.

I wish you'd let me come down there.

No. I don't . . . I can't. Not yet.

I had the apartment redecorated.

Oh.

It looks really nice. You'll like it.

Yes.

When you come home.

I don't . . . I can't, Michael.

You can't what?

That place. I couldn't go in there. Never ever again.

Jen—

Never, Michael. Never.

The white Honda turned off Alameda and headed up Kinsley Drive toward Altamira; the BMW followed it. Gaines nodded. No doubt about it now.

Wait a minute. The last rape to occur in Santa Rita had been the attack on Jennifer Skelton, July 15. According to the personnel file, Richard Hoffman had left town on July 19 for a two-week seminar in San Francisco. Had he been stalking Leona Flynn and whoever it was lived in the Seaview Heights condo since he got back, since the first of the month?

Was he getting ready to strike again?

Leona Flynn's car took the right turn into Joshua; Richard Hoffman went past and took the next turn, Redwood. He would double back into Joshua from there the way he had done before. Gaines turned left into the lower end of Joshua and parked with his rear toward the hill. After a minute, the shark nose of the BMW came over the rise at the top of the road and slid to a stop above the house where Leona Flynn lived. He checked his watch—4:42.

Slightly more than an hour later, Gaines saw a white Mercedes 190 turn into Joshua Road and park in front of the garage of the Flynn house. A man in a dark suit carrying a briefcase got out; from a distance he looked to be in his middle forties, slightly overweight. He opened the front door with a key and went in. A few moments later, Hoffman started his car and drove off.

Think like the rapist. He stakes her out so he knows

where she works, what time she leaves, what time she arrives home. He knows there's a husband, and when he gets back. There's an hour between the two. More than enough time. Hello, little pig.

Trailing discreetly, Gaines followed Hoffman's BMW back down Kinsley and across the bridge over the Alvarado Highway, taking Espanola Drive to Beach Avenue. Seaview Heights, he bet himself. Hoffman's car slid to a stop at the curb and Gaines watched as he got out and went across to the entrance of London House. He had been here before; this was the condo building where . . .

Jesus Christ, wait a minute!

Could it be? Think, think. Her photograph had appeared in the paper the day following the Riker verdict. He felt a chill of premonition. Was Kathryn Mackay the rapist's prey?

Because if she was, he couldn't tell her.

30

"I don't know how to do this, Doc," Dave Granz said. "Gaines is my friend. Just thinking about it makes me feel like shit."

"You don't have a choice," Morgan replied. "Friend or no friend, you can't sit on it any longer.

And if you don't do it, I'm going to have to do it for you."

"He's not just a good cop, Doc," Dave said. "He's a good human being. There's a hundred women out there owe their sanity to him."

"That was never in question."

"If it's true . . . if he did this it's because he was driven to it. By what happened to Jenny."

"I know that too. But his motives are not our concern. He may have killed four men, Dave. We can't look away."

"I know. I just hate to be the one to roll over on him. It's the worst thing one cop can do to another."

"No, Dave," Morgan said. "The worst thing a cop can do is act as if there's one law for the cops and another for everyone else."

"I know, you're right," Granz said wearily.

"Tell me what the Frazers told you."

"They were home. Jenny called them from her apartment, hysterical. When they got over there they found her sitting in a chair naked, rocking herself. She was black and blue and there was blood all over her, the bastard hadn't just raped her, he'd bitten off one of her nipples. They didn't know what to do. Ellen Frazer wanted to call the police but Jenny wouldn't let them. She made them promise. No one else was to know. No one."

"Not even Michael?"

"Especially not Michael. She was afraid of what he would do. She got hysterical when they suggested calling him, if anyone even went anywhere near a phone. In the end her father drove over to the home of their family doctor, swore him to secrecy, then brought him back to the house. The mother had stopped the bleeding by compressing the wound. The doctor wanted to send Jenny to the emergency room, but she wouldn't go. He stitched the wound, dressed it and left."

"Why didn't they send for Gaines anyway?"

"How's this for irony, Doc—Gaines had a date with Jenny that night. He had to call it off because he was called out on a rape."

"And while he was there . . . ?"

Granz nodded. "I got the feeling the old man blames Gaines for what happened to Jenny, like, if he'd been there it never would have happened. You and I know the rapist would just have come back some other night, but it wouldn't be any use telling Frazer that. He's the type who'd view rape as sex, not violence. I got the distinct impression he felt that by being raped Jenny had become worthless, you know, like she was something valuable that got damaged. Maybe he felt it shamed the family. Hell, who knows. Whatever the reason, they didn't call Michael."

"How long before they told him?"

"He didn't find out about it until two days later. From what the Frazers said, Jenny was very guarded when she described what had happened. He wanted her to report it, but Jenny made him swear to keep it a secret."

"And he agreed?"

"God alone knows what it cost him, but yes, he agreed. You want my opinion, I think he probably figured she'd already begun to bury it, she *wanted* to bury it."

The syndrome was known as "silent reaction." The victim did not, perhaps could not, deal with her feelings about and reactions to the rape, and internalized all the agonies, psychological as well as physical.

"From what Ellen Frazer told me, Gaines nearly went crazy trying to get Jenny to deal with it, but nothing he did was any use. She just kept slipping further and further away from him. The harder he tried, the more she regressed. It was like she needed him to believe she had never been raped, and nothing else would do. And the more he persisted in trying to make her face the fact she had, the more she retreated."

"He should have got her into therapy."

Dave shook his head. "If she wouldn't talk to him about it, no way would she talk to anyone else, Doc."

"I guess," Morgan said. "So what happened in the end?"

"The Frazers told him they were sending Jenny to La Jolla. She would have plastic surgery on her breast and then have a long rest at her aunt's home."

Morgan shook his head sadly. "A long rest. Did they really think that was all it would take, that she was going to come to terms with the rape on her own, without help?"

"To be fair, I think Ellen Frazer thought she was doing her best for Jenny," Granz said. "As for the old man, he just wanted it to go away. The pain, the hurt, the shame. Especially the shame. So they concocted some story about her working too hard on her doctorate, and told everyone she was going to stay with her aunt."

"And in effect told Gaines it was all his fault," Nelson said, shaking his head. "Jesus, he must have been torn apart. Bad enough trying to handle his own feelings about what happened, bad enough coping with Jenny's trauma. Then on top of that the father blames him for not being there to prevent it from happening . . ."

"I keep thinking, here's the best damn rape investigator we've got and when someone rapes his sweetheart, instead of letting him do what he's good at, her father cuts his balls off."

"You've got a man buried in guilt," Morgan said. "Thinking if only he hadn't broken their date, if only he'd been there, if only there was some way to get the guy who did it."

"You've got to tell Kathryn," Morgan said.

"I know, Doc," Granz said wretchedly. "I just don't know how."

"How isn't important," Nelson said.

Dave nodded glumly. "You're right," he said. "I'll call her."

He picked up the phone and dialed Kathryn's number, heard it ring four times followed by the opening hiss of the answering machine. He hung up quickly before the message broke in.

"Nobody home," he told Morgan. It seemed to the older man there was a note of relief in his voice, as if he was glad of the reprieve, however temporary.

"Don't you want to leave a message?" he asked.

Dave shook his head. "I'd rather tell her in person anyway."

"Fine," Nelson said. "But do it."

The Corcorans left for Tahoe a little after 5:30; in a way Kathryn wished she had accepted their invitation to join them for the weekend, but something told her it would do Emma more good if she was with someone her own age for a few days. After the goodbye hugs and kisses, she felt strangely bereft and found herself reluctant to go back to the empty condo. Instead she got into her car and drove across to the Linda Vista Mall, trying to remember how long it had been since she had gone shopping other than for necessities.

She spent a pleasant hour wandering through the department stores and browsing in the B. Dalton bookshop, vacillating over whether to buy the new Scott Turow or the new Patricia Cornwell. In the end she bought both.

After a quick capuccino and a croissant at the French bakery, she called Dave's apartment from a public phone, but there was no answer. She bought a shirt and the new pair of jeans she had been promising herself since forever. Then she piled her purchases into the back of the Mazda and headed for home in the gentle warmth of sunset.

There was washing to do, a pile of ironing; half a dozen reports to read. The hell with it all. Tonight she was going to indulge herself, have a long, lazy soak in the bath, with bubbles. A glass of wine, even. Then something to eat and an early night in the company of Kay Scarpetta, she decided. The prospect, and the probability that there would be a message from Dave waiting on her answering machine made her smile in anticipation.

There were only two little pigs this time around. He had discarded the third almost as soon as he began to check her out. Her name was Nancy Rigg; she was a hair stylist in a downtown salon, and she lived in

Outlook Heights, not far from the main western entrance to Cabrillo Park. In the course of several careful preliminary checks he made on her apartment, there always seemed to be someone arriving or leaving; Nancy led a very busy social life, with friends likely to drop in without notice at any time. She also had a live-in lover who was some sort of writer or journalist; he was around a lot during the day and almost always at night. He discarded her and decided to concentrate on the other two.

He had to have one soon. The fantasies weren't enough any more. The porno videos were useless, all grunt and groan. The dark, burning, aching urge pounded inside his head and his body all night. Nothing made it stop. Nothing would, except doing it. Going out, hunting. At night, in the daytime. Waiting, waiting, watching. And while you were waiting and watching, remembering. Reliving all the other ones. And then, when you found one, imagining. When you would do it. How you would do it. What you would do. Thinking about the twisting, struggling, shuddering body beneath you. Hurting it.

The throbbing urge that was always there inside his head grew stronger, more insistent. Begin, begin, begin, begin. Begin the stalking. Begin the ritual. And then do it. One of them. It doesn't matter which. The one in Altamira looked good, but she had a husband. The one in Espanola looked good too, but the problem there was the daughter. Never mind. Begin. Begin.

He drove over to Altamira and parked a block over from Joshua Drive; he had been seen there often enough already. No use encouraging some nosy old biddy with nothing better to do than watch out the window to call the police. Putting on his new Armani jacket, he sauntered down the hill. Leona Flynn was outside in her garden, deadheading roses. She had on a halter top and shorts. Begin, begin. He smiled at her.

"Pleasant change from selling books, right?" he said.

"Right," she said, smiling back. "And a lot less hectic."

"That was a nice piece they did about you in the Gazette.*"*

"They made a window display of it," a male voice chimed in. Shit. It was the husband, standing at the corner of the house. His name was Raymond. T-shirt and jeans, fortyish, pot belly, going bald. Shit, shit, shit.

"Yeah, I saw it. Looks like you folks got plenty to do here."

"Come by tomorrow," Leona Flynn said. "We'll have it finished."

"Maybe I will," he smiled and walked on, showing no sign of his inner rage. He turned right at the bottom of the hill and made his way back to his car. No point waiting. The goddamn husband was going to be home all weekend. He looked at his watch; almost 4. He got in the car and headed for Espanola.

Neither Leona Flynn, her husband, nor Hoffman noticed Gaines as he walked down the hill on the other side of the street. He got back into his car and waited. After a while Hoffman came down the hill and walked to his own car. You had to hand it to him: for sheer effrontery the scene Gaines had just witnessed took some beating. The bastard was actually having a friendly little chat with a woman he had very probably targeted to rape. Stopped to check her out, to see if her husband was around. And when he found he was, abandoned the plan.

Hoffman's BMW slid past him and he moved in pursuit. If Leona Flynn was off the agenda, that quite possibly put Kathryn Mackay on it. Well, wait and see. From Altamira, Kinsley Drive ran almost due south. On the other side of the Alvarado Highway it became Espanola Drive. Gaines took the inside lane at the Bay Avenue junction, coming to a stop alongside the BMW. Hoffman glanced at him without interest, waiting for the light.

When they moved off, Gaines made a left on Escalona and cut through to Seaview Heights so that he would be in position before Hoffman, who went the long way around.

Gaines parked in the same place as last time and watched as Hoffman arrived and went through his routine. First he would go down to the garage to check if Kathryn's car was there. If it was not, he would go to the main entrance and push buttons till someone buzzed him in. If the Mazda was in its slot he would return to his car. If she came out he would follow her. If not he would wait, watching who came, who went.

Today he came back to the car, got in, waited. That meant—if she was the target—Kathryn was home. At a little before 5, Gaines saw her red Mazda come out of the garage entrance; a moment later, Hoffman's BMW glided off in its wake. The clincher: why else would he be going after her?

Gaines followed at a distance, making no effort to get close. Kathryn drove north on Lighthouse, under the highway bridge, then east on Laguna. She pulled to a stop outside a big house on Ridgeway Drive facing the Laguna Golf Club. Hoffman drove past as she and her daughter got out and went into the house together, coming to a stop perhaps fifty yards further up the road. Gaines parked out of sight and walked over to where he could watch the house.

About fifteen minutes later Kathryn and her daughter came out with a man, a woman and a little girl about the same age as Emma. Emma was carrying a Labrador puppy. That must be Sam, Gaines thought. Kathryn got his dog bed and Emma's sleeping bag and put them in the trunk of the car, a sleek Jaguar XJ6. The girls got in the back together, the adults in front, and he heard Kathryn calling goodbye, have a good time, waving to Emma as the car drove off.

When it was out of sight Kathryn got into her Mazda. By the time Gaines swung into Ridgeway, Hoffman's BMW was following her down the one-way street to the intersection of Lighthouse. From there she headed for the Linda Vista Mall; two and a half hours later, with the sun reddening the tiled roofs of the big houses on Escalona Drive, Kathryn Mackay led the little procession back to Seaview Heights.

Gaines watched the BMW pull over and stop down the hill in its usual place. Hoffman got out of his car and headed for the main entrance of the building. During the time they had been in Linda Vista he had changed his clothes. Instead of the casual shoes and gray silk jacket he had worn earlier, he now had on Nikes and a dark sweatshirt and was carrying a small canvas bag.

Jesus, Gaines thought, is this it? Is he going to do it?

He got out of the car and crossed toward London

House, reaching the doorway just as the release buzzer sounded. Richard Hoffman nodded and smiled politely as he held the door open; the bastard had nerve, Gaines thought, as they waited for the elevator in silence. When it came, Gaines waited until Hoffman pushed the button for the third floor and then pushed the fourth. Neither of them spoke. He noted that Hoffman turned right on leaving the elevator. That was where the stairs were.

The moment the doors opened on the fourth floor Gaines ran cat-footed along the corridor and down the four flights of stairs to the second floor. He knew the layout because he had been here before: Kathryn's condo was 22-A, at the far end on the ocean side. Drawing his gun, Gaines eased along the corridor on silent feet. The door of 22-A stood ajar.

He could feel the now-familiar tightness in his groin, the hard pulse of hatred in his brain. Everything was perfect, as if it had been planned, the child going on vacation, the puppy gone, the little pig all alone. When he reached the door of her condominium he put on the nylon stocking mask and the surgical gloves, his going-in outfit. The door was easy; he left it slightly ajar for easier escape. He slid inside, every sense alert. There was no sound. Then he heard the faint splash of water. Bathroom. She was in the bathroom.

Smiling his wolf smile, he tiptoed across to the breakfast bar on his right and disconnected the telephone; there was another in the bedroom, he remembered. He stopped as he passed the bathroom door. The sound of moving water and the scent of soap told him what he wanted to know: she was taking a bath. He had never had one in a bath before. This would be new. Different, exciting. He went silently across the room, tugged the telephone wire out of its socket and closed the door.

One, two, three, four, five steps up. He crossed the living room and opened the sliding glass doors leading to the balcony. It was a drop of about fifteen feet to the soft ground below; an emergency exit he was confident he would not need. He leaned against the wall, the feeling of power rising in him like the red roar of an incinerator. Now. Now. He took hold of the door handle and turned it very slowly. Then he opened the door and stepped into the steamy warmth.

"Hello, little pig," he said.

31

On his way over to Espanola, Dave rehearsed what he was going to say. He was pretty sure what Kathryn's reaction would be: disbelief at first, anger because he had taken so long to confide in her, to trust her; and then sadness.

Bad enough that Gaines would undergo the humiliation of an investigation: the arrest, the media coverage, the trial, the conviction. But if what he suspected was true, even if Gaines escaped the death penalty, his life would be forfeit from the day he went to prison. No matter which prison he was sent to, putting a cop in prison was like passing a sentence of death on him. The inmates would fight for a chance to kill him. And sooner or later, one of them would be successful.

As he headed east on the Alvarado Highway, Dave put in a call to Kathryn on his car phone. To his surprise the answering machine did not cut in after the fourth ring. After ten rings he hung up, frowning. Kathryn never disconnected her answering machine unless she was in the condo: she had to be available twenty-four hours a day, seven days a week, for call-out to any homicide or rape. If she was home she always picked up before the fourth ring; if not, why hadn't the machine cut in?

He dialed County Comm and asked them to page her. A few minutes later when the dispatcher advised him she was not responding to her pager, a faint chill of unease touched his nerve endings. Checking the mirror, Granz pulled into the fast lane and speeded up.

As if by the flick of a switch, the warm water in which Kathryn was lying felt clammy cold. Naked and unprotected, she could feel the inside of herself shrinking, curling up in fetal fear as she stared at the masked man in the doorway. She could see features, but nothing more, through the nylon stocking covering his head and face. The knife in his hand looked as big as a bayonet.

"Hello, little pig," he said, and then she knew who he was. And what he was. Her eyes flickered desperately around the bathroom for something she could defend herself with, scissors, a bottle, anything. Her automatic was in her purse, on the floor in the corner of her bedroom. It might as well be on the far side of the moon.

"Don't make any noise," he hissed, and stepped forward. "Just do what I tell you and you won't get hurt."

She nodded, her eyes on the knife. If she could get out of the bathroom, into the bedroom, there might be some way she could get to her gun. In here, there was nothing. No chance.

"Don't do this," she said. "Don't."

He squatted by the side of the bathtub. She could smell his sweat. His eyes were like dark holes burned in wood. He laid the cold knife against her breast and she flinched. She tried desperately to remember everything she had read, everything she knew about this man, about attack and response.

"Afraid, little pig?" he said, his mouth twisting with derision.

"No," she said, trying hard to keep her voice level. Her throat felt taut, dry. "I know about you. Why you're here."

"Do what I tell you and you won't get hurt," he said. "Get out of the tub. Get out. Lie down on the floor and spread your legs."

She stood up and stepped out of the bath, water sluicing in heavy slaps on to the floor.

"Down!" he said. "Lie down!"

"Wait," she said. "Listen. I won't fight you. I know I can't stop you. We can go in the bedroom. But let me get a condom first."

She saw him hesitate, torn between puzzlement and excitement. Was it a trick, or was she really going to let him do whatever he wanted?

"You're an intelligent man," she said. She held her voice down, neither defiant nor abject, trying hard not to shiver. "If you use a condom there'll be no semen. No DNA. Nothing to tie you to me."

He made a gesture with the knife. "Where?"

"In my purse," she said, gesturing toward the bedroom. "In there."

"Show me."

He clamped a hand on the back of her neck and propelled her into the bedroom. Then he hurled her forward on to her hands and knees, following up, towering over her.

"Get it!" he shouted. "Hurry up, piggy!"

She crawled to where her purse lay on the floor, top gaping open the way it always did, a jumble of papers sticking out. Her hand closed on the gun and she turned around with it in her hand. When he saw the weapon he shouted something inarticulate and came at her. He was only a couple of feet away. She fired without thinking and she heard the heavy thwack of the slug going into him. He stopped in his tracks, dropping the knife.

"Bitch," he said. Then louder, "Bitch!"

He sprawled backwards against the bed, one arm draped over it, a widening stain of blood on the left side of his body. Kathryn already had her portable phone in her hand. She scurried to the far side of the room, keeping the rapist covered, punching in the three digits and telling the operator who and where she was.

As she put down the phone she felt a draught of

cooler air as Michael Gaines threw open the door, came down the steps into the bedroom half-crouched, gun in hand.

"Michael!" she shouted. "It's all right, Michael, he's down, it's under control!"

It seemed to her that everything started to move in slow motion. She saw the rapist try but fail to get up off the bed. Then Gaines fired his gun twice and she felt her eardrums flatten and saw the top of the rapist's head move, as if a vagrant breeze had ruffled his hair, and blood spattered the wall behind him. His body contorted and then stretched out in a long, final movement. Gaines went past her and knelt down by the still figure, gun ready, his eyes as empty as glass.

"He's dead," he said emotionlessly.

He took off his jacket, draping it around her shoulders. She was shivering now, but it was not from cold.

"Are you okay, Kathryn?" he asked gently. "Did he—?"

Kathryn shook her head. "No. I didn't . . . I'm all right. It's all right. I just don't understand. Michael, he was . . . I had it under control. I called 9-1-1. Why did you shoot him?"

"Not now," he said. "Let's take care of you first. I'll get your robe."

"I'll get it," she said.

She went to the bathroom and got her robe, then came out tying it. As she did, Granz came through the bedroom door in shooting stance, the gun in his hand leveled at Gaines. He saw Kathryn facing him and held up his left hand, stay.

"Put the gun down, Gaines!" he snapped. "Put it down. Now!"

In the middle of the room Gaines looked down at

the gun in his hand, as if he was surprised to see it still there.

"It's okay," he said, frowning as if he could not understand why Granz was acting this way. "He's dead, Dave. No sweat."

"Put down the gun!"

Granz raised his voice to a shout this time, and Gaines put the gun down on the nightstand to his right, lifting his hand away from it as if it were hot.

"Dave, what's wrong, what are you doing?" Kathryn said, "Michael just—"

"He's not here by accident, Kathryn," Dave cut in. "Are you, Gaines?"

Michael said nothing.

"Tell her," Dave gritted. "Go on, tell her. Or tell me I'm wrong."

Still Michael said nothing, his eyes desolate.

"He's the vigilante, Kathryn," Granz said tersely. "Aren't you, Gaines? You killed them all. Croma, Bitzer. You strangled Harry Bosendorf. Did he fight back? Is that how your blood got on his sheets? Then you threw George Zabrowski off Lover's Leap. Didn't you, Gaines?"

"Michael?" Kathryn whispered. "Michael, was it you?"

"Tell her, Gaines," Dave said, keeping Gaines covered as he moved to Kathryn's side and put his arm around her shoulder. Gaines shrugged.

"Then it's true?" Kathryn said. "You killed all four of them?"

"And this one as well," Dave told her. "This one was special, wasn't he, Gaines?"

"If you know that, you know why," Gaines said

dully. "And you also know the bastard had it coming."

Sirens cut the air in the distance.

"Who was he, Gaines?" Dave said.

"A pile of shit named Hoffman," Michael said. "He raped Lisa Hernandez, Stacie Percell, Jennifer Skelton. I can prove it. He raped them all."

"And one other," Gaines said. "One that wasn't reported. Go on, Gaines, tell her."

"He raped Jenny, Kathryn," Gaines said. "My Jenny. He beat her and tore her body with his teeth. And she's . . . she'll never . . ." Tears misted his eyes and he shook his head to clear them. "He broke her. Everything that was lovely. They said she won't ever be . . . she won't ever come back to me. Never. And that's why, you see. You can understand that, can't you?"

"No, Michael," Kathryn said. "We live by law. You can't set yourself up as judge and jury and executioner."

"You do when the law doesn't work," he said defiantly. "That was why . . . after Jenny, I decided. Somebody had to make it work. Me. I was the one who saw them out there—broken, torn, bleeding. The one who tried to talk them back to sanity. I figured I had the right."

"No one has the right, Michael," Kathryn said softly. If he heard her he gave no sign of it. The sirens grew louder as the approaching police cars came up the hill.

"Dave," Gaines said and looked at Granz.

"No," Dave said. It was not denial, Kathryn thought. It was regret.

"What was it you guys used to say? 'Here's to us, who's like us?'" Gaines said softly. "Remember?"

"I remember," Dave said.

"Way it's got to be, Dave," Gaines said. He picked up his gun off the nightstand and Dave made no move to stop him. Kathryn started forward but Dave held her back.

"No, Kathryn," he said. His voice was like iron. Michael Gaines went past and out of the door without looking at either of them.

"Dave, stop him!" Kathryn said angrily, struggling ineffectually against his grip. "We can't just let him—"

Amplified by the space of the stairwell, the shot sounded very loud. Kathryn looked up at Dave in horror. His eyes were bleak, his face a graven image.

"It's over," he said.

32

The half-hour dog obedience sessions were held weekly in the yard of the kennels at Espanola. Emma took them very seriously. It didn't seem to bother her that she was the only young person there. Or that some of the dogs looked big enough to eat Sam as a snack.

Tonight they were doing "Stay" and "Come."
Barbara, the owner of the kennel who was also the
instructor, provided a long extending lead, which was
fastened around the neck of each animal in turn. The
dog was told to sit. Then its owner would walk
backward away from the dog, telling it to stay.

The first pupil was a middle-aged man with a
golden retriever named Rafe. "Sit, Rafe," he said.
"Sit."

The dog ignored him.

"Sit, Rafe."

Barbara knelt by the dog, her arm around its neck.
She had bits of cookie for bribes. She got Rafe to sit.

"Now walk backward, walk away," she told the
owner. "Say his name. Get his attention. Tell him,
Stay."

The man walked backward, paying out the lead.

"Rafe," he said. "Rafe."

The dog ignored him and got up, licking Barbara's
face. She gave it another cookie, got it to sit again.

"Rafe," the man said. The dog looked up. "Stay,"
the man said. "Rafe, stay."

Rafe stayed. "Very good," Barbara said. "All right.
Now call his name again. And this time, c-o-m-e."

"Rafe, come," the man said and the dog bounded
happily over to his side. Barbara looked relieved as
she started over with the next owner. Emma stood
patiently waiting her turn, Sam sitting obediently by
her side. He already knew how to sit. He was still
having a little trouble with stay. He preferred to romp
with Emma.

"She looks happy," Dave said. "The weekend away
did her good."

"Maybe she's turned the corner," Kathryn said. They were standing over by the chain-link gate near the road. It was warm and still. "Started to come to terms with her grief."

"Yeah," Dave said. There was sorrow in his tone and she knew he was thinking about Michael.

"What did he mean?" she asked softly. She didn't need to say who she was talking about. "What was it he said, 'Here's to us' or something like that?"

"It was a long time ago," Dave told her. "The detectives, we had a toast. 'Here's to us, who's like us? Damned few—and most of them are dead.'"

"I still can't believe he's gone."

"He was a deputy coroner then. He used to come in to investigations. He looked up to us, the great detectives."

"Don't be bitter, Dave. He wouldn't want that."

"I know. I just wish . . ."

"So do I," Kathryn said, slipping her hand into his. "We all do."

"He was a good cop," Dave said. It was as fitting an epitaph as any, she thought, and a lot better than most. They stood silently, holding hands, knowing their words were a goodbye of sorts, a way of letting go.

"Look," Kathryn said. Emma stepped forward proudly, with Sam cavorting about her ankles. She held up a finger and told him to sit. He sat at once, his head cocked to one side, watching her. Then Barbara told her to take the long extending lead. Emma knew what to do without being told.

"Sam," she said firmly. "Stay."

Sam wagged his tail and looked up at Barbara.

"Sam," Emma said, backing away. "Stay."

"Will you look at that kid?" Dave said.

Emma was about fifteen feet from Sam now. He was watching her intently, ears forward.

"All right, Emma," Barbara said. "Now say his name, and then tell him c-o-m-e."

"Sam, come," Emma said and the dog scampered across to her.

"Well done, Emma, terrific!" Barbara said.

"Good boy, Sam," Emma said, ducking her head as if she didn't want anyone to see her smiling.

The final exercise was making the dogs lie down, all the way down flat. Then the lesson was over and people started to leave, calling good night to each other and to each other's dogs. Emma came toward Dave and Kathryn, her eyes shining.

"He was a good dog, wasn't he, Mom? Wasn't he, Dave?"

"He sure was, Princess," Dave said. "You two are a great team. I think she deserves a treat after all that hard work, Kathryn, don't you?"

"You mean like ice cream, Dave?" Emma said. "You mean like maybe triple chocolate passion?"

"We-e-ell," Dave said.

They both looked at Kathryn. She shook her head. "You two," she said.

They got in the car and drove over to the Baskin-Robbins ice-cream parlor in the mall. Sam stayed in the car while they went in. Emma got her double scoop of triple chocolate passion. Dave preferred butter pecan. Kathryn chose espresso and cream.

"You want to get a lid for that, Princess?" Dave said. "In case Sam wants to share it with you?"

"It's okay," Emma said. "Sam can have some if he likes. He's part of our family."

She gave her ice cream to Kathryn to hold, put one hand in hers and the other in Dave's.

"Let's go home," she said.